INHERITANCE

A DEADLY CURIOSITIES NOVEL

GAIL Z. MARTIN

INHERITANCE

DEADLY CURIOSITIES, BOOK FOUR

By Gail Z. Martin

eBook ISBN: 978-1-939704-97-9
Print ISBN: 978-1-939704-98-6

Cover art by Lou Harper
SOL Publishing is an imprint of DreamSpinner Communications, LLC

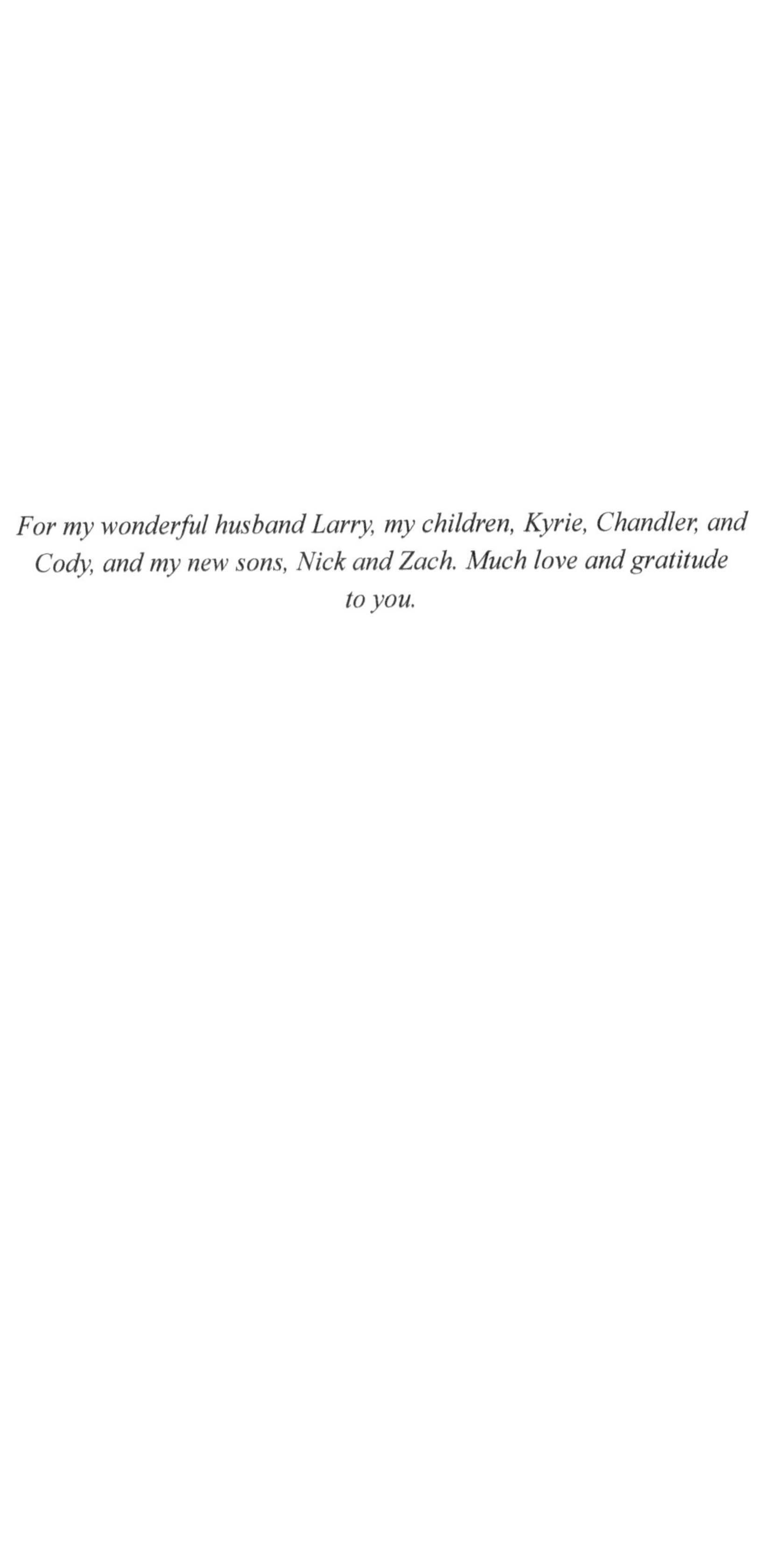

For my wonderful husband Larry, my children, Kyrie, Chandler, and Cody, and my new sons, Nick and Zach. Much love and gratitude to you.

CHAPTER ONE

"I HAVE A PROBLEM ANTIQUE I'D LIKE YOU TO TAKE A LOOK AT." THE man on the other end of the call sounded rattled. I recognized his name —Alfred Stone, from Stone Auctions—but I didn't think we had ever spoken, let alone met.

"What kind of 'problem' does it present?" I asked. A number of possibilities came to mind. "Questionable provenance? Not sure how to authenticate?"

"I think it's trying to kill me."

Well, damn. *That* kind of problem. "All right, Mr. Stone. Try to stay calm."

"I just told you, it's trying to kill me. I heard you…know…about these things. Please, help me."

Across the store, Teag Logan glanced up to make sure everything was all right. I nodded, and he went back to helping a customer.

"I can come now. Are you at the showroom?"

"Yes. Thank you. And…please…hurry."

I ended the call and sighed. This might be the first time Alfred Stone had an antique try to kill him, but that made it just another day here at Trifles and Folly.

I'm Cassidy Kincaide, and I own Trifles and Folly, an antique and curio shop in historic, haunted Charleston, South Carolina. The shop has been in my family for more than three hundred years. While we're known as a great place to buy high-quality antiques, the shop is also a cover for the Alliance, a coalition of mortals and immortals who save Charleston—and the world—from supernatural threats. I'm a psychometric, which means I can read the history and magic of objects by touching them. Teag is my assistant store manager, best friend, and sometimes bodyguard—and he's also a talented Weaver witch. Sorren, my business partner, is a nearly six-hundred-year-old vampire. Together with some other friends with very specialized abilities, we do our best to keep the world safe from dark magic and things that go bump in the night.

"Problem?" Teag asked when the customer left.

"I'm not sure," I replied. "Alfred Stone just called—from the auction house. He says he's got an item that's trying to kill him."

"You want me to go with you?" Teag pushed a lock of dark hair out of his eyes. His skater-boy haircut and skinny jeans made him look younger than his late twenties. "Maggie can handle the store."

On cue, Maggie—our lifesaver of a part-time associate—waved to agree from the other side of the store. She was sporting a new bright pink streak in her short gray hair, and it matched her sweater, a reminder—as if I needed one—that she believed in taking risks and living large.

I reached up to slick my humidity-frizzy strawberry blond hair back into a ponytail and shook my head. "Let me go see what the problem is, and I'll figure out what to do from there. It's not far away, in case I need to give a shout."

"Just let me know," he said, with a look that told me I'd better not get myself hurt. "I can be there in ten minutes. If in doubt—call."

"I promise." I appreciated Teag's concern, but I had proven my ability to hold my own against some pretty nasty creatures, and while I didn't intend to push my luck, I didn't know enough about Stone's "problem" to call in the cavalry just yet.

As I drove over to Stone Auctions, I tried to remember what I knew about the man and the business. While Trifles and Folly had enough of a reputation in the area that a lot of people sold their items directly to us, Teag and I sometimes bought from auctions and estate sales. Occasionally an item would be listed that we knew would be a perfect fit for our typical customers, who were tourists looking for a one-of-a-kind souvenir, interior designers searching for just the right piece, or antique enthusiasts hunting down the perfect addition for their collection.

More often, we bought pieces because they were cursed, haunted, or so tainted with bad mojo from long-ago tragedies that we needed to make sure nobody got hurt.

Usually, we spotted a dangerous piece ourselves or got a heads-up from someone in our network of friends. This time, whatever had spooked Alfred Stone had enough juice to get his attention, even though he didn't have insider knowledge about just how much of a spookapalooza Charleston really was. That told me the item might be especially dangerous.

To my surprise, Stone was waiting for me near the front desk. He looked like he had probably hovered behind the poor receptionist since he called me.

"Cassidy Kincaide?" he asked, extending his hand. "I'm Alfred Stone."

Stone was a stocky man who looked to be in his fifties, and he stood only a few inches taller than my five-foot-eight height. He had a twitchy energy that I suspected was a combination of caffeine and hustle. The man also had a black eye and a gauze bandage on his forehead, like he'd been in a fight. His once-over glance told me that I looked younger than he expected. I'm close to Teag's age, but don't look it. Someday, that may be an advantage. Now, it's more of a liability. I gave Stone credit for not mentioning it.

"Good to meet you, Mr. Stone. I've attended some of your events, but we've never had the opportunity to meet."

"Alfred, please."

I smiled, trying to set him at ease. "Cassidy." Now that we were on a first-name basis, I hoped we could get down to business. "How can I help?"

Alfred led me down a hallway, away from the reception area. "If you've been to some of our events, then you know Stone Auctions has an eye for the unusual, the off-beat. Our repeat buyers know they can come to us for pieces that are, if not completely unique, then at least unlikely to pop up everywhere." He tugged at his collar, trying to hide his discomfort. "Sometimes, we end up with pieces that are…unsettling. We've had items made from bone, and odd taxidermy pieces, mourning jewelry, that sort of thing. But I've never sensed anything dangerous—until now."

I didn't have the heart to tell him that was because Teag and I bought the malicious items from prior sales before they had a chance to hurt anyone. Since he hadn't recognized their negative juju, then whatever it was that freaked him out had to be hella bad.

Which, given the kinds of things I've seen since I took over the store, could go anywhere from soul-sucking demons to end-of-the-world Viking sorcerers. Never a dull moment.

"How did you come to purchase it?" I asked. Not that I expected Alfred to give up his sources—those were a trade secret in this business—but I needed something to go on, and finding out where a piece came from usually told me a lot about what to expect.

"Through a seller's representative," Alfred replied. "Fairly common, for someone who wants to sell a piece but doesn't wish to handle the sale directly. I'm sure you've done acquisitions that way yourself."

I had, but rarely. Given our particular specialty at Trifles and Folly, I liked to know exactly who I was dealing with. Sometimes that could be a life-or-death detail.

"Anyhow, this gentleman assured me that the piece had been in the collection of a very wealthy man from an old family, whose will directed that the pieces be sold after his death," Alfred said.

"Did he give you a name? Of the man or the family?" I had a bad feeling about this. There was a thin line between discretion and deception.

"No, although the paperwork all seemed to be in order," Alfred replied, shaking his head. "And before you ask—I tried to reach him when the … problems…began, but his number has been disconnected."

His cheeks colored, telling me that he knew exactly how bad that sounded.

Great. So it's not just a secret…the piece was probably stolen.

There could be situations in which a representative could not disclose the former owner. That was rare because an item's history—the fancy word is "provenance"—usually increases the price. A common object that was owned by a famous person is worth far more than the item itself would fetch. Keeping the ownership and history a secret hurt the representative's ability to get the best price for the client—unless the history would raise a scandal.

Or, as I suspected happened here, the item was hot.

"I know what you're thinking," Alfred said, with an embarrassed expression. "I may have left myself open to legalities. A rookie mistake—and I assure you, I'm no rookie. But…the piece wasn't terribly expensive, although it was unique. And it called to me. I realize how that sounds."

It sounded exactly like what would happen if a cursed object saw the perfect victim.

"What you're describing isn't that unusual when an object has troublesome energy." I'd learned to use phrasing that didn't come right out and mention ghosts and magic to set people at ease, people who wanted to go back to their ordinary lives and forget that they ever got a glimpse of the supernatural. Sometimes the lucky ones could do just that.

Usually, it wasn't that simple.

We reached the door to the storage area, where items are checked in, cataloged, and tagged while awaiting their turn in the spotlight during an auction. While the auction theater is luxurious, like good seats at the symphony or opera, the room Alfred led me into was utilitarian, with functional wooden racks and plenty of shipping boxes. We crossed to the far corner, to a small room with a steel door and a reinforced glass window.

"It's in here." Alfred sounded less than excited about getting close to the troublesome piece. He unlocked the door and gestured for me to go inside. While I was ready for danger, I had to admit to being curious—especially since Alfred seemed to swing between fear and chagrin.

"That's it."

All right, then. Now, I understood—at least a little more. It wasn't every day when a well-to-do business owner was forced to admit he was terrified by a framed mosaic made up entirely of seashells.

"It's a 'sailor's valentine,'" I said, recognizing the style. I leaned closer, careful not to touch. While the idea of an intricate design crafted from shells sounded like a kitschy souvenir, antique sailor's valentines could be true works of folk art and fetch thousands of dollars. This one was particularly well done, with a floral rose inside a nautical wind rose, enclosed in a detailed decorative border, and all of it painstakingly pieced together from naturally-colored seashells.

"We can authenticate the original ownership," Alfred asserted, probably hoping to regain my professional respect. "It's old—the date on the back says 1845, and the appraiser confirmed that the materials are consistent with that period. The writing next to the date reads, '*To my darling Millicent, undying love from Joseph.*'"

"Do you have any idea who Joseph and Millicent were?"

"Unfortunately, no," Alfred admitted. "The representative said that it had been given by a sailor to his fiancée when he returned to port." He cleared his throat. "Unfortunately, it was a parting gift, because the sailor had already married someone else. After that, the piece passed through various hands until it was acquired a few decades later by the family of the late owner."

I walked around the piece, which was secured on an easel. The mahogany frame appeared to be in good shape, and despite the age of the piece, the shells had not discolored or come loose from their glue, and the glass had no chips or breaks. The shell work itself was a wonder, using a variety of types—common cockles, beaded periwinkles, baby's ears, bubbles, jingles, and more—in an array of colors and sizes. I could understand why it could catch someone's eye.

Assuming they couldn't feel the psychic reek of malevolent energy that made me recoil. *If it has that much resonance when I'm a foot away, I really don't want to know how it feels to pick it up.*

When an item gave off vibes that were that strong, I could usually get a read without having to touch it. I closed my eyes, aware that Alfred was watching, and reached out with my psychometry, stretching my gift toward the piece but not getting any closer than necessary.

Hatred and vengefulness hit me like a punch to the face. After all this time, the resonance was so powerful that I caught my breath and took a defensive step back. I saw everything, like a movie in fast-forward. Millicent's happiness that her beloved had returned from the sea, and her delight in the beautiful gift. Joseph's admission of betrayal. Her shock, turning to grief and then cooling into anger. A heated argument, and the swing of a candlestick in rage, leaving Joseph in a pool of blood. Fear, remorse, loss, and guilt, and then a knife blade that Millicent used to open veins and let herself die beside her faithless lover.

The vision ended as abruptly as it had begun, leaving me breathless. I might have spared some sympathy for Millicent, despite her reaction, if I didn't feel the temperature drop and know from the prickle on my skin that Millicent's spirit still clung to the tragic gift.

"Get back!" I reached into the pocket of my jacket and grabbed a handful of the loose salt I kept there for situations just like this. As Millicent's spirit began to take shape and the air around us grew freezing cold, I hurled a handful of salt at her ghostly outline, making her flicker and vanish.

"Run!" I grabbed Alfred by the arm and dragged him with me as I sprinted toward the storage room door. I'd disrupted Millicent's manifestation, but it wouldn't take a spirit that strong long to regroup.

I slammed the door and reached into my large tote. In this business, it never paid to leave home without tools of the trade. I grabbed a canister of salt and a small bag of iron filings. "Go over there," I ordered, and Alfred was all too happy to put distance between himself and the small room. Then I laid down a line of salt across the threshold and sprinkled iron filings on top. As an extra precaution, I hung a small, blessed silver chain from the door handle.

"What are you doing?" Alfred sounded skeptical but curious.

I straightened and put the items back in my bag. Just to be safe, I palmed an iron dagger and the old wooden spoon I used as an athame to channel my touch magic defensively.

"Keeping Millicent in the storage room until we can send her on her way," I replied.

His eyes widened. "So, you saw her too?"

"Yep. Throwing salt at her bought us time to get out, but it won't stop her from manifesting again. And the line at the door will only hold her for a while. I think we need to talk, while I call in a consult."

Alfred seemed lost in thought as he led me to his office. I paused in the hallway to call Father Anne Burgett.

"Cassidy? What's up?" Father Anne knew I didn't call to chat.

"Got a vengeful ghost I could use some help with. Are you free?"

She chuckled. "Give me the address. I'll be there as soon as I can," she replied. I rattled off the information and walked to the front desk to let the receptionist know I was expecting someone. When I came back to Alfred's office, he was pacing and looked like he could use a stiff drink.

"I called in a priest who can help the spirit move on—I hope," I told him. "And I'd like you to send everyone home, so no one gets hurt from Millicent acting up. But before my priest friend gets here, I need to know everything—including how you got that black eye."

Alfred stopped pacing and sat. He glanced toward a side cabinet with a look that suggested it was probably the liquor cabinet. "I should have known something was wrong when the damned thing seemed irresistible. I'm not usually an emotional buyer."

I shrugged. "We all are, whether we like to admit it or not. And the piece is well made. It could fetch a good price."

He shook his head as if he hadn't quite made himself clear. "This was different. It wasn't just strongly liking the piece. When I saw it, I *had* to have it. And then afterward, I wasn't sure what came over me."

I had a suspicion, but it could wait. "Did Millicent give you that shiner?"

Alfred reached out to touch his sore eye, looking chagrined. "She packs quite a punch—for a ghost. I was alone with the piece, and all of a sudden the air got very cold and I felt shivery. And then I saw a gray woman in an old fashioned dress appear out of nowhere. She rushed toward me and knocked me into the wall. I tried to get away, but she slid furniture into my path. I tripped and fell, and that's how I hit my head."

"You said she tried to kill you."

He nodded. "When I was on the floor, I felt like there was a heavy weight on my chest. I couldn't breathe. And I heard a voice say, 'you'll pay for what you did.'"

"How did you get away?" I asked, as my theory grew stronger.

"Thank God one of the appraisers heard all the thumping. Kristen opened the door to check on me, and the weight on my chest vanished. I made up a story about toxic fumes from the glue in the artwork and asked her to put it in the side room. I figured if the ghost went away when Kristen came, she might be able to move it without getting attacked."

"Did Kristen notice anything odd about the piece?"

He shook his head. "No, and nothing strange happened when she moved it. I watched her."

Lucky for him, although Kristen would have found it hard to file a workplace safety claim against a ghost if something had gone wrong. I leaned forward, anticipating his reaction to my next question.

"Have you been unfaithful to your partner?"

Alfred's head jerked up, and for a moment before he regained control, his eyes were wide with fear. "What did you just say?" he sputtered, but I already had my answer.

"Ghosts that cause problems often have an agenda. In this case, Millicent punished her unfaithful fiancée and killed him. I suspect that, if we could find the provenance of the art, it's caused quite a few deaths over the years. Did the representative show you other pieces you declined?"

A sheen of sweat dotted Alfred's forehead, and he refused to meet my eyes. "I…I mean…" He sighed as if all the fight had gone out of him. "Yes. He showed me two or three other items, but once I saw the sailor's valentine, nothing else interested me."

I nodded. "I suspect that Millicent chose you as her next victim. That's why you felt the strong attraction to the piece."

He licked his lips nervously. "I'm getting a divorce," he admitted. "It isn't public knowledge yet. I fooled around on my buying trips, and she found out."

"With anyone here at the auction house?" I doubted Millicent would take pity on someone she perceived as a homewrecker. Since Kristen hadn't been touched, I ruled her out immediately.

"What? No. No one here." Understanding dawned, and he caught his breath. "Because you think she'd hurt them?"

"I'm sure she would."

Alfred ran a hand through his thinning hair. "And she'll try to kill me again."

"Yes. But we're not going to let her do that."

His phone buzzed, letting him know I had a visitor, and he told the receptionist to send "him" back and then close up. A few minutes later, Father Anne walked in. I knew immediately she hadn't been what Alfred pictured when I said "priest."

With short, spiked dark hair, a clerical collar over a black T-shirt, protective tattoos that peeked from beneath the shirt sleeves, black denim, and Doc Martens boots, Father Anne didn't fit most people's mental image. She's the rector at St. Hildegard's Episcopal Church, but more importantly—for me—she's also a member of the St. Expeditus Society, a secret group of priests who take on demons, monsters, and other supernatural riff-raff. Including, fortunately, vengeful ghosts.

"Thank you for coming on short notice," I greeted her, and made introductions. "We've got a haunted picture with a dangerous spirit attached to it."

"Let's do it," she replied, with a grin like she was looking forward to the challenge.

I turned to Alfred. "Wait here." I walked a circle around him, laying down a line of salt and iron filings. "Don't leave the circle, no matter what."

He swallowed hard and nodded.

Father Anne had a duffle bag with her gear shouldered, and she stood by the door, ready to go. "Hang in there. We'll be back," she told Alfred, and then we headed to have a come to Jesus moment with Millicent.

On our way, I filled Father Anne in on the particulars.

"Do you think the 'representative' knew the piece was haunted?" she asked.

"I think the representative knew that the items for sale had a questionable chain of ownership," I replied. "I'm betting they were stolen —whether by outsiders or from family, by family. Hence the mysterious, vanishing broker."

Father Anne snorted a laugh. "Yeah. That's not sketchy at *all*."

"Millicent is powerful enough to make herself visible and throw objects. She knocked Alfred around and kept him pinned. If she's been killing unfaithful lovers for a century or more, she might feel like she's on a mission. I'm not betting that she'll be excited about going into the light."

"There's a rite for that," Father Anne replied. We stopped a few doors down from the storage room, and she set the duffle on the floor and unzipped it. I already had my iron knife and athame handy, and while I'd left my tote in Alfred's office, I had salt in my jacket pockets and some small bits of iron, too. I wore a silver and agate necklace and an onyx and silver bracelet, since I never left home without my protective jewelry,

Father Anne took out a piece of rebar, a flask of holy water, and the sacramental stole she wore to administer Last Rites. She tucked that last item into a pocket and pulled a silver cross on a chain from beneath her T-shirt, putting the protective charm in full view.

"Ready?" I asked, moving to the storage room door. She gave me a curt nod in reply. I opened the door, taking care not to break the salt line. I didn't want Millicent getting loose.

The room was quiet when we entered. Millicent's sailor's valentine sat on its easel, deceptively pretty, waiting for the next victim.

"It's time to move on, Millicent," Father Anne called out. "We know what happened with Joseph. He hurt you, and you killed him, then yourself. Other people too, since then. Now it's time to rest."

I didn't trust Millicent. Whatever had turned her spirit vengeful meant she wasn't likely to go quietly. Especially if she saw herself as the protector of wronged women, carrying out a trail of vengeance, one dead lover at a time.

"He deserved it." The disembodied voice sounded scratchy, like a bad recording. Ghosts didn't usually have the power to say much, if anything. I guessed Millicent saved her energy to tell us what mattered the most.

Father Anne and I watched as Millicent's ghost took form. She stood beside the shell art, and her face contorted in rage.

"Joseph was wrong to lie to you. He hurt you. But you didn't have the right to kill him—or any of the others. There have been others, haven't there?" Father Anne asked, refusing to let the ghost bait her.

Instead of trying to reply, Millicent charged at us, arms outstretched, hands clawed. I sliced through her form with my iron knife, and she blinked out.

"Start the rite!" I yelled. "I'll keep her busy."

Father Anne spread a handful of salt around where she stood—not as secure as a circle, but better than nothing on short notice, and pulled the ceremonial stole from her pocket. She placed it around her neck and began the prayers to break Millicent's connection to this world and send her to the next.

"Depart, O Christian soul, out of this world; In the Name of God the Father Almighty who created you…" Father Anne began the litany.

Millicent shrieked and appeared again, this time in front of Father Anne. She tried to close the distance, but the salt on the floor held her back, so she wheeled on me once more.

I didn't need to hear Millicent's voice to understand the fury in her eyes. Joseph had betrayed her, and so she had made vengeance for wronged women the cord that bound her to this world. Since Father Anne and I were trying to stop her, that made us betrayers, too.

I blocked out the rise and fall of Father Anne's voice. To keep Millicent from killing me, I needed to stay focused on her, without distractions. Millicent circled, watching the iron knife in my left hand.

That meant she wasn't considering the wooden spoon, gripped handle-out, in my right hand to be a threat.

She came at me from the right. I focused my touch magic, drawing on the resonance of all the love and memories of my grandmother that her spoon represented and felt the energy spark. Millicent's ghost lunged for me, but the cone of white light from my athame reached her first, shining through her and scattering her image like cinders in the wind.

"Hurry!"

Father Anne gave me a look, wordlessly reminding me that sacred rites can't be rushed.

For as many times as I'd heard Father Anne read through the liturgy, I couldn't remember how much more she had to go. A spirit as stubborn as Millicent's wouldn't leave quietly. I turned slowly, alert for tricks.

The easel with the sailor's valentine crashed to the floor, taking the artwork with it and shattering the glass. In the next moment, shards of glass and loose shells rose into the air, and I knew what Millicent intended before I saw the glass hurtle toward us.

I raised my athame and let loose a blast of cold, white energy, intercepting the sharp glass and sending the pieces flying toward the other side of the room. I slowly moved to put myself in front of Father Anne, and she turned to face the opposite direction, so we were standing back to back. Since she knew the rite by heart, her hands were free to use the iron rebar or splash holy water.

We just had to keep Millicent at bay until the rite ended, and her spirit moved on. Maybe Millicent thought her work on earth wasn't finished, or perhaps she was afraid of where she might end up on the Other Side. But no sooner had Father Anne and I positioned ourselves than the glass shards rose again and were flung toward us like a hail of knives.

I got off another blast from my athame, but some of the shards got past me. I closed my eyes and threw one arm in front of my face, but splinters lodged in the sleeves of my shirt and my hair, opening tiny cuts where they reached skin.

Millicent tackled me before I could safely see, and we crashed to the floor. I felt glass and sharp shells crunch beneath me and knew I was bleeding. A heavy weight pressed me down, making it hard to breathe, each inhale more difficult than the last.

"Deliver Millicent, O Sovereign Lord Christ, from all evil, and set her free from every bond; that she may rest with all your saints in the eternal habitations; where with the Father and the Holy Spirit you live and reign, one God, for ever and ever. *Amen!*" Father Anne's voice rang out, defiant and commanding.

Abruptly, the weight on my chest vanished. Millicent let out one long, furious wail at being denied her vengeance, and then the sound cut off, and the energy in the room shifted.

Millicent was gone.

"Cassidy!" Father Anne's boots ground the glass beneath them to powder as she squatted next to me. "Are you okay?"

"I need to pick the glass out of my skin and rinse it out of my hair," I replied, hesitant to move and scared to open my eyes.

"Stay still," Father Anne commanded. She'd had her back to the last rain of glass, and I hoped that meant she had avoided quite as much exposure. I heard her leave the room, and several minutes later, she returned.

"I'm going to pull you up," she told me and reached down to grip my wrist. Once she had me on my feet, she guided me out into the hallway and into the bathroom.

"Let me clean you up." From the concern in her voice, I stayed still and didn't argue. Blood trickled down my neck and cheek, and I felt like a pincushion.

"I'm going to wrap a wet towel around your hair until you can shower and get any glass out." Moments later I heard water running.

"Let's rinse your arms under the water, and your face, too."

The water sluiced away the splinters, and I resisted the urge to rub, not wanting to push more shards into my skin. Father Anne helped me splash my face again and again until I could run my fingers over the skin without finding anything sharp. Only then did I dare open my eyes.

"Wow." Thin trickles of blood mingled with the water on my face, arms, and hands.

"Give it a minute, and you'll stop bleeding. Fortunately, it doesn't look like you've got any serious gashes." Father Anne produced a stiff brush that she'd found somewhere and began to whisk it over my clothing, followed by a quick swipe of another wet towel.

"There. I think that should do it," she said.

"Are you all right?"

She chuckled. "Thanks to you heroically throwing yourself in front of me, I'm fine. I also had my back to the worst of it." Father Anne handed me the brush, and I dusted off her back and shoulders, just in case.

"Is Millicent really gone?" I asked, as the adrenaline from the fight drained away.

Father Anne nodded. "Yeah. You couldn't see it, but when I finished the rite, she vanished, and the whole room felt cleansed."

"Thank you." I blotted my face gingerly, removing the worst of the blood.

"All in a day's work. Unfortunately, the shell art didn't survive."

"I didn't think we should leave it behind. A century of being haunted by a killer ghost has to leave a psychic stain," I said. Of course, explaining that to Alfred might not be quite so easy.

"Come on. Let's clean up the pieces, go report to the auction guy, and get out of here. I think we could both use a shower." Father Anne shouldered her bag, and we headed back to the office.

We found Alfred sitting where we'd left him, and he had obviously been freaking out.

"Is it over? Is she gone?" He looked at me with wide eyes, and I guessed I hadn't washed off all the blood.

"Millicent is gone," I reported. "She attacked us, trying to stop the rite, and in the fight, the art piece got broken." I shook the garbage bag that contained what was left of the shell valentine.

"I never want to see that awful thing again," Alfred replied with a shudder. "Please, take the pieces with you and…burn it or bury it or… just make it go away."

"We can do that," Father Anne said. She shot me a satisfied glance.

"Thank you." Alfred looked from one of us to the other. "I don't know what I would have done without your help."

I smiled and shrugged. "Happy to help." From the abashed look on Alfred's face, I didn't think I needed to add any warnings about buying art from shady brokers or avoiding pieces that "spoke" to him. He probably wouldn't be handling any new acquisitions himself for a long time.

We found a box to safely transport the ruined art.

"I'll get rid of this," she said, taking it from me when we walked out to the parking lot. "Thanks for having my back in there."

I grinned. "What are friends for?" I groaned when I glanced at the time. "Crap. I need to get home and clean up. I'm supposed to have dinner with Kell tonight, and it would be nice not to look like an extra from a horror movie."

My boyfriend knew about the *other* side of my work, and he'd been part of some big showdowns. It didn't hurt that he ran a paranormal investigation group, meaning I didn't have to convince him that spooky stuff was real.

"Go. Have fun. I'll burn what's left of the art while I write my homily for Sunday," Father Anne said. "I'm thinking that this week's message will be about keeping your promises," she added with a wink.

"Sounds like a winner. Might be a nice touch to add something about letting go of grudges," I replied with a wan smile. Given what we deal with, if we couldn't share some dark humor, we'd probably all go nuts.

"Good idea. Now go—get cleaned up for your date. And call me if you find out anything else about the artwork. If it's stolen, there might be more where it came from."

I felt a chill at her words, despite the warm Charleston temperature. As I waved goodbye and got in my car, I had the feeling she was right —and that trouble was headed our way.

CHAPTER TWO

"The food is fantastic—and I love the atmosphere." I looked around Elwood's and felt right at home. The restaurant where Kell had gotten us a reservation was located in a converted old house just off King Street and named for the owner's childhood dog. A statue of a Shetland sheepdog sat on the front porch, and dog pictures, paintings, and cartoons hung on the walls. Shelves displayed dog-themed bric-a-brac, and the menu assured us that asking for a "doggy bag" was no problem.

Kell grinned and gave my hand a squeeze. "I know how crazy you are about Baxter," he replied, naming my adorable Maltese, "and I figured you'd enjoy it here." He leaned in as if to share a secret. "I bet Bax would appreciate it if you brought him some of your meal in one of those bags. Just sayin'."

"I'll think about it," I replied with a laugh. "And if we let him have some popcorn when we watch a movie, I think he'll get over not being invited to come along." Baxter loved snuggling on the couch with us while we watched TV, and popcorn was a favorite treat.

Kell Winston and I had been an item for over a year now, and I liked how comfortable we were together. It helped that Kell knew the truth about my "side gig" stopping spooky threats and that he'd been a believer in the supernatural before we met.

"How's the video business?" I asked. By day, Kell ran a production company that shot commercials, corporate training films, and even some independent TV shows. At night, he ran SPOOK, the Southeastern Paranormal Observation and Outreach Klub, a team of paranormal investigators that chased ghost stories all over the Lowcountry. That was how we met, since Teag and I ended up running into the SPOOK folks more than once tracking down dangerous haunts.

"It's been good," Kell replied, doing his best to stifle a yawn. He downed his cup of coffee and signaled the server for a refill. After a terrific meal of fried green tomatoes with homemade chutney, award-winning fried chicken, and house specialty mashed potatoes that had local foodies all abuzz, we were waiting for dessert—a Sundrop pound cake that promised total sugar overload.

If he was fighting off a food coma, I could understand the yawn. We'd been having fun, so I knew I hadn't put him to sleep. But now that I really looked, I could see the dark circles under his eyes.

"Burning the midnight oil on a big project?" I teased. It wouldn't be the first time. Neither of us kept regular hours.

He shook his head. "Not exactly, although business has been good, thank God. It's just that lately, Charleston's ghosts have gotten downright weird."

I finished my sweet tea, and the server refilled my glass before I had a chance to ask. Between the tea and the pound cake, I might be wired until morning.

"Weird, how?" We tried not to talk shop on dates, but given how passionate we both were about what we did, it was hard not to break that rule.

"I don't know whether it's just the full moon or Mercury in retrograde, but we've had double the usual number of emails and posts to the blog reporting ghost sightings," he replied. "And they're not the usual Charleston ghosts. If you know what I mean."

Odd as it might sound, I did. Charleston was known for being one of the most haunted cities in the U.S. Given its history, we had plenty of ghostly pirates, smugglers, rum runners, jilted lovers, unlucky dualists, Confederate soldiers, and criminals. Every ghost had a story rooted in the city's long history.

"What's so unusual?"

Kell downed another cup of coffee. "Some of the places people reported seeing ghosts have a history of being haunted, but they've been quiet for years. Now, apparently, they've woken up—orbs, moaning, footsteps, cold spots, shadow figures. But why?"

"Any area in particular?" I couldn't shake the feeling there was more to the story than we knew.

"Mostly down toward the waterfront," Kell replied. "A lot of Charleston's shady history took place near the port or the old Navy Yard, or the bars, rooming houses, and brothels that catered to that crowd."

I'd had some run-ins with ghosts in those locations, and knew how crazy it could get. But Kell was right—most of those places had been quiet for a while. What had riled up the ghosts?

"Last night, I talked to a man who said he and his friends were chased by a rolling cow that was dragging clanking chains. He swore the cow tried to knock them into the Ashley River."

"Okay, that's different." I'd run into the ghosts of serial killers and people killed by witches and cursed objects, but I'd never dealt with a ghostly killer cow before.

"You're not kidding," Kell said. "The thing is—I believe the guy. He and his buddy had been drinking, but they weren't drunk, and they were legit terrified. I don't think he made it up. I mean, if you were just doing it for the attention, that kind of story is more likely to get you trolled than get you on TV."

"Anything else?"

"Believe it or not—yeah. Two men said they were walking back from one of the bars that's just off the historic district when this sexy woman in a long dress came on to them. They remember her having a hat that was angled so they couldn't see her face. They weren't interested—turns out, they were already a couple. That's when she lifted her hat and showed what one guy called a 'monster face,' and then she chased them. That's not even the strangest thing," he added.

"When she was running after them, they said that they could see through the slit in her skirt that one of her legs looked like a cow leg." He leaned back with an expression that dared me to top that tale.

"What is it with cows?" I asked. "That's definitely strange. Do you think they were drunk—or high?"

Kell shrugged. "Like the other guy who called, they sounded really scared. I don't know what to think."

"Are you going to investigate?" As bizarre as the stories were, I had a hunch they needed to be looked into.

He grinned. "Want to come with me? Before I haul the whole team out, I want to interview the people who phoned in the reports, so we don't go on a wild goose chase. Not only does that waste time, but it's a lot of work setting up a shoot. And since they were on public streets, there would be a lot of red tape involved.".

"With no guarantee the ghost would show," I said, thinking out loud. "Sure. I'm in." I chuckled. "And just when I thought that it couldn't get weirder than a killer 'valentine.'" I'd filled Kell in on the incident at the auction house when he first picked me up because I had to explain the tiny little cuts that dotted my face and arms.

"Good," he said with a big smile. "I'm supposed to meet the first two men for coffee tomorrow morning, and the second two guys after that at the diner by the cargo port at ten. They only have a couple of days in town because they work on a ship."

That got my attention. "What kind? One of the cruise ships?"

"I'm not sure," Kell admitted. "They just said that it would have to be tomorrow because their leave is up the next day."

My thoughts were spinning, already wondering if the fact that all four men were crew members mattered. I looked up at Kell. "They all work on ships. They're sailors. And the shell art piece at the auction house was a type of mosaic called a 'sailor's valentine.' Think it's just a coincidence?"

Kell's eyes widened. "Maybe? Although, Charleston's a major port. There are a lot of ships and a lot of sailors. And while we've had more calls than usual to SPOOK, we haven't had enough to account for every sailor in town."

I had the feeling something important was eluding us. Maybe once we talked to the sailors who had seen the strange ghosts, we could see a pattern. "Sounds like we've got a busy morning ahead of us," I said. "Let's go enjoy some downtime while we can."

"I'll make the popcorn. You and Baxter can pick the movie," Kell replied with a grin.

~

DESPITE THE SUGAR rush of the Sundrop cake, we both fell asleep during the movie and dragged ourselves to bed sometime after midnight. The alarm went off far too soon, and then I remembered we had early meetings.

Kell groaned and muttered something about reminding him not to make appointments at the crack of dawn. By the time we'd showered and made it to the kitchen, the coffee pot I'd set the night before had a steaming pot of fresh java ready.

"I'm gonna need that coffee to wake me up enough to go get more coffee with the ghost guys," Kell said, still looking rumpled and adorable. He was tall and lean with light brown hair, blue eyes, and a dark summer tan, a combination I found hard to resist.

"Mornings are evil," I agreed. "Teag and Maggie are going to open the store. And I sent Teag a picture of the sailor's valentine piece from the auction house. He's going to do a little research and see if he can find out anything helpful."

Neither of us were morning people, so the ride to the coffee shop was quiet. I thought Kell looked a little better rested, despite the early wake-up call. Then again, he hadn't been up all night on a stake-out for ghost sightings.

We walked into the Waffle House near the port area and looked around for the men Kell had agreed to meet. I hoped that, once they sobered up, they hadn't decided to skip out on the interview. But a man at one of the back tables hailed Kell, who had apparently given him his description.

Both men were in their early thirties, I guessed. They looked like they did hard work for a living, with muscles that didn't come from a gym. The man on the right had a shaved head and wore a single silver earring. I could make out the bottom edge of a tattoo against his dark skin beneath one shirtsleeve. The man on the right wore his hair military short, and I wondered if he'd been Navy. I caught a glimpse of ink on his right forearm, but not enough to make out the design.

"Thanks for meeting us so early," Kell said as we joined the two men at their table. "I'm Kell, and this is Cassidy. She's part of the team." We'd agreed that was the easiest way to explain why someone who ran an antique shop was asking questions about ghosts.

"This isn't really that early for us. After all, the sun's up," the bald man said. "I'm Marcus, and this is Deshawn." The other man gave us a curt nod. Neither of them looked like the kind of men to drunk dial a paranormal investigator with a made-up story.

Kell ordered coffee for both of us, and we waited for our cups before getting into the conversation. "Tell me what you saw the night you contacted me," Kell said, leaning forward with interest.

The two men exchanged a look. I was afraid they were going to say it was all a mistake, but Marcus clasped his hands on the table in front of him and lifted his chin as if challenging us to doubt him.

"We went over to Mick's Bar to play some billiards," he said, naming a place not too far from the docks. "We had a couple of beers each—*just* a couple. We both got over carousing a long time ago. Hurts too damn much in the morning. We're not teenagers anymore."

Marcus cleared his throat and went on. "The weather was nice, so we decided to save the price of a ride-share and just walk back to the ship. When we got near the river, we were crossing the parking lots, and we heard this weird clanking noise."

"Like chains in a bucket," Deshawn added.

"I've been around ships for a long time," Marcus went on. "What we heard wasn't a normal sound for the docks. So we turned around and saw this…"

"Cow," Deshawn said. "It was a ghost cow, dragging a chain. And it was rolling toward us, across the parking lot."

"Rolling?" I echoed, having trouble imaging the scene.

Deshawn didn't break a smile. "Yes, ma'am. It had its legs folded up, and it rolled right for us, making that awful clanking noise."

"I know it sounds strange," Marcus admitted. "I've spent half my life at sea, and I've seen a lot of strange things. Deshawn here served in the Gulf, in the War." Dashawn nodded. "What I'm saying is, we don't scare easily. But we both just knew that haint meant us harm. So we ran."

"Except it kept changing its path, cutting us off," Deshawn picked up the story. "And then we realized, it wasn't just trying to keep us from getting back to the ship. It meant to force us into the river."

"What did you do?" Kell was caught up in the tale.

"We were running out of dock," Marcus admitted. "And I wasn't about to jump in the river. So I turned toward the ghost, and I grabbed the charm my mama gave me when I went to sea, and I told it to be gone because we were protected."

"I did the same thing," Deshawn said. "My gran swore when she gave me that necklace that it would keep me safe, and I told that ghost it had no hold on me."

"Then what happened?" I asked. I didn't doubt their story. Both men had such quiet dignity that I couldn't imagine that they would risk ridicule by making up a tale. There was nothing to gain, and the very real possibility of losing respect.

"I thought it was going to roll into us, but it just vanished," Marcus said. "It was there one minute, solid enough to knock us into the water, and gone the next. No cow, no clanking chain. Just gone."

"Have you ever heard of such a thing happening to someone else?" Kell asked. I could tell he took them seriously and was trying to figure out the strange apparition.

Both men shook their heads. "I've heard a lot of ghost stories in my time, but I'd have remembered a rolling cow," Marcus said. "And I know it sounds funny, in daylight. But let me tell you, at night, in those big empty parking lots? It was plenty scary."

"Would you mind telling me about the charms—medals—you used for protection?" I still had no idea what we were dealing with, so I wanted all the details I could get. I'd learned from experience that little things could turn out to be very important.

Marcus pulled a chain from beneath his shirt. On it hung a silver anchor with a cross-piece near the top. "It's a St. Clement's cross," he told me. "For protection against evil."

Deshawn did the same, but a different medallion hung from his chain. The oval charm had an image of a man in monk's robes standing in front of water and a lighthouse. "St. Brendan the Navigator," he explained. "Patron saint of sailors."

I didn't know much about either saint, but I intended to do some research as soon as we got back to the store.

"What ship do you sail with?" Kell asked. I noticed he'd gotten so engrossed in the story that he let his coffee go cold.

"The *Caribe Queen*," Marcus answered. "It's a cargo ship. We make the Charleston-Bermuda-Caribbean run. It's mostly bringing stuff like sugar, rum, bananas, and mineral ore up from the islands, and coming back with things they can't make there, which is pretty much everything from the mainland. Parts for machinery, industrial supplies. It's not exciting, but it's a living," he added with a shrug.

Kell dug out business cards and handed one to each man. "We believe you. If anything else weird happens, please call me or email me. Whatever came after you might attack someone else—and they might not be so well prepared."

When we had paid the bill and gotten coffee to go, Kell and I headed to the car.

"What did you make of that?" he asked me as we sat with the AC on, sipping our drinks.

"I believe them. They seem like reliable witnesses. They don't gain anything by making up stories. It'll be interesting to see what the other two people have to say."

We had some time before our next meeting, so while Kell glanced through email on his phone, I called my cousin, Simon.

"Cassidy! Great to hear from you. What's up?" Simon's a psychic medium who runs Grand Strand Ghost Tours in Myrtle Beach, and he works with the police there—and his homicide detective boyfriend—to solve supernatural crimes. Before he moved to the beach, Simon earned his Ph.D. in folklore and mythology and taught at USC. He was on my shortlist of people to ask about legends and lore.

"I need your help," I replied. "Can you spare a moment?"

"I've always got time for my favorite cousin," Simon assured me with a laugh. "Tell me what you need."

"Hold on while I put you on speakerphone. I'm with Kell." I changed the setting and put the phone between us while Kell and Simon exchanged greetings. "What do you know about rolling cow ghosts with clanking chains?" I asked. "Or a ghostly woman with an ugly face and one leg that has a hoof?"

"You don't fool around, do you? Okay, anything else unusual, besides the obvious?"

"The men who saw the ghosts were sailors, and the ghosts showed up in a waterfront area," I told him. "And medals for St. Clement and St. Brendan the Navigator worked against the cow ghost."

"I'm going to bet those are Caribbean ghosts," Simon replied. "The woman's ghost sounds a lot like the legend of La Diablesse. There are plenty of variations, but the monstrous face and animal leg are always part of the description. As for the rolling cow…my bet is a duppy."

"A guppy?" Kell echoed. I was just as lost, because that's what I heard, too.

"Duppy," Simon repeated. "It's a type of restless spirit that shows up in the folklore of Jamaica, Barbados, and some of the other nearby islands. Has its roots in African lore. The rolling cow is a common story."

"Maybe even the ghosts get into a little too much rum down in the islands," Kell said. "I wouldn't have believed the cow could be scary if I hadn't heard Marcus and Deshawn tell their story."

"There are some pretty weird ghosts in folklore," Simon replied. "And they're all dangerous. If you'd been brought up with the legends, they'd be your boogiemen."

"So, how do we banish them?" I asked. Simon didn't know the full story about the kinds of big threats we'd dealt with here in Charleston, but he did know Teag and I got rid of haunted and cursed objects and busted troublesome ghosts.

"Rice," Simon said. "Duppies are a little OCD. If you throw rice in front of them, they have to stop until they count every grain. Salt can weaken them, and a salt ring can contain them—for a while. Those saints you mention are protectors of sailors and particularly revered in the islands."

"How about getting rid of the ghosts for good?" Kell asked.

"I'm going to have to look into that and call you back," Simon admitted. "Usually, there's a personal reason the duppy attacks someone. La Diablesse might go after a man who is unfaithful. The rolling cow may chase someone who has evaded justice."

"We can check, but I don't think that's the case here. Is there anything that might make a Jamaican ghost randomly attack people hundreds of miles from the Caribbean?" I was afraid I might already know the answer.

"When ghosts don't act the way they ought to, my bet is on some kind of curse or a haunted object," Simon said, confirming my suspicion. "Do you know if all four men were crew on the same ship?"

"Not yet," Kell said. "We're heading over to talk to the other two men next."

"There could be someone else on the ship who is under a geas," Simon speculated. "Some kind of supernatural obligation that hasn't been fulfilled. A deal with a witch or a demon, or unfinished business. The ghosts the men saw might have been 'spillover'—-manifestations caused by the cursed or possessed person, not really meant for them. Or—"

"Or?" I was really hoping there was another alternative.

"There could be something on the ship that is haunted, something that's attracting the spirits, or brought them along for the ride."

"It's a container ship," Kell said, looking up from his phone where he'd done a search on *Caribe Queen.* "Finding a cursed object on a ship like that..." He didn't have to finish his sentence. Even if we could get access—which didn't seem likely—it would take forever.

"You might be able to access the manifests," Simon suggested. "If you knew where the cargo originated, you could be able to narrow down the possibilities." He paused. "And I'm just going from what I studied or learned from books. You know Lucinda Walker, right? The folklore professor? She might be able to tell you more. Duppies don't have anything to do with Voudon, which is Lucinda's specialty, but a lot of the folklore from those islands overlaps."

"Thanks, Simon," I said. "You and Vic need to figure out when you can come down here for some time off. It's been too long since we've gotten together."

"That sounds like a great plan," he replied. "Once the current unpleasantness is over, let's make it happen."

I ended the call and looked at Kell. "Duppies, huh?"

"Let's go see the other two guys," he replied. "And then I'll check on the manifest."

"I'll call Lucinda, and try to catch her after classes," I replied. "Simon knows Lucinda from academic circles when he used to be a professor. He knows that she's a mambo, but not that she's helped us actually fight monsters."

Lucinda was a close friend and a powerful ally. As an experienced Voudon mambo, she could call on the Loas themselves in dire circumstances. She'd helped us defeat demons, deadly curses, even rampaging Nephilim. The Caribbean was her area of expertise. If there was a way to dispel the duppies, Lucinda was our best bet to find out.

We were both deep in thought as we headed to the diner to meet up with the guys who had encountered what Simon called La Diablesse. When we pulled up, two men in leather jackets were waiting in the parking lot. I would have made them for bikers, but I could imagine them as sailors, with a hint of pirate on the side. One was tall and broad-shouldered, with shoulder-length black hair and two full sleeves of tattoos. His partner stood a few inches shorter, with a slender, wiry build, and ropy arms also fully covered in tats.

"I'm Kell. This is Cassidy," Kell said.

"Tom," the bigger man said. "And this is my husband, Pete."

"Thanks for meeting us," Kell said. "Let's get a table. We want to hear your story."

The diner smelled of coffee, bacon grease, and fried food. Given the hard-working customers—all of whom looked like they bench-pressed small cars for a light workout—I figured the food had to be good. No one would risk having these guys riot over bad burgers. All the same, I found I didn't have an appetite. I was starting to have a bad feeling about the duppies. What had begun as a ghost hunt looked like it might be quickly turning into something more serious.

Tom and Pete found a booth and sat down, and we slipped in on the other side. "So, you're a ghost hunter?" Tom asked, looking Kell up and down.

"We both investigate paranormal phenomena," Kell replied.

"That's really something people do?" Pete asked, his expression skeptical and fascinated at the same time. He leaned forward. "Do you fight the ghosts, like those guys on TV, or do you walk around old houses with those night vision cameras looking for ghosts?"

The truth was actually "both," but that was more than Tom and Pete needed to know.

"Mostly the cameras," Kell admitted. "But we do have some resources to banish ghosts that cause problems. It's not quite as exciting as fighting them, but it keeps people from getting hurt." I'd seen Kell go full shotgun on dangerous spirits, but I wasn't going to mention it.

Pete looked a little disappointed. "Oh. Okay. I guess that makes sense."

Tom sighed with fond exasperation. "He binge-watches hit shows when we can get a signal." He glanced from Kell to me. "So why did you want to meet up?"

"The ghost you mentioned in the email sounds dangerous. It's the kind of thing we try to dispel," Kell replied.

"It sure seemed dangerous enough to us, at the time," Pete muttered. Tom bumped his shoulder supportively.

"We were leaving John Swann's," Tom said, naming a popular bar named for an infamous gay pirate, "and we'd each had a few beers, but that's not even enough for a buzz. We were going to take a walk before we called a ride back to the ship. Nice night, and all that. There were still a fair number of people around on the main streets. We turned down a side street—and all of a sudden, there she is."

"She had a big, broad-brimmed hat, angled down so we couldn't see her face, and she was wearing a clingy dress slit almost to the hip," Pete took over. "Very curvy—if you like that sort of thing."

"She picked the wrong guys to proposition," Tom added. "Not that it doesn't happen in other ports. I guess some ladies see it as a challenge. But we told her very politely that we weren't interested, and just kept on walking."

"That's when I heard this *clip-clop* sound, like hooves," Pete said. "I thought maybe one of those carriage tours was coming, and we should move to the side. But what I saw—" He shuddered, and Tom laid a hand on his arm.

"She tipped her head up. Her face looked like a zombie, all rotted and bones showing," Tom picked up the story. "And when she ran, her skirt flared out, and we could see that one leg…it wasn't human. It looked like something from a cow, or a deer, or maybe a horse. With a hoof at the end."

"How did you get away?" I asked.

"We ran to the end of the street," Pete said. "And there was a church. Those are usually safe—on TV. We went up the steps and banged on the door. It was closed, but when we turned around, she was gone."

"Consecrated ground," I said. "Many darker spirits can't follow you there."

"I don't know what she would have done if she'd have caught us, but it wouldn't have been anything good," Pete replied.

"What ship are you on?" Kell asked.

"The *Caribe Queen*," Tom replied. "Why?"

"We just talked to a couple of other sailors from that ship who were chased by a different ghost. Both their ghost and yours are spirits associated with the Caribbean islands. Do you know if the ship picked up any unusual cargo on this last trip?"

Tom shrugged. "It's all just big boxes to us. Pete and I have been doing that run for a couple of years now, and nothing like this ever happened—not that we've heard about. And I'm pretty sure there'd have been talk, if this happened a lot. Sailors are superstitious. I don't think Captain Ellison would have taken on a shipment if he thought it would cause problems."

"He might not have known," I mused. "Especially if whatever-it-is got handled by intermediaries."

"But why haunt us?" Pete asked.

"Maybe it wasn't haunting you in particular," Kell said. "Maybe you were just in the wrong place at the wrong time."

"I'm glad we had those tats," Pete said quietly.

"Which tats?" I hoped I wasn't overstepping. Ink can be a very personal topic.

Tom and Pete slid up their shirtsleeves to expose more of the tattoos on their forearms.

"That's my compass rose," Tom said, pointing to a design that reminded me of the multi-pointed star on a map. "It's supposed to protect sailors."

"And this is my hen and pig," Pete added. "They're supposed to be lucky because they can swim."

"Well, they worked," I said. "Keep on believing in them. They certainly could have helped turn the ghost away."

"What are you going to do about her?" Tom asked, tugging at his sleeve.

"See what we can find out about the cargo that got off-loaded here in Charleston," Kell replied. "That's a starting point." He handed them both business cards. "If you hear about anything strange being in the containers on this last run, call me. It might be important."

"Were there any big crew changes, coming up from the Caribbean?" I asked.

Tom and Pete thought for a moment. "People always come and go, depending on their contracts," Tom said finally. "But Captain Ellison is a good man, and people aren't trying to change ships the way they do when the captain is a son of a—"

Pete cleared his throat loudly, and Tom caught himself. "—gun," he finished with a smile. "In fact, we've said that we like how little turnover there's been with the crew on this ship. If you've got good people and they get along, it's rare."

"Were there any unusual incidents during the last leg of the trip?" Kell asked. "Anything hard to explain?"

Pete nodded. "Yeah. Like Tom said—sailors are superstitious. Talking about something makes it real, so people just don't say anything. But there was some strange shi—stuff—going on. Odd knocking sounds on bulkheads. Voices, where there shouldn't be anyone. Singing at odd times and places."

"Nobody said they saw a ghost," Tom added. "But the guys who work in the hold and the lower decks started going down in pairs this trip. I thought it was some new safety rule, but maybe they didn't like being alone. It's creepy on a good day."

"And that guy at the port, when we left," Pete said quietly.

Tom nodded. "I forgot about him." He looked at Kell and me. "No one shows up to wave goodbye to cargo ships. It's not like a cruise ship. We leave at all hours. But this last time, when we left Barbados, there was an island man in a white shirt and pants who stood back from everything, just watching. Didn't say anything, didn't bother anyone. It was strange. And when we started to pull away from the dock, he was still there and he waved. But…the look on his face was more like 'good riddance' than 'have a nice trip,' if that makes any sense."

It did—if the man was a witch and knew that bad mojo was leaving his island. *Or a ghost.*

"We'd better let you get back to your ship," Kell said. "Thank you for talking to us. We're going to do everything we can to keep people safe."

"Thanks for taking us seriously," Pete said. "I hope you figure out how to stop that thing so no one gets hurt."

When we got back to the car, I had a text from Lucinda, letting me know when she would be back in her office. "Do you want to head over with me?" I asked Kell.

"I need to finish a video for a client," he said with a sigh. "I should get home. Call me and let me know what you find out, okay?"

I promised to fill him in on the scoop, and he drove me back to my house so I could get my car. He leaned in for a kiss before I got out, and his smile made my heart beat a little faster. "See you for dinner tonight?"

"I'll pick up Chinese take-out on the way," he said. "You want the usual?"

"Surprise me." I got out and waved as he drove away, then headed for my car and drove to the College of Charleston.

"CASSIDY! Come in and have a seat. It's always good to see you." Dr. Lucinda Walker welcomed me into her office. Bookshelves lined the walls of the small space, with folk art carvings, pottery, and other decorations. Most people would see them as colorful souvenirs, but I knew, even from a distance, that they carried magical resonance. I spotted several Voudon *veves* among the art pieces and recognized the intricate designs as being sacred to Papa Legba and Erzulie Dantor, two of the most powerful Loas.

Lucinda's pumpkin-orange jacket complimented her dark skin, and the batik-print blouse beneath it set off the handmade necklace that was as much protective amulet as decoration. She and I both knew what lurked in the shadows, and we made sure not to leave ourselves unprotected. My fingers touched my silver and agate necklace, which was my own protective amulet.

"Good to see you, too," I agreed, taking a seat in front of her desk. She smiled and came around to sit next to me, which spared me flashbacks of visiting my advisor from my college days.

"I'm guessing this isn't a social visit."

"I wish it were," I replied. "By the way, Simon says hello."

"Tell that boy he needs to call me," Lucinda replied with a sparkle in her dark eyes. "Now that he's got himself a man of his own, he doesn't stay in touch."

"From what I gather, he and Vic have had their hands full with some supernatural problems up in Myrtle Beach."

"Humph," she dismissed my comment. "That's no excuse. But I'm not surprised he's become a protector. With those gifts of his, he just needed to be in the right place to put them to use." She smiled. "Does he know about what you and Teag do here?"

"Not really," I confessed. I knew I'd have to come clean to Simon at some point, given how often I called him for information. I had just wanted to protect him from the dark truth for as long as possible. Lucinda gave me a look that told me I should let him know sooner rather than later.

"Now, what brings you here?" she asked.

"What can you tell me about duppies?"

She raised an eyebrow. "Well, now. That's interesting. Why do you ask?"

Lucinda listened while I told her about the haunted shell picture, the rolling cow ghost, and the appearance of La Diablesse, then finished with our conjecture about the cargo on the *Caribe Queen*.

"I think you're right," she said after I finished. "Since we haven't seen those ghosts here before, their appearance when the ship docked is too convenient to be coincidence."

"Is there a way to dispel the ghosts so they don't hurt anyone?"

Lucinda paused, thinking, then shook her head. "Without dealing with whatever's called them? No. They're the symptom, not the real problem. You were able to stop the ghost who haunted the sailor's valentine because you could destroy the object she attached to. But having a piece like that show up at the same time the other ghosts manifested? There's probably a connection if you know where to look."

"Kell intended to ask Teag to help him find the manifests for the *Caribe Queen*. Even if we can't find out the exact contents of each crate, I'm hoping that there will be some kind of information on the owners or origins that gives us something to work with," I replied. "I hate having to wait until someone else gets hurt to make the next move."

"The duppies aren't Voudon, but both have their roots in old African beliefs. And until we can figure out what has energized the ghosts, perhaps we can keep them at bay with protections from the same traditions."

"Both of the attacks happened in public places," I reminded her. "That makes it harder to lay down salt lines, or wash down the area with Four Thieves vinegar," I added, referencing the Hoodoo protection our mutual friend, Mrs. Teller, often recommended.

"Maybe, maybe not," she replied. "I'll give Ernestine Teller a call and see what we can come up with when we put our heads together. It won't banish the ghosts, but we might be able to drain their power so they can't do real harm. And meanwhile, you chase down what came in on that ship and who owns it."

If anyone could figure out a way to deal with the ghosts, it would be a mambo and a powerful root worker. I knew Lucinda and Mrs. Teller were up for the challenge.

"Thank you. I can't shake the feeling that there's more to this than a few haunted objects. My gut tells me that it's going to require some time to unsnarl this mess."

"Then we'd better get started," she replied with a grin. "Since ghosts wait for no one."

CHAPTER THREE

"You didn't miss much," Teag told me when I arrived at Trifles and Folly that afternoon. "It's been a pretty slow day."

Slow days are rare at the store. Charleston's tourist traffic is year-round, and some people want a unique souvenir, like a piece of estate jewelry or a vintage cup and saucer. Design professionals come in looking for just the right item to complement a client's project. And locals stop by looking for the perfect gift for the person who has everything. Since Teag and I go over every item with our magic before it's offered for sale, our customers never end up taking home bad juju with their special treasure.

I take pride in running a profitable business, but the truth is the salary that Teag and I are paid compensates us for the risks of our supernatural activities as well as our duties at the store. My business partner, Sorren, is a nearly six-hundred-year-old vampire who founded the store with my ancestor back in the 1600s and is a leader of the Alliance. So while the traffic at the store might have been slow, my morning with Kell was anything but.

"Nice for you," I said, stepping behind the counter to give Maggie a break. "My day just keeps getting crazier."

At the moment, there were no customers in the shop, so we could talk without being overheard.

"I hate to continue your streak, but between walk-ins, I did a little digging on the questions you sent me," Teag said. His Weaver magic means he can weave spells into cloth, but it also gives him a magical edge in weaving data into information, making him one hell of a hacker. "Why don't you tell me what you and Kell learned, and then maybe I can fill in some of the blanks."

I caught him up on everything that had happened, including my visit with Lucinda. "After that crazy ghost with the shell valentine, now we get two more spirits with ties to the islands—ones that I don't ever remember hearing about popping up in Charleston." I shook my head. "There's got to be a connection."

"Charleston's had a lot of trade with the Caribbean over its history," Teag mused. "Probably even more in the past than it does today. I agree that there has to be a common thread."

"Tell me what you've found," I said, taking a seat on one of the tall stools behind the counter.

"I can't solve your ghost problem just yet, but I'm trying to solve the mystery of the *Caribe Queen's* manifest. I don't think that the paperwork they provided to the customs inspectors was completely accurate."

"You think they're smuggling?"

He shook his head. "No. At least, I don't think the crew is involved in anything like that. More like some of the owners of the cargo containers and the contents that are listed don't check out. There are discrepancies I'm still looking into, both in some of the containers' origins and in the total number of containers. Which is pretty much what you'd expect if someone was bringing in something that was magically 'hot.'"

"All right. That sounds like our best lead."

"If I can't turn something up by tonight, I'm going to see if Seth Tanner can find anything through some of his connections."

"The hunter?" I hadn't met Seth in person, but I knew that Teag and Simon helped him with research chasing down the dark warlocks he had sworn to stop.

"Yeah. He's a 'white hat' hacker, so he gets hired by companies to find their security flaws. He doesn't have my magic, but he has some pretty impressive skills. And he knows how to spot bad magic."

"Whatever works," I replied. "Anything else?"

"Funny you should ask." Teag's grin told me I was in for trouble. "I have alerts set on some of the sites I monitor in case anything that's our kind of strange turns up. Things like unusual attacks, odd disappearances, or weird deaths. And there have been three autopsy requests in the past week that definitely fall under 'weird.'"

"How weird?"

"Well, one man died of nitrogen bubbles in the blood. That's usually referred to as 'the bends,' because it happens to divers who go down deep and then surface too quickly. But this guy hadn't left his house."

"Definitely strange," I agreed.

"Then someone else got stabbed through the heart," Teag continued. "Except that the coroner found odd residue in the wound and sent it in for analysis. The lab identified cells from the horn of a narwhal. But the dead woman was found in her office, nowhere near the ocean. Police report said the body hadn't been moved. So when did narwhals start killing people on dry land?"

"Okay, that's a whole new meaning to 'land shark,'" I said, and Teag grimaced at my bad joke. "How about the third one?"

"Just a guy who drowned—in his living room, in front of witnesses. Autopsy found seawater in his lungs. Witnesses said he had a normal day—until he started coughing up water and died."

"I'm amazed they've been able to keep those out of the news."

"The autopsy reports haven't been made public yet," Teag replied. "And what reporter wants to break a story that's going to either start a panic or make them a laughingstock?"

"So we've gone from odd ghosts to some type of supernatural killer. And we don't know if they're connected, or whether we should be looking for a witch or a creature or a cursed object," I summed up. "And Kell says that there's been a spike in sightings."

"So someone—or something—could either be spooking the spooks or juicing up their energy." Teag and I had run into both scenarios in the past, and they spelled trouble.

"Lucinda said it's not Voudon. Do you think we've got a renegade witch?"

Teag shook his head. "Rowan would have given us a heads-up," he countered, mentioning a gifted practitioner who had helped us out a number of times.

"Unless the coven wanted to handle it on their own."

"That doesn't feel right," Teag argued. "I think we're missing something."

"All right," I agreed. "See what you and Seth can hack. I'll give Kell an update. Maybe he's got any new information. I wish Sorren wasn't out of the country." Sorren had a network of shops like Trifles and Folly all around the world. He'd been in Europe dealing with problems, and I didn't feel right about calling him until I had something more concrete to report.

"We'll figure it out," Teag assured me.

"When you're looking into the manifests for the *Caribe Queen*, can you check when it came into port?"

"Three days ago," he answered. "That means it wasn't anywhere near here when the weird deaths happened."

"Damn. So, whatever might be on the ship isn't behind *all* the strange happenings."

"Apparently not. But that doesn't rule out another type of connection."

I hated feeling useless, and right now I had hit a dead end. "Okay. Just let me know when you find something."

We got hit with a gaggle of tourists just then, which brought the conversation to a halt and helped me put the problem out of my mind, at least for the moment. By the time they finished shopping, and we rang up their purchases, it was time to close for the night.

"Is Anthony working late?" I asked after Maggie bid us goodbye.

"Not tonight. He finished up a big case, and he's coming up early. I think we'll go out and celebrate," Teag replied. Anthony Benton was Teag's long-time partner. They'd been a couple for a while now, and we often double-dated. Anthony came from a well-connected old Charleston family, and he was a lawyer in the family firm.

"Have fun. Kell promised to bring Chinese take-out when he finishes up the project he was working on. You know Baxter will want to steal all the broccoli." My little Maltese loved vegetables. Go figure.

"Give Bax a hug for me," Teag said. "And tell him I'll bring him carrots the next time I come over."

"I SWEAR they have the best General Tso's chicken in town," I said when Kell and I finished our meal. Kell's beef with broccoli gave him plenty of treats to slip to Baxter, and we made quick work of the egg rolls and steamed dumplings. Baxter planted his little furry white butt on my feet, giving me pleading looks, hoping for more treats.

"That's why the restaurant keeps winning awards," he agreed, surveying the empty containers that littered the table.

We had just started cleaning up when his phone rang. Kell glanced at the number and frowned, giving me a shake of his head to indicate he didn't recognize the caller. He pressed the speaker button so I could hear.

"Hello?"

"Kell Winston? Grace Winston's son?"

His expression turned wary. "Who is this?"

"My name is Miranda Adams. I'm a friend of your mother's. And...I need help. I think a ghost killed my husband."

WE SHOWED up at Mrs. Adams's home fifteen minutes later. Any plans for a relaxing evening had ended when the call came, but Kell could hardly turn down her plea for help, and he wanted me to go with him.

"Thank you for coming on such short notice," she said, ushering us inside. The townhome was South of Broad, in a pricy and desirable section of Charleston. Antiques and expensive accent pieces set off a home that had clearly been decorated by a professional. Her casual slacks and twinset were designer-label, and her stylish haircut didn't come cheap. The Adams's had money. And, apparently, a ghost problem.

As soon as I stepped inside, my magic triggered. When there's a strong enough resonance, I can pick up on the energy just from standing in a place. Right now, I registered old, foul magic and recent death.

Kell gave me a look that said he saw my response and recognized what it meant. I nodded, letting him know I was all right. I reached for my silver and agate necklace, and as soon as my fingers closed over the amulet, I felt calm and strong. Still, something with powerfully bad juju had been here, so I intended to be very careful about what I touched. Getting a full-blown vision might give me important information, but it came at a high toll—headaches, nausea, and sometimes passing out. Kell knew how to handle me if that happened, but the recovery sucked.

"I didn't realize that my mom talked about SPOOK," Kell said as Miranda brought us into the living room and gestured for us to have a seat.

"She thinks it's pretty interesting—and brave," Miranda replied. "She's always telling us about what you've posted on your blog. I should have called you right away, but I was just so shaken by this."

"How can we help? I'm Cassidy Kincaide, and I'm often part of Kell's team."

Miranda's half-smile vanished, and despite her stoic exterior, I could see the grief and loss in her eyes. "My husband, Edward, died last week, and the circumstances weren't normal. The coroner said it was nitrogen bubbles in the blood, and asked if Edward was into any strange drugs or fetish play." She rolled her eyes. "Neither of those were Edward's thing. I told them that, but they just gave me a look that said they think he was up to something behind my back."

My pulse raced as I realized this was one of the weird deaths Teag had discovered. "We're sorry for your loss," I replied. I knew that not everyone was comfortable showing their grief in front of strangers. Miranda struck me as a very private person.

"You think it was something supernatural behind his death?" Kell asked.

She nodded. "Edward was a collector. We traveled all over the world, and he loved to bring home unusual items. He also scoured the internet and was always buying pieces from obscure sites. I warned him that he could get into trouble, but he didn't listen."

"What kind of trouble?" Kell asked.

Miranda hesitated and then answered. "Edward wouldn't have knowingly broken the law. He always declared his purchases when we came back from abroad. But not everyone on the internet is who they say they are. I was afraid that he'd end up buying something that was a fake—or worse, stolen or dangerous." She bit her lip. "And I'm scared that I was right."

Kell and I exchanged a look. "Had Edward bought new items recently?"

She nodded. "That by itself isn't strange. We have money. Edward liked to shop. There were worse ways he could have spent his time, so I didn't complain. The pieces I liked, we put in the main rooms. The ones that were a little more…unusual…he put in his den."

"Define 'unusual,'" I said.

Miranda shrugged uncomfortably. "Some of the artwork gave me the willies. They didn't seem to bother Edward, and I didn't want to spoil his fun. But I wasn't sad when he sold off a few of the pieces. When he got the new items, I stopped going in the den."

"But these new pieces didn't make Edward uncomfortable?" Kell asked.

"No. If anything, he was fascinated with them. That last week, he spent more time in his den than usual. I had to knock on the door or text him to get him to the dinner table. That was odd, but I figured he was just admiring his new 'toys.'" She looked pensive. "If I'd have known they were really dangerous, I would have made him get rid of them. I wish I'd have just thrown those boxes out when they showed up."

"Would you mind showing us Edward's den?" Kell asked. "We might learn a lot from seeing the pieces."

Miranda nodded, and her expression told me she was plucking up her courage. "Yes. And I can tell you which ones are the newest. But after what happened, I never want to go in that room again."

"I'm sorry to ask, but can you tell us what happened the night Edward died?" I asked. We needed to know, but I hated to put Miranda through reliving the event.

She took a deep breath and nodded. "I'd started trying to get Edward out of the house more. We're retired, so that doesn't happen without some planning. I thought it improved his mood, and it got him off the computer and interacting with real people," she said with a sad smile.

"We had gone out for lunch and run errands, regular stuff. He wanted to take a walk when we got back, so we went down to White Point Garden and walked along the Battery, then sat and looked out at the ocean." Miranda wiped away a tear, and we waited for her to collect herself.

"He talked about selling the house here and moving to our beach house full time. The property in town is expensive to maintain, and it's more than we need. It's something we've discussed for years, but this time I think Edward was serious. He even said he'd sell off most of his collection, so he didn't have to pay to store it when we moved to a smaller house. I told him I was ready to go whenever he was."

"What happened next?"

Miranda looked past me, staring over my shoulder as she relived that night in her mind. "We ate dinner out and then came back to the house. He was in good spirits. Everything seemed fine. It was still early, so I went into the kitchen to run the dishwasher, and he went into his den. We were going to watch TV, and I went to remind him. I got worried when he didn't answer the door."

She swallowed hard and paled at the memory. "I went in and found him on the floor. He was having a seizure," Miranda said. "His skin was mottled, and he had trouble breathing. I called 911 and tried to help him, but he passed out before the ambulance came. He never woke up."

"I'm very sorry," Kell said. "Did Edward have any medical conditions that might have caused those symptoms?"

Miranda shook her head. "No. He was in good health. A little high blood pressure, but it was controlled. None of his medicines were unusual. That was one of the first things I went over with his doctor in the hospital. They couldn't explain it."

I couldn't tell Miranda that the autopsy results Teag had hacked included a toxicology screen that came back negative. Edward hadn't been shooting up designer drugs. That made a supernatural cause look like the prime suspect.

"Let's go see his den," Kell suggested. "Maybe we'll get some ideas from that."

Kell and I had taken precautions before we came to the house. We had bags of salt and iron filings in our pockets, and we wore silver jewelry along with carrying onyx and agate charms. I had a very old agate spindle whorl in my pocket that held some powerful protective magic. Just in case, my athame was tucked in my tote bag.

Even with all those protections, I could feel a dark resonance. Like the thrum of a bass beat on a subwoofer, it was a low vibration that jangled my nerves. I couldn't imagine how Miranda lived with the sensation. Even without any magic of her own, I'd imagine it might still make it hard to sleep or concentrate.

"Follow me," she said. "Just forgive me for not going inside. I just...can't."

Miranda led us through a beautifully furnished house with tasteful —if eclectic—decor. I could see a collector's hand in the choice of artwork and accent pieces, and knew enough about several of the items to recognize that they were fairly rare and valuable.

"Did your husband's collections have any particular theme?" I asked as she led us down a hallway.

"Not really. He liked to buy things in the countries we visited, and we've done a lot of traveling. He just said certain pieces spoke to him.

And until the last one he bought online, I was happy to let him do what he wanted," Miranda replied.

The house itself had been carefully preserved. Like many of the showplace homes South of Broad, it was more than a century old, and its owners had taken good care of the signature features like plaster-work designs on the ceiling and beautiful woodwork. The closer we got to the den, the harder it was to sense any other resonance, but I didn't think that the house itself had bad vibes. I hoped that meant that whatever Edward had dragged home hadn't awakened some dark, dormant presence in the house itself.

"In there," Miranda said, pointing at a door on the left. She stepped to the other side of the hallway to let us pass and stared at the doorway as if it might bite.

Kell reached for the door with his right hand and slipped his left into a pocket of his jacket. I knew he had a bag of salt in that pocket, as well as other protective items, and as I moved to back him up, I gripped my silver and agate necklace.

The door swung open, revealing a room furnished in dark wood and leather. Floor-to-ceiling bookshelves covered the walls, and the smell of cigar smoke hung in the air, along with the faint scent of expensive cologne. Under other circumstances, I might have paid more attention to the pricy antiques, original oil paintings, and rare knick-knacks. But right now, all I could feel was a malevolent power that covered everything like a black stain.

"Can you pick anything up, or do you need my EMF meter?" Kell asked. His SPOOK team had all the latest gadgets to read electromag-netic frequencies and faint audio, the usual way of recognizing a super-natural presence. My psychometry wasn't high tech, but it was never wrong.

"Give me a minute," I murmured. "I'm trying to figure out the source." I didn't want to walk into that room, but someone had to deal with the evil that had cost Edward his life, and that made it my respon-sibility.

The dark resonance permeated everything in the den, like a spreading rot. I doubted that the other pieces Edward had collected were malicious, even if they did possess a bit of mojo that attracted his attention. But his newest acquisition had taken root, corrupting everything around it.

"There." I pointed to a carved figure of a leaping dolphin. The artist had polished the mahogany until it shone, and the piece was beautifully fashioned. I could understand what had caught Edward's eye—although it was impossible to overlook the taint of its curse.

"That's the newest piece," Miranda confirmed from where she stood in the hallway. "Is it haunted?"

"There's certainly a dark presence to it," I said, unsure how to break it to her that her husband had more likely been murdered by magic than by a vengeful ghost.

"Can you deal with it?" Kell asked me in a low voice.

I shook my head. "Not alone. We need to call in an expert."

Kell and I backed out of the room. I wasn't sure whether the carving was capable of "noticing" us, but I definitely didn't want to draw its attention. More likely, I thought, it was some kind of dark magic that affected someone the longer they were nearby. If my guess was right, then Miranda had been very lucky not to be affected so far, but that luck wouldn't last forever.

We reached the hallway, and Kell pulled the door shut. I felt a physical sense of relief at having a barrier—however flimsy—between me and the cursed statue.

"Do you know what happened?" Miranda asked.

I hesitated, wondering what to say, but I saw something in her eyes that made me think she would believe the truth.

"I think that the dolphin statue is cursed," I said. Kell looked surprised at my candor, but Miranda's expression was relieved.

"So, that's it," she whispered. "I thought I was crazy."

I shook my head. "No. You're not. Magic is real, and it can be good or bad. What's attached to that statue is old and evil."

"Are you going to call a priest?" she asked.

"No. A witch." I expected her to object. After all, Charleston had earned its name as the "holy city" for its hundreds of churches.

"All right." She spoke so softly I almost couldn't hear her. "If that's what it takes. I just don't want that awful thing in the house—and I can't let it hurt anyone else."

The look on her face as she turned away gave me a flash of insight. "There have been a couple of other strange deaths, recently. Did you or Edward know the people who died?"

Miranda nodded, and her expression was guilt-ridden. "We ran in the same circles—collectors, you know? Either bidding against each other—usually good-natured competition—or comparing our most recent 'find.' Shannon Hendricks bought off-beat art pieces for her interior design customers. Brett Langdon was like Edward—he loved the thrill of the chase when it came to bidding on an item. I used to joke about them being the 'three amigos' because they would go to estate sales and auctions together and then come home crowing over their trophies."

"Did they all buy something from the same place Edward got that dolphin?" I felt a cold chill. Out of the corner of my eye, I saw that Kell had pulled out his EMF meter. Even with the volume turned off to keep it from squealing, the light display flashed all red.

Miranda bit her lip to keep from crying. "Yes. I didn't pay much attention at the time. It was always something with those three, and I let them have their fun. It was harmless, I thought." Her voice broke.

"You couldn't have known." I offered what comfort I could. Most people could go their whole lives without encountering a cursed object. Haunted items were more common, but even so, ones with lethal mojo were, thankfully, fairly rare. Edward's taste had been eclectic, but from what I saw, he hadn't purposefully sought out occult pieces.

No, the fault here lay with whoever sold the statues, just as it had with the dangerous sailor's valentine. We needed to track down the dealer and find the source of the malicious magic before more people died.

"Do you have a way to track the purchase?" Kell asked. "Credit card receipts? Emails? If we could find where they bought the items, we could shut down whoever sold this to them—and maybe save other people."

Miranda's eyes widened. "Do you think the seller knew the figures were dangerous?"

I couldn't substantiate my gut feeling that the answer was "yes," so I shrugged. "I don't know—but if we know who sold the statues, we could find out where they bought them, and track the source. That dark magic didn't happen by accident."

Miranda nodded absently, and I couldn't tell whether she was reconciling our confirmation that magic was real or was just overwhelmed by guilt and grief. "Okay," she said quietly, and I wasn't sure if she was talking to herself or us.

She seemed to pull herself together. "I can see what I can find in the credit card records. Can your witch friend come out tonight? I don't want to spend another day with that awful thing in the house."

"I'll find out," I said. "And when it is cleansed…what do you want done with the item?" Given the rest of the collectibles in the house, I couldn't imagine the dolphin carving had been cheap. I didn't want to leave it here, but I couldn't just take it without her permission.

"Burn it. That's what they do on those TV shows, isn't it? Throw it in the ocean. I don't care how much it's worth—it cost Edward his life. Destroy it, so it can't hurt anyone else."

"All right," I told Miranda. "When it's gone, there are a couple of ways to also cleanse the house. We'll talk about that later, but I thought you'd want to know."

"That would be good," she replied and gave a bitter laugh. "Edward and I have never been religious. I don't think he ever took it seriously when there would be something on TV about a piece having any supernatural power. I guess we were wrong." She turned before I could answer and headed back toward the front of the house.

"You're going to call Rowan?" Kell asked.

I nodded. "Lucinda said the ghosts weren't Voudon or Hoodoo, so they're not in her wheelhouse. Father Anne could help with a demon or a ghost, but I think this kind of magic is more of a witch problem." Fortunately, I had a lot of talented friends on speed dial.

Kell and I retreated down the hall, needing to put some space between us and the den. He watched the doorway like he expected something to charge out, and I'll admit that made me feel better. I wasn't sure what kind of spell or curse would cause the kind of awful deaths that Edward and his friends had suffered, and I knew that underestimating its power would be dangerous.

Fortunately, Rowan answered after the first ring. Given my friends' abilities, I never know whether to credit luck or premonition for something like that.

"Rowan, we've got a situation that's killed three people. I think it's your kind of thing. Sorry to ask on short notice, but can you please come take a look?"

Kell glanced my way, and I nodded to indicate Rowan's willingness to help. He showed me the address from his phone's GPS, and Rowan promised to join us shortly. I ended the call and let out a long breath.

"Are you okay?" Kell asked, worried.

"Sort of. Even out here, I can feel that something really bad is in that room."

"You're planning to go in there with Rowan, aren't you?"

Kell knows about my magic, and he's seen me hold my own in a supernatural fight. Maybe because he understands the dangers, he worries about me, and he'll protect me if need be, but he trusts me to know my limits. That's one of the many things I love about him.

"Yes. Rowan's plenty powerful, but we don't really know anything about the carving, except that it can kill. So I want to back her up."

"Do you need me to call Teag?"

I thought for a moment and shook my head. "No. This isn't his kind of magic. If Rowan can't handle it, she'll say so. Let's not borrow more trouble than we already have."

Miranda hadn't returned. I didn't know if she needed some time to gather her wits and adjust, or if searching through Edward's purchases was just time-consuming, or perhaps both. Kell and I moved closer to the front door, so we could let Rowan in when she arrived. She must have understood my urgency because she got there quicker than I expected.

We barely said hello before her nose wrinkled in disgust. "Wow. I can feel the magic from here. Fill me in."

Kell and I took turns telling the story, as Rowan listened intently. "It's old magic," she said when we finished. "I can tell by the feel. The power feels odd. If I had to guess, I'd say it's a blend of magical traditions—European and African."

"That would make sense, if it came from the islands like the ghosts," I replied.

"Can you remove the magic?" Kell asked.

Rowan frowned. "I'm not sure. But between Cassidy and me, I think we can contain it long enough to put it in the lead box I brought." She nodded toward a heavy gray metal box by her feet. "At worst, we can let Sorren deal with it." Sorren had been handling supernatural problems for hundreds of years, and he had connections who were good at neutralizing dangerous items.

"Does the curse transfer to whoever has the box in their possession?" I asked. "Because that would be bad."

Rowan thought for a moment. "Doubtful, or else who sold it to these folks? And we're not buying it—we're removing it. Technically, there is no owner right now. The man who bought it is dead, and his estate hasn't been settled."

Odd as that sounded, magic could be incredibly technical. I was willing to trust Rowan's judgment. Kell looked skeptical but didn't argue.

"What can I do to help?" Kell asked. I know it bothers him that, without magic, he can't always be on the front lines. He's gotten good with a shotgun full of salt rounds and other weapons against ghosts, but none of those items would work against this particular threat.

"Keep Miranda safe," I said. "Put down a salt circle, and make sure you both stay inside. Just please, both of you stay away from the den. I can't keep my attention on backing up Rowan if I'm worried about you two."

I could tell from the look on his face that Kell didn't like it, but he knew I was right. "Okay. But you both better come back safe," he said, meeting my gaze. His eyes said everything that he didn't say aloud, and I nodded, making a silent promise.

"We'll do our best," I answered. Then I turned to Rowan. "Ready when you are."

When I first started channeling my gift with my athame, I got a white blast of power, good for knocking things over and throwing bad guys out of the way. I've been working on control—Rowan's helped a lot with teaching me—and on managing to pin something with the energy instead of putting it through a wall.

Now, I really hoped I could do this right so that I didn't get us all killed or put a big hole in Miranda's paneling.

I focused my will, drew on the strong resonance of the athame, and sent a controlled flare of cold energy toward the dolphin carving. It swept the piece off the desk and pinned it to the wall, making a dent but not a hole, containing it within the light. I'd take that as a win.

"Go!" I told Rowan through gritted teeth.

Rowan began to chant a nullification spell, which might not take away all of the carving's power, but would hopefully reduce it long enough for us to get the cursed statue locked away.

Still chanting, Rowan picked up the box and moved toward the figure slowly, as if it were a wild animal that might bite.

I drew from the good memories and positive emotions that made up the resonance of my athame, which had been my grandmother's favorite wooden spoon. That's when I realized that the statue was sending its own impressions and memories back down the energy stream, trying to crowd into my thoughts and flood my mind.

I felt the malice of the person who created the carving, how he layered ill intent into the piece with every cut of his blade. The air around me grew warm like the tropics, and I heard thunder in the distance, a gathering storm. Edward wasn't the first person this statue had killed, and I sensed that its power grew each time it spilled blood.

"Hurry." I struggled to hold my focus and keep back the flood of dark images. It wanted to show me the faces of the people it killed, make me feel their deaths. My head throbbed with the effort of holding the assault at bay, and I knew I couldn't last much longer.

Rowan's chant had grown louder and more defiant as she closed the distance, and by the time she reached the carving, she was shouting. She positioned the spelled box beneath the dolphin figure, just below where my athame's blast held it pinned to the wall.

"Now, Cassidy! Let it fall!"

As the energy torrent from my athame winked out, Rowan spoke a command, and the wooden piece dropped into the containment box. She slammed the lid shut, and the sigils etched into the metal glowed as her magic activated the binding spell.

She sagged against the wall, spent from what the magic had cost her. I dropped to my knees, with my head throbbing, exhausted from keeping the killer carving immobilized and also throttling the flow of psychic sludge it tried to throw at me.

"Cassidy! Rowan! What's going on?" Kell shouted from where he and Miranda waited. I heard the worry in his voice, but he kept his word and stayed inside the salt circle.

"We're all right," I called back, although my voice shook and sounded reedy to my own ears. "Stay where you are. We'll bring the box out."

I glanced to Rowan. She gave me a tired, but victorious, smile and pushed off from the wall, clutching the spelled box in both hands. "Let's get out of here," she said. Despite her bravado, I could see the strain on her face from the powerful magic she'd worked.

"Sounds like a great idea to me." I got to my feet, took a moment to steady myself, and then Rowan and I walked out of the room together.

"It's safe to come out now," I shouted to Kell and Miranda. They walked around the corner a minute later. Kell gave Rowan and me a worried once-over, and I nodded to let him know we were all right.

"I'll hang onto this until Sorren gets back to town," Rowan said, looking at the box with distaste. "I've got a place to store it that will keep the magic contained."

"There are two more pieces, like that one," I told her.

Rowan sighed. "All right. I can help you get rid of them. But not tonight. I need to find more of these boxes and strengthen the containment warding. I'll call when I've got everything ready." With that, she took the box and headed out.

Kell and I walked Miranda to the living room. "How are you feeling?" I asked. To my heightened magical senses, the house already felt cleaner, as if we had stopped a flood of supernatural sewage.

"Like it's easier to breathe," Miranda said.

I nodded. "You can help purify the house by burning sage. If you have a faith tradition, you might want to ask to have the house blessed or cleansed. It will probably take some time before the den loses its stain, but the rest of the house should clear pretty quickly."

"Thank you," Miranda shook our hands. "I took a chance, contacting you, but I didn't know where else to turn."

"Glad to help," Kell replied. We turned down payment and assured Miranda that her thanks was all we needed. She promised to contact the other owners of the other carved figures and put them in touch with us as soon as possible. Leaving her house seemed a bit surreal as we waved goodbye at the curb as if we had come over for tea instead of waging a supernatural battle.

Kell didn't say anything until we were on our way back to my house. "It would have killed her, wouldn't it?"

I nodded. "If she stayed in the house, near it? Yes. If the curse is linked to the owner, then probably when the estate was finalized, if not before."

"Do you think Rowan can keep the box safe?"

"I think she and the coven can protect it until Sorren and Donnelly get back," I replied. Archibald Donnelly was a powerful necromancer, and he had gone with Sorren to handle the problems in Europe. "We've never come up against something that the two of them didn't know how to contain." *And I hope we never do.*

Teag called just as we walked in the door. I scooped Baxter up in my arms, juggling the phone, as Kell closed the door behind us and went to pour us both some wine.

"Everything okay?" he asked. I recounted what happened at the Adams's house, and smiled my thanks as Kell gently took Baxter and handed me a glass of Cabernet.

"That's a little more excitement than I was expecting," Teag replied. "I'm glad it all worked out. And I'll be glad to go along as backup when you and Rowan go to handle the other two pieces. But here's why I called—I found out where Edward and the others bought the carvings."

I put the call on speaker and followed Kell and Baxter into the living room, so happy to be safe at home. "Someplace local?" I asked.

"No—a sketchy site on the Darke Web," he replied. The "Dark Web" was a part of the internet known for cryptocurrency, illegal activities, and content banned from the sections of the web most people visited. The "Darke Web" used ensorcelled encryption to keep itself hidden, catering to members of the supernatural community.

"Interesting. I didn't think Edward and the others were particularly into occult items," I mused.

"All it takes is one bad tip," Teag said. "Anyhow, the site is like a sketchy eBay—if eBay were located in an abandoned warehouse in a bad section of town and everything it sold was stolen."

"Wow. Edward was really slumming it. Was he a regular?" Somehow, that didn't fit what Miranda had told us, or anything we had found out about the man and his friends.

"I don't think so," Teag replied. "He might have been sent there by a malicious contact. It would be hard to stumble on the site, but maybe whoever gave him the tip thought they could blackmail him, or control him."

"You said a lot of the merchandise was stolen. Any idea where the carvings came from?" Kell asked.

"Seth and I are still hacking the site," Teag said. "But the owners aren't as clever as they think they are. We'll get in. Of course, everyone is using an alias. But here's something interesting—the same day that you said Edward bought the carvings, several other pieces also went up for sale. And they all have a Caribbean connection."

"Do you think they came in from the *Caribe Queen*?" Somehow, I didn't think it was that easy.

"No. Because they were uploaded before the ship docked. Maybe the items on the shady site came from the same source as whatever was on the ship that caused the ghosts to appear," Teag answered. "I'm still working on it. But I thought you'd like to know."

"Thanks." I started to feel the events of the day as exhaustion took hold. "Keep me posted."

"See you tomorrow." Teag ended the call.

I set the phone aside and sipped my wine as Baxter wriggled his way between Kell and me on the couch. "You know, I'm probably going to be asleep again before the end of the movie," I warned him as he picked a movie we had both seen before.

"That's fine," he assured me, drawing me closer. "We're here together, you're safe, and we had a win tonight. Enjoy the moment while it lasts."

CHAPTER FOUR

After all the excitement at Miranda Adams's house the night before, I was looking forward to a normal, quiet day at Trifles and Folly. Teag and Seth were running programs to crack the encryption on the Darke Web collectibles auction site, but they hadn't gotten in yet, so we had to wait. Rowan and her coven were preparing the other two containment boxes, but good magic takes time, and they weren't ready to go get the remaining two killer carvings. Just to be on the safe side, the spouses of the other two people who were killed by the items from the Darke Web site went to stay elsewhere until we could take care of the problem.

I went in to work excited about not having any excitement, at least for a day. The morning flew by quickly with a steady stream of shoppers, and that kept Teag, Maggie, and me hopping and too busy to think about Caribbean ghosts and murderous knickknacks.

I should have known it wouldn't last.

We were just finishing up lunch when my phone rang. "It's Alistair," I said with a glance at Teag. "I'll put it on speaker."

"Hi, Alistair," I said. "What's new with the museum?" Alistair McKinnon, the curator of the Lowcountry Museum, is a professional friend, and someone Teag and I help out when items with bad mojo find their way into the exhibits. I doubted this was a social call.

"Hello Cassidy, Teag," Alistair said. "And Maggie, too, if you're there. I'm afraid I need to ask you for a consult—and not the appraisal kind. We have a new bequest that worries me. I think it's haunted."

"What's giving you that idea?" I asked.

"It keeps moving around the museum at night on its own."

Teag and I exchanged a look. *That would do it.*

"I can handle the store," Maggie spoke up. "Go see what's going on. It won't do to have exhibits wandering around loose."

Alistair chuckled. "That's one way to put it. And...thank you. The first couple of times, we thought it was moved by mistake or as a prank. But I'm afraid it's more than that, and the staff is very uncomfortable."

"We'll head your way right now," I said. "You caught us at a good time." The call ended, and we cleaned up the cups and wrappers from lunch as I mulled over what Alistair said.

"Do you think there could be a connection with the other weirdness?" I asked Teag as we headed for my car.

"I vote for suspecting there is until we prove there isn't," he replied. "Whatever started this Caribbean mess, it's got scary power. I think we play it safe and assume it's all related."

I'd come to the same conclusion, but it helped to hear Teag say it. The drive to the museum didn't take long. I found a spot to park beneath one of the big live oaks, and we headed inside. The receptionist recognized us and waved us in. We knew the way to Alistair's office, but to my surprise, he was pacing by the entrance to the first exhibit room, waiting for us.

"Thank you for coming. I'm just not sure what to do about this," he said quietly.

Alistair didn't fluster easily. I'd seen him handle big donors with ease, charm his way through major media events, and navigate the treacherous currents of Charleston high society without a second thought. But haunted and cursed objects go with the territory for museums, although you'll never hear that said on the record. Alistair had seen firsthand how dangerous a haunting or bad magic could be, and I was pleased that he trusted us enough to ask for help.

"Fill us in on this wandering bequest," I said as we followed him into the area that was under construction for a new display that would open soon.

"We're doing an exhibit on the Triangle Trade, and its impact on Charleston," Alistair said as we walked past half-assembled kiosks and empty glass cases. "Back in the early days, that was the trade that went from Boston to Charleston to the islands. Most people associate it with molasses, rum, and slaves—and that was a big part of it. But there was so much more."

"Like what?" Teag had been all-but-dissertation on his Ph.D. in History before he took a summer job at Trifles and Folly. He decided he liked putting his knowledge to use stopping supernatural threats, researching antiques—haunted or not—and learning how to use his Weaver magic. So, I knew he and Alistair would be going full geek on the subject.

"You can see the Caribbean influence in the sugar plantations, the architecture styles, and even the furniture and decorative influences," Alistair answered. "Not to mention the family ties. British families moved to the islands, and then some of their descendants took up residence in Bermuda—and Charleston. The island trade was a big deal during the Civil War when some of the British in the islands backed the Confederacy and the blockade runners," he added. "And during Prohibition, the rum runners made a fortune in bootleg Caribbean rum."

Charleston is a beautiful city built on rivers of blood. Enslaved individuals toiled in the plantations that created the city's wealth, and their labor built many of its landmarks. Indentured servants and desperate Irish immigrants were often treated only slightly better than slaves. Add to that hurricanes, outbreaks of Yellow Fever, Cholera, and other tropical diseases, pirates and duels, and there's a reason that Charleston is one of the most haunted cities in the country.

"...some of those old Caribbean families have kept ties to Charleston to this day," Alistair was saying when I zoned back in.

"Wait, what?" I asked. "Which old families?" Somehow, I hadn't realized that Charleston's ties to the islands remained that close, even now.

Alistair turned away from the half-finished diorama he had been pointing to and looked at me. "Quite a few of the prominent families had a 'Caribbean branch' that handled their land holdings in Barbados, Jamaica, Haiti, Cuba, and the Dominican Republic," he replied. "Not to mention their pirate connections to havens like Antigua and Tortuga and the Bahamas. Respectable families don't always mention that, as late as the 1830s, some of their wealth came from piracy or privateering."

Teag and I exchanged a glance. *Here we go with the Caribbean connection again.*

"Are you naming names in the exhibit?" Teag asked. "Or would that upset your donors?"

Alistair chuckled. "Now that the movies have romanticized pirates, people are more willing to claim that part of their heritage. The families we approached for the exhibit were excited about loaning us all kinds of items and documents. No treasure maps, unfortunately," he added with an exaggerated sigh.

"Is the wandering bequest part of the pirate exhibit?" I looked around, but nothing in sight struck me as likely to go walkabout on its own.

"Yes. Right this way." We followed Alistair to a locked glass case with a blinking light to show an active alarm system. Inside was a black cane.

"This is the piece," Alistair said. "It's a gentleman's walking stick, made from woven sugar cane fibers. Beautiful work—it took a real artist to create the spiral pattern you see. But somehow it gets out of a locked case without tripping the alarm and turns up in other parts of the museum. Not every night, but three or four times so far. Enough to have the staff…unsettled."

Teag bent down for a closer look. "It's gorgeous. The weaving is very tight and regular. I didn't know you could make something three dimensional like that."

"It's from the early 1800s," Alistair said. "Belonged to Chapin

Etheridge, the patriarch of the Etheridge family. I trust you recognize the name."

We nodded. The Etheridge family remained prominent in Charleston social circles and politics, but I'd never linked them to magic.

"At the height of their wealth, the Etheridges had large sugar cane plantations and distilleries in the British West Indies. They were the sworn enemies of the Pendlewood family, which was equally wealthy and who made their money in sugar, rum, and piracy."

"I don't recognize the Pendlewood name. Did they die out?" I asked. Epidemics were common back in the day and sometimes killed entire families.

Alistair shook his head. "They abandoned their land here in Charleston after the Civil War and left the manor house empty. For a while, they let the phosphate miners dig up the grounds, and when that ran its course, just let the whole place fall apart. Sad, really. Aside from some financial ties, the family has kept to its island properties since then. They haven't been a force here in the city for quite a long time."

"Why the bad blood between the Etheridges and the Pendle-woods?" Teag asked, staring at the old cane. I was sure that with his magic, he could feel its resonance as strongly as I did. Either the cane itself had a curse or a ghost attached to it, or the piece had been in close proximity to someone with a lot of strong juju.

"That depends on who you ask." Alistair pointed toward a display that was only partly finished. "We'll talk about the rivalry on that wall. Some say it was over a broken engagement. Others swear it was a business deal gone wrong. There's even a version that says a Pendlewood cursed an Etheridge, over a lost card game."

"Cursed?" My ears pricked up at that.

Alistair nodded, giving me a knowing look. "New Orleans has its Voudon—and I know Charleston does, too. But that wasn't the only kind of magic in those islands. Some sorts were darker than others. And while the plantation owners wouldn't admit it, they all dabbled—to the point that there were rumors of weather witches and hexed competitors, and ships cursed to sink."

One of my ancestors, Dante, had been a privateer in those days, working with Sorren and the Alliance even then to intercept dangerous objects. Family history held that Dante was a weather witch himself. I wondered if he'd ever had a run-in with the Etheridges or the Pendlewoods.

"And you think that the walking stick might be a relic from that feud?" Teag asked.

"I'm afraid so." Alistair looked around before he said more. "The truth is," he added, dropping his voice, "we didn't really want the bequest. Antiquities people talk, you know. I'd heard some stories from someone who was called in to appraise the Etheridge estate when one of the old-timers died. He had some tales that would turn your hair white. Swore up and down it was a regular haunted mansion, for real."

"Do you know what happened to the rest of the items from that estate?" I wondered if this was the connection we'd been looking for.

"Most went to family members or were bought by museums," Alistair replied. "As for the more…questionable…pieces, I heard they were all bought by a wealthy Dutch collector who took them out of the country."

Score one for Sorren. My boss had started out as a jewel thief in Antwerp back in the 1400s. I didn't doubt he'd stepped in to get the dangerous Etheridge legacy off the market. But if the cane was still here, had he missed some pieces? And were they somehow responsible for the Caribbean chaos we'd been experiencing?

I looked at Teag. "I guess we do a stake-out and see where it wanders."

He shrugged. "Sounds like a plan to me."

"Can we stay after closing?" I asked Alistair. "Because I don't think it's going to wander off while it's daylight and we have people around."

Alistair nodded. "We have insurance coverage for 'special access.' Just try not to incinerate anything we can't replace."

Teag cleared his throat. "About that…we might need to destroy the walking stick to stop it from rambling. How much trouble would that cause the museum?"

"It's a bequest, not a loan, so no one will be expecting it to be returned," Alistair said with a wan smile. "Although, it's a very nice specimen, so if it's possible to…deactivate…it without ruining it, that would be nice."

"We'll see what we can do," I said, although I suspected Teag's scenario was more likely. Even without touching the glass case, I could sense that the cane had power. It wasn't likely to go quietly.

Teag set up his laptop. I took pictures of the walking stick and sent them to Rowan and Lucinda. Then I went to get us coffee and sandwiches from the museum cafe, to get us through the evening. I was hoping we really didn't have to spend the night. Museums are a strain on my touch magic under normal conditions, and I didn't expect that to get better after dark. Alistair promised he would come let us out as soon as we called, so we wouldn't trip the alarms. That was a small comfort, but we had to defeat the stick's magic first.

"It's a coco macaque," Teag told me when I got back with the snacks.

"Sounds like a fancy coffee drink."

"It's a lot more dangerous, unfortunately," he said, accepting the coffee. "Not only can it move on its own, its master can send it on errands, according to legend. And if the master of the cane strikes someone with it, they'll die by morning."

"Lovely."

"Just saying—don't get hit."

"I'll keep that in mind." I found a chair and pulled it over beside Teag. "But who's its master now? Alistair said that the man who owned it died. If the family let it come here as a bequest, no one else laid claim to it. And if someone did want it, what's the point of having it here in the museum?"

"No idea. But the other thing that worries me is, why are we just now finding out about two powerful magical families?" Teag asked.

"Well, for one thing, they were in the islands, but they hadn't been active in the Charleston magical community for a long time," I replied, thinking out loud. "So, they hadn't caused problems here since I took over the store—maybe even before my Uncle Evann ran it."

Teag nodded. "Sorren probably never had a reason to mention it. Actually, that doesn't make me sleep better at night, since who knows how many supernatural hazards are out there that we don't know about?"

I thought about Sorren's long existence, most of it spent fighting dark magic, vengeful ghosts, and creepy creatures. Not to mention all the horrors of human history he had witnessed. I didn't envy him his immortality, and I wasn't sure I wanted to know everything he knew.

"One nightmare at a time," I said, eyeing the cane in its locked case. "That's enough to handle. Did you find anything that said how to destroy it?"

Teag leaned back and took a long drink of his coffee. "Fire works."

"Fire works on most things, but burning down the museum isn't an option."

"Yeah, there's that. Since the cane is woven, my Weaver magic might be able to counter it," Teag mused. "Whoever created it had to weave their magic into the walking stick. If I knew how it was made, I might be able to unmake it. But..."

"What?"

He shook his head. "I think that there's more than magic involved. The walking stick was made from strips of sugar cane. Those cane plantations were brutal. The workers didn't last long, and the conditions were inhumane. So, it's not just the evil intentions of the weaver. The materials used to make the cane could have absorbed the evil of the people around it."

My phone buzzed with a message from Lucinda. "She's heard of a coco macaque, but she doesn't know how to destroy it, aside from the usual." By that, I was sure she meant fire, maybe with some blessed oil thrown in and some incantations for good measure. A text from Rowan moments later said much the same.

"I wonder how long it'll take until it decides to act up?" I watched the cane as I spoke, but it didn't do anything unusual.

As if on cue, we heard an announcement that the museum was about to close. The workers in the exhibit area had left more than an hour ago, but that hadn't fooled the walking stick into thinking it was alone.

"I guess we'll find out," Teag replied.

At closing time, the quiet background music turned off. We heard footsteps in the hallway as the last of the staff filed toward the door. Both Teag and I looked up when Alistair stuck his head in.

"I'm heading out, but I'll have my phone on," he said. "Good luck and…be careful."

Even though we couldn't see the parking lot, I could tell by the feel of the building when everyone else was gone. The emergency lighting kept the museum from being completely dark, and I figured Alistair left a few extra lights on in the exhibit hall for our sake.

"What are you picking up?" Teag asked.

"I'm trying to figure that out," I replied in a hushed voice. It was silly to whisper. No one could hear us, and I doubt the walking stick was listening. Still, the resonance of the history surrounding us weighed on me, and I knew that the cane wasn't the only item with magic and dark memories in the building.

Teag waited as I got my bearings. I'd learned to shut down part of my gift whenever I visited the museum to keep from getting overwhelmed. Before I figured out how to open and close the throttle, so to speak, I had some embarrassing moments, passing out and throwing up when the resonance was more than I can handle. But I'd gained a lot more control since then, and learned a lot about my abilities. I hoped it would be enough.

When I reached out with my gift, I could feel where the haunted and magical objects were. A teapot in the "Lowcountry Living" exhibit still carried the ghost of its mistress. Pottery vases held a trace of the long-ago enhanced talents of their enslaved maker. Hot spots showed up on my mental radar, alerting me to pieces in the museum's collection that were more than they appeared.

Over the years, Teag and I had worked with Alistair to remove anything that was a danger to the staff or public. Sorren had removed the worst pieces, and we'd managed to neutralize the others that were too powerful. What remained showed up to my magic, but most people would never notice.

I could sense the walking stick. It felt unsettled, jittery. Ready to move on. Maybe it missed having a master. Perhaps when its last owner died, the bond with the cane hadn't been shut down correctly. Whatever the cause, the cane wanted to be somewhere else.

"There's nothing else in here that's going to hurt us," I said finally. "Or help us."

"I guess, considering the possible ways that could have gone wrong, that's a good thing."

"You can weave power into things. Can you weave it out?"

Teag and I stared at each other for a moment. "I'm not sure. I've never tried to de-magic an object without just destroying it."

"How would you do it, if you did try?"

Teag stared into the distance, thinking. "When I put energy into a piece of fabric, I use my will to weave it in like another strand of thread. If I concentrate on the walking stick, I can see the magic. But when I reach for it, it slips away."

A rattling sound made both of us turn toward the glass case. The walking stick twitched back and forth in the cabinet, and I expected the panels to shatter. Then the lock popped, and the cane righted itself, hopping down and pogo-sticking its way across the room.

"It's showtime," I murmured.

Teag and I had brought a duffle bag filled with weapons and ingredients for spells and protections. Silver, iron, salt, holy water, as well as blessed blades and sanctified amulets. We wore our usual protective charms, but I wasn't sure what effect they'd have on the coco macaque.

Teag pulled out a net made from silver mesh. I had another rope net soaked in colloidal silver. We closed in on the hopping cane from both sides, ready to trap it, hoping silver worked against the enchantment.

"Watch out!" The stick bounced high, then sent itself spinning, aiming at Teag's head. It might have other nasty surprises for us, but we knew that getting hit was a one-way ticket to dead.

I let my athame fall down my sleeve into my hand and loosed a blast of cold power, knocking the stick off its path, sending it careening away. Teag threw his net, but the walking stick slipped beneath it, and the silver fell harmlessly to the floor.

"I've got it!" I ran toward the cane, hoping it couldn't suddenly change direction and threw my net. This time, it hit the target, and the silver-soaked rope and the cane fell to the floor.

Teag sprang for it, with a silver knife clutched in one hand. He threw himself on the net, stabbing and ripping with the blade, as he chanted an incantation for protection that Father Anne had taught us.

I closed the distance between us, with my athame at the ready in case the coco macaque got loose, and I needed to blast it again.

The walking stick fought back, bucking like a wild thing beneath the net, nearly rolling Teag off of it or squirming as if it intended to wriggle out through the gaps between the silver-soaked ropes. Teag's knife strokes missed as often as they hit, and I chanted with him, reinforcing the power of the incantation.

Finally, the cane stopped struggling. Teag ripped his knife down through the mesh of fibers and cut off the woven ball at the top. He sat back on his haunches, sweat-soaked from the fight, wary but hopeful.

"I think we got it."

I edged closer. "I didn't get a chance to read the shell valentine before we destroyed it, and I didn't dare touch the carved dolphin. But if I can get a sense of the power that created the walking stick—and what it's witnessed—I might have some insight into who, or what, we're actually up against."

"That usually goes hard on you."

I shrugged, although I knew he was right. "I'll stay on the silver net, to dull the power of the pieces that are left." I hoped that would give me the magical equivalent of watching a movie with the surround sound turned off, providing information without the full immersion experience that could be overwhelming—and sometimes, dangerous.

"All right," Teag replied, although I could tell he didn't like the idea. Still, he always had my back. "I'll be right here, and if anything starts to go wrong, drop the pieces, and I'll get you away."

We exchanged places, and Teag stepped back. He gathered the silver chain net and held it ready, still gripping his knife, just in case.

I wasn't sure about how this would turn out, but the walking stick might give us a clue about the origin of the run of Caribbean-linked problems we'd encountered, and I figured it was worth a shot. Before I could second-guess myself, I reached out and laid my hand, palm down, over the ripped sugar cane strands that poked through the holes in the net.

Immediately the scene in front of me changed, and I "saw" the memories imprinted on the old walking stick. I felt the oppressive heat of an island summer, caught the scent of tropical flowers, and heard the rhythmic thwack of machetes chopping down endless fields of sugar cane.

The images shifted, and I saw a well-dressed older white man whose intimidating stance and grim expression made it clear he was not to be disobeyed. From the man's breeches and vest and the style of his buckle shoes, I guessed it to be the late 1700s.

Fear, rage, and loathing coursed through me as I experienced what the cane's maker felt. At the same time, I felt crushing shame, guilt, and frustration at being unable to choose my fate. I watched the maker's ebony fingers weave the thin cane strips into the cane, a process that often mingled his own blood into the weaving when the sharp edges cut his skin.

Once more the view changed, and this time, I saw through the eyes of the walking stick's owner. He feared nothing, sure of his power, filled with the importance that his money, status, and magic imparted. He bent the cane's energy to meet his needs, sending it out at night as a warning to frighten the servants or to spy on family members or rivals whom he suspected were conspiring against him.

The memories streamed by me, a montage of lifetimes. Each of the walking stick's owners added layers of greed, paranoia, and obsession. The final images were of an old man whose pale, skeletal body neared death, his bony fingers locked around the magic cane as the death rattle slipped from his lungs.

I came back to myself with a gasp, as if I had been beneath the water for too long. My heart thudded, and my head ached, and for a moment, all I could do was breathe.

Teag led me away from the net and the remains of the walking stick, guiding me to a chair and pressing a bottle of water into my hand. We'd done this kind of thing enough times that Teag knew the drill. He watched over me, staying close until he was certain I wouldn't faint. Then he went back to gather up the shreds of the coco macaque, still wrapped in the silver netting, and stuffed it into a bag made from cloth into which he had woven protections and binding spells.

I had finished the water, and my hands had stopped trembling by the time he came back.

"Are you okay?" he asked, giving me an assessing once-over.

I nodded, and for once I wasn't faking. "Yeah. I am."

"Want to tell me about it?"

"How about I give you the short version while we wait for Alistair to come let us out, and I'll tell you the rest tomorrow, once I've had a chance to sort through it all."

"Deal."

I waited for him to call Alistair, and then we gathered up our things and headed for the museum entrance.

"The coco macaque itself wasn't really evil," I said, "not like some of the malicious objects we've dealt with in the past. But it was created from bad intentions, and the men who commanded it were very bad. That leaves a stain."

I tried to put the things I'd seen into words. "The cane was woven by a slave. I'm guessing he'd been a shaman or a witch of some sort. The plantation owner forced him to weave the walking stick against his will. He was afraid—of punishment, or maybe for his family. He did what his master ordered, but all of his anger and his hatred for the man who enslaved him went into the weaving."

Teag nodded. "That makes sense."

I swallowed, dry-mouthed at the memory. "I saw glimpses of the men who owned the walking stick over the years. All of their malice and selfishness made an imprint. They used the cane's magic to do bad things. More than once, they made it kill." I shuddered.

"You don't have to tell me everything tonight," Teag said, laying a hand on my arm supportively. "I get the idea." We looked up as headlights flared and Alistair drove up. "Let's get you home, and we can talk about this some more in the morning."

I was glad I'd let Teag drive us to the museum because I still felt unsteady. Once I was home, I gathered Baxter into my arms, guzzled a glass of water, and barely peeled off my clothing before I fell across my bed and went right to sleep.

CHAPTER FIVE

"ANTHONY REALLY WENT ALL-OUT FOR HIS BOY'S BIG DAY, DIDN'T he?" Kell said as we pulled up to the valet parking for Conrad's. The restaurant was a Charleston landmark, mentioned regularly on all the where-to-eat blogs and featured frequently for its award-winning chefs. It was an old-Charleston favorite, where the long-established families dined when they weren't at the Country Club, the kind of place where the regulars acknowledged each other with a nod and a wan smile.

"He said he wanted to do something really special for Teag," I replied as a valet came to get the car key.

"Renting out the private room here certainly counts. My cousin checked their prices for her wedding and decided she'd rather have a down payment on a house."

Anthony Benton came from money. He had a partnership at Benton Connor Hawthorn, one of Charleston's most prestigious law firms. His family lived in a home on the Battery that had belonged to a Benton since before the Civil War. He was an odd match for Teag, who had grown up in middle-class suburbia and put himself through college and grad school.

But somehow, they were perfect for each other.

I slipped my arm through Kell's as the valet drove his car away. "I ate here once with my parents, before they moved to Charlotte," I said as we walked toward the door. "The food was good, but mostly I was worried about using the wrong fork."

Kell chuckled. "I promise not to turn you in to the etiquette police."

Anthony had asked my opinion on who Teag would want to invite, and I knew the friends here tonight wouldn't care about things like forks, but they cared a lot about Teag. I wanted to get to the restaurant early so I could see the look on Teag's face when the two of them arrived.

"We're with the Benton party," I said to the Maître'd, who led us to a large room in the back roped off with a sign that said "private party." I thought we'd arrived early, but it looked like everyone else had the same idea, because we weren't the first ones there.

"Cassidy! How come I haven't seen you down at the Market lately?" Ernestine Teller greeted us as we walked inside. She gave me a warm hug, as did her daughter, Niella. Mrs. Teller and Niella sold beautiful sweetgrass baskets down at the Charleston City Market, each one carrying a touch of their Weaver magic, and perhaps a bit of Hoodoo protection, too.

"We've been crazy busy," I explained. "I'll have to make sure to head over soon. I haven't even been down to Honeysuckle Café for my favorite coffee."

Mrs. Teller gave me an appraising glance and shook her head. "You need to *take* time, girl. Live a little," she added, giving Kell a wink and a broad smile.

I spotted Father Anne across the room, deep in conversation with Lucinda. Maggie, our part-time assistant, was laughing with Alicia Peters, a psychic medium who helped us out a lot. In the far corner, Alistair McKinnon from the museum was chatting with Mrs. Morrissey, who ran the Historical Archive.

The sound of ticking made me turn. "Chuck! I'm so glad you could come!" I greeted Chuck Pettis. "And this must be your great-uncle Robert," I added, acknowledging the octogenarian beside him.

Chuck was in his mid-fifties, ex-military from a supernatural special ops organization that hunted the kind of creatures we did. He'd played a big role in some of our hardest cases, but he'd been absent for a while, helping Robert get settled after his retirement. The ticking came from the inside of Chuck's jacket, which I knew was covered with wind-up watches. Chuck's PTSD manifested in the firm belief that if his watches ever all wound down, he would die. He was an odd bird, but a tough fighter.

"You're Kell, right?" Chuck said, extending his hand. "You treat her right, you understand? I'd hate to have to kick your ass," he added, keeping a straight face until Kell's expression made him laugh.

"Don't mind my great-nephew," Robert said with fond exasperation. "He's always been like this."

"How do you like Charleston? It's quite a change from Cape May," I said.

"I miss my store, Trinkets, but it's in capable hands," Robert replied. "You and Sorren advised me well on choosing my replacement. I do believe Erik Mitchell will be a good fit."

Robert's store, like Trifles and Folly, was an Alliance outpost in the never-ending war against dark magic and supernatural threats. Robert looked to be in his eighties, but I suspected that his long association with Sorren had extended his lifespan, perhaps by decades. That had been true for my Uncle Evann, who left Trifles and Folly to me because I shared his psychometry. I wondered if I, too, would outlive my contemporaries. The thought made me shiver, and Kell squeezed my hand.

"You all right?" Kell murmured.

"Yeah. I just must have caught a draft," I fibbed.

"I am looking forward to it cooling off a bit," Robert went on. "I was happy to put Cape May winters behind me, but I didn't realize I'd be moving to the jungle."

"The tropics," Chuck corrected. "Not the jungle."

"Feels like the damn jungle to me," Robert replied. "Speaking of which, let's go see if the bar makes those fruity drinks I like. The ones with the little umbrellas." He nodded a farewell, and then made for the bar, with Chuck hurrying after him.

"Do you think Robert can get Chuck to give up all his watches?" Kell wondered aloud as we watched them go.

"I doubt it. But it'll probably be good for Chuck to have Robert move in. Chuck's been on his own since his wife died. They certainly make an odd pair."

The private event room had glass walls that looked out over Charleston Harbor, and strands of twinkling lights made a canopy over the patio just beyond the French doors. A trio of musicians off to one side played lively Zydeco music, a favorite of Teag's. Kell and I dropped off our presents at the gift table, then made our way to the hors d'oeuvres, where plenty of scrumptious finger foods tempted my self-control.

Kell snagged us both flutes of champagne from a passing server and handed one to me. "To birthdays," he said, lightly clinking his glass to mine.

"To birthdays," I replied with a smile. Despite everything else that had been going on with the Caribbean ghosts and the cursed statues, at the moment my heart felt lighter than it had in a long time. We were surrounded by good friends, here to celebrate Teag's special day, and I refused to let dark thoughts take any of the shine off the evening.

"Make sure you get some of those crab puffs," Maggie said, coming up beside me. "They're amazing!" I glanced at her plate, piled with goodies that included cold shrimp, little soufflé bites, and fried green tomatoes with a fancy chutney topper.

Maggie had the business sense of Steve Jobs and the fashion sense of Stevie Nicks. Her blue kerchief-hem dress was made from recycled sari silk, and I recognized her vintage earrings as ones she'd recently purchased at our store. Somehow on Maggie, it all worked.

"You've never steered me wrong about appetizers before," I confirmed, as Kell and I began to fill our plates.

"When are Teag and Anthony going to get here?" Maggie asked, excitement shining in her eyes. "I can't wait to give him my present. He's going to love it!"

She had already confided to me that she had bought him a bamboo loom shuttle marked with protective runes and blessed by Tibetan monks. That was as quirky-perfect as the hand-turned cypress wood drop spindle I'd commissioned from a woodworker with some magic of his own. The agate spindle whorl I'd added to the gift wasn't nearly as old as mine, but it held strong, positive energy.

"I got him a gift card for that specialty taproom down by the Market," Kell said, grinning. "Sometimes, simple is best."

"I wish Sorren and Archibald Donnelly could be here," Maggie said after she'd polished off another crab puff. "Even if Sorren can't really enjoy the food." Vampires could eat, but they didn't need to, and Sorren had told us that one of the downsides of the Dark Gift was that food never tasted as good as it had in his mortal days. Donnelly, our resident necromancer, would have loved the posh spread since he had a reputation for a hearty appetite.

"Sorren sent a package for Teag to the store," I told her, glancing toward the gift table. "Knowing him, it'll be unique." Sorren had a penchant for giving either protective amulets or arcane weapons. No one in this crowd would bat an eye at either one.

I glanced around at our friends and felt warmth and gratitude at our unusual found family. As an only child, I always longed for the sprawling extended families my friends had, and when my parents moved away, I'd felt adrift. That was when I'd just taken over the shop, and Baxter and I seemed all alone. But one by one, all these wonderful, gifted people had not only come into my life, but they'd become friends and allies, people I knew had my back even against nightmares and monsters. I wouldn't trade that for anything.

"Penny for your thoughts," Kell teased, holding up a piece of pickled okra for me to take a bite.

"Just happy to be here, surrounded by friends. And my best guy." I stretched up to give Kell a peck on the lips.

"I was just thinking that we've got most of Charleston's major magical players in one room. It's got to be the safest place in town," Kell said.

"You've got that right." Rowan walked up with Alicia Peters a step behind. "And to make sure, Lucinda and I put down some wardings earlier today. Just in case."

I thought I'd felt a frisson of power when we walked in, but I'd convinced myself I'd imagined it.

"The ghost of the restaurant's original owner is hanging out in the lobby," Alicia said. "He promised to keep an eye out for anything weird. Spirits make the best security guards."

I glanced around the room, mentally counting heads. Lucinda's cousin—and fellow Voudon practitioner—Caliel had joined the party. So had Ryan Alexander, a friend whose urban exploring often overlapped with Kell's SPOOK investigations and several of the cases Teag and I had worked on. Everyone was here—except for Teag and Anthony.

"They're here!" Maggie called out from near the door. "Places, everyone!"

I had to chuckle at Maggie's exuberance. This wasn't really a surprise party since Teag knew we'd all be here, but I suspected he might not have realized the lengths to which Anthony had gone to make the gathering special.

Anthony ushered Teag through the doorway and stopped just a few steps inside.

"Happy birthday!" We all called out in unison. Teag's eyes went wide, and he clutched Anthony's arm.

"This is...this is amazing," he managed, looking a bit overwhelmed. "Wow. Thanks for being here."

Teag and Anthony made their way around the room, making sure to greet everyone. Maggie threw her arms around Teag and gave him a gleeful embrace. I wrapped an arm around his waist for a side hug. Anthony stood beside him, grinning at Teag's expression.

"Were you surprised?" I asked.

"God, yes. I mean, I knew Anthony got everyone together, but I didn't think..." He looked happily gobsmacked.

"Don't I always take good care of you?" Anthony asked.

"Sure you do. We take care of each other," Teag replied, taking Anthony's hand.

With his blond hair, blue eyes, and broad shoulders, Anthony looked every inch the prep school former rowing captain that he was.

His Tommy Bahama shirt, khakis, and Sperry's were a contrast to Teag's geek chic combination of a plum shirt beneath a black jacket over dark skinny jeans and Converses. Teag was X-Games to Anthony's GQ, but it worked for them.

The servers arrived to herd us toward the tables. Everyone was talking and laughing, trading in-jokes and references only those who ran in our circles would understand. Most of the time, when we got together, we were holding off the gathering doom or saving the world. I liked seeing everyone happy and relaxed for a change.

Kell and I sat across from Teag and Anthony. Teag gave me a look. "Did you know this wasn't just a casual little get-together?"

I smiled. "Maybe."

"And I thought besties didn't keep secrets," he teased.

"Good secrets don't count," I replied with a laugh.

The servers brought out the homemade cornbread, house-made pickled watermelon, okra, and black-eyed pea salad, and kept everyone's drinks full. Entrées came out soon afterward—artisan pit-smoked pork barbecue, shrimp and grits, or Conrad's fried chicken, the meal all the foodie magazines raved about. We'd had the chance to pick our meals when we sent the RSVP, so soon the conversation quieted as we all dug into the delicious food. By unspoken agreement, everyone kept the topics light, although given this group's shared interests, there was no avoiding comparing notes and discussing the finer points of magic and lore.

By the time we got to dessert, I leaned against Kell's shoulder, stuffed and happy. The servers cleared the table and brought over Teag's presents while they got the cake ready.

Teag looked a bit overwhelmed and teary at the pile of gifts. Anthony stood behind him and laid a steadying hand on his shoulder.

"Y'all really shouldn't have," Teag protested. He looked around the table with a fond smile. "Just having all of you here is the best present. I don't know what to say."

"Say you'll open them, so we can get to the cake!" Maggie teased, and everyone laughed.

Like Kell, Ryan had gone for a gift card, but everyone else's presents reflected the very special interests of our group of friends. Mrs. Teller presented a handmade scarf, and Niella gave him one of her sweetgrass baskets, both items specially woven with protective magic. Lucinda and Caliel gave silver medallions with the *veves* for Papa Legba and Damballah, two powerful and protective Loas. Father Anne had located a hard-to-find book on Weaver magic, while Alicia Peters gave a small carved piece of jasper that provided protection against shadow people.

Rowan, knowing Teag's martial arts background, gave a rune-carved staff made from ash wood. Mrs. Morrissey and Alistair went together on a gift certificate for Teag's favorite rare book store. I wasn't surprised when Chuck and his uncle, both former special ops with CHARON, gave Teag a blessed antique knife made with Damascus steel. And, of course, Maggie and I had our gifts among the presents to be opened as well.

That left Anthony. He pulled an envelope out of his leather messenger bag and handed it to Teag. "Sorry—it wasn't easy to wrap," he said.

Teag met his gaze for a moment, then opened it and let out a gasp. "Oh, my god! We're going to England for Christmas!" He waved the paper at us. "And we're staying in a real castle!"

Anthony cleared his throat. "That's just part of the present," he said, and something in the odd tone of his voice made us all quiet down. He reached into his bag again, then sank down on one knee.

"Teag Logan, will you marry me?" Anthony held out a small velvet box, and we were close enough to see the beautiful brushed platinum ring with a single, embedded baguette diamond. Knowing Anthony, I felt certain he'd had the ring custom-designed.

"Yes. Yes, yes, yes!" Teag cried.

Anthony slipped the ring on Teag's finger, then Teag threw his arms around Anthony's neck, and we cheered as they kissed.

Teag and I had gone into battle together against some high-powered supernatural bad guys and been badly injured, but in all that time, I'd never seen him cry. Now, happy tears rolled down his face, and I was crying with him. Maggie openly sobbed with joy. Everyone gathered around Teag and Anthony to give them hugs, wish them well, and see the ring.

When the door opened, we all looked up, expecting a serving cart with birthday cake.

Instead, a wild-eyed man in his early thirties burst into the room. "I need to find Sorren! Where is he? I've got to warn him."

Chuck and Kell moved toward the man cautiously, and I could see that, despite the festive nature of the dinner, Chuck had drawn a silver knife and held it at his side. Several of the others stood, ready to take action if the situation required it.

"Hey, buddy. This is a private party. Sorren's not here," Chuck said. "You need to leave."

The stranger shook his head, looking even more desperate. "You don't understand. There's a lost demon who wants vengeance for three hundred years of servitude. I'm Beckford Pendlewood, and it's all my family's fault."

CHAPTER SIX

"Sit down, boy. Your demon can wait. Why don't you join us? We're about to have some cake." Ernestine Teller's gravelly voice carried a note of command, and it cut through the stranger's panic. Chuck and Kell escorted Beckford to a seat at the table, and Anthony overcame his surprise with aplomb, leaning out of the door to signal a server to bring dessert.

Beckford Pendlewood looked like a man at wit's end. His chestnut brown hair was mussed as if he'd been running his hands through it. The monogrammed button-down shirt was bespoke, his jeans were a pricy luxury brand, and his boat shoes were Prada. A vintage Rolex watch glinted beneath his cuff on his left wrist. He obviously came from wealth, but it certainly hadn't brought him peace of mind.

Everyone else had taken their seats, except for Chuck, who hovered behind Beckford's chair. Rowan pointedly cleared her throat.

"What? Pendlewoods are trouble," Chuck growled.

"And I think the folks gathered here are more than up to the challenge," Rowan countered. Chuck took his seat, although he continued to glare at our new guest.

"I'm sorry," Beckford said as if he only now realized he had barged in on a party. "I should go."

I exchanged a glance with Rowan. Neither of us thought letting Beckford leave was a good idea.

"Stay," Teag said. "It's my party, and it's okay if I say so."

Beckford looked uncertain, but he didn't bolt for the door. Two servers wheeled in a large white sheet cake decorated with candles and a sparkler. When we all serenaded Teag with "Happy Birthday," Beckford seemed unsure whether to join in, so he hummed along quietly. When a server placed a piece of cake in front of him, he hesitated, until Teag nodded for him to eat.

Everyone raved about the excellent cake, but the newcomer's arrival put a damper on the conversation. I remembered that the Pendlewood name had come up in the context of the two warring plantation families who had branched out into the dark arts. Looking at the man who picked at his cake with downcast eyes, I had to admit that it was difficult to picture Beckford as the evil wizard type. But evil can be most effective when it looks appealing and harmless, and I resolved to handle this new development with care.

When we were finished with the cake, Anthony bumped my leg under the table, with an unspoken question in his eyes about what to do next.

"Why don't you take the birthday boy and his presents home, and we'll wrap things up here," I said. "How long do we have the room?"

"Until midnight," Anthony replied. "I wanted to make sure we didn't feel rushed."

That gave us two hours to sort things out with Beckford because I didn't want to bring him inside the wardings at Trifles and Folly, and I certainly wasn't going to bring him home with me. Without having to ask, a glance at the others around the table yielded nods, letting me know they were onboard with settling this issue here. I took comfort from the fact that Lucinda and Rowan had put down wardings around the restaurant, so if Beckford had gotten through them, the magic didn't see him as a threat.

Or he had more power than they did. *So much for feeling reassured.*

"Are you sure?" Teag asked, cutting his gaze to Beckford and then back to me.

"Positive," I told him. "I promise to fill you in. Go enjoy your birthday. We'll handle this."

Ryan stood to help carry the gifts and said his goodbyes. Teag made another loop of the table, thanking everyone again and giving hugs. Chuck and Robert were the hold-outs on hugging, although Robert gave Teag a firm handshake, and Chuck clapped him on the back and did the forearm grip brothers-in-arms thing. Teag gave me a peck on the cheek when he got to our end of the table. "Thank you," he whispered. Then he looked to Kell. "Just make sure she gets home safely," he warned.

"Absolutely." Kell reached over to take my hand.

Alistair, Mrs. Morrissey, and Maggie also wished Teag well, thanked Anthony, and gathered their things to go.

When the door closed behind them, everyone turned to look at Beckford.

"Maybe you should begin at the beginning," I said. The man looked scared to death, but I didn't know whether he was afraid of us or something else. From what he'd said when he crashed the party, I had a feeling we were the least of his worries.

Our unexpected guest raised his head and looked out at the admittedly wary faces staring back at him. "My name is Beckford Pendlewood, of the Barbados and Charleston Pendlewoods." He took a sip of water and gathered his nerve.

When he squared his shoulders and set his jaw, he almost looked like the kind of guy whose casual outfit cost a couple of grand. Almost, if it weren't for the haunted look in his eyes and the dark circles, and the fact that those expensive threads looked like he'd slept in them.

"My father, Ellis Pendlewood, is—was—the next-to-last direct descendant of Wilfred Pendlewood, the man who made our family fortune and brought the family curse down on us," Beckford said. "He shot himself on his fiftieth birthday three weeks ago. That's what Pendlewood men do. And now…I'm the last of the direct line."

"There's no love lost between your family and Sorren," Robert

Pettis said in a voice like ground glass. "So why come here looking for him? Because I know, boy, that we've had dealings with Pendlewoods over the years, and we didn't part friendly." The fire in the old man's eyes made me suspect that he gave up his shop in Cape May because he wanted to, not because of a frail mind or body.

"Would it surprise you if I said that I'd have been rooting for you?" Beckford didn't back down, even though he looked out at us as if we were a firing squad. "I want nothing to do with the family legacy, the magic, or the money. But I can't break the curse on my own. That's why I'm here. I need your help."

"I have the feeling you jumped into the middle of this tale," Ernestine Teller said in a slow drawl that underscored her words. "How 'bout you start at the beginning. We have time." She leaned back in her chair and clasped her hands on the table, fixing Beckford with her gaze.

Beckford swallowed nervously, then nodded. "Yeah. Okay. It's complicated." He took another sip of water while he collected his nerve. I glanced at the rest of my tablemates. Chuck and Robert still looked like they might jump Beckford in the parking lot. Mrs. Teller and Niella were wary but open to hearing what our strange newcomer had to say. Rowan's mouth was a thin slit, and her eyes had narrowed. There had to be some history there, none of it good. Lucinda and Caliel looked angry. Beckford had his work cut out with them.

Father Anne appeared intrigued, and I saw her surreptitiously pull out her phone to text someone below the table. *Interesting.*

"My great-something grandfather, Wilfred Pendlewood, fled the witch hysteria in Europe in 1640," Beckford said. "He settled in Barbados, where he founded a sugar cane plantation. He also bought property in Bermuda and Charleston for shipping and the social connections, but Barbados has always been the heart of things…until now.

Beckford took a deep breath. "Wilfred fled the witch hunts because he was a witch. So, in addition to sugar cane and rum, he added smuggling occult objects." He met my gaze. "I believe his ships had more than a few run-ins with an ancestor of yours, a privateer named Dante."

That startled me, a little twist I hadn't seen coming.

"Wilfred became rich, but it wasn't enough. He bound a soucouyant, and locked it in a sugar chest to make sure we'd always be wealthy." Beckford's voice dripped with loathing.

"A what?" Kell couldn't help asking.

"It's a Caribbean vampiric demon," Lucinda supplied. "Nothing to mess with."

Beckford nodded. "The black magic needed to keep the demon bound brought a curse on my family, and the risk of catastrophe if he ever gets out. To compel the demon, all those in Wilfred's direct line had to learn Solomonic magic."

"There's a reason Solomonic magic is heavily restricted," Rowan said. "It's good for little except summoning and commanding demons."

"The Pendlewood heir controls the demon through a signet—the Ring of Ornias. Mastering that kind of magic strengthens the demon and takes a toll on the heir's soul."

"Is that why your father killed himself?" Kell asked.

Beckford shook his head. "No. The demon keeps my family rich. But the deal is that the heir to the power dies on his fiftieth birthday, mad, by his own hand. And for a long time, generations, my family was fucked up enough to think they got the good end of that deal. Back in the day, fifty was a ripe old age. But now…not so much."

"So, you're the new heir, and the job comes with a demon side-kick?" Father Anne gave Beckford an appraising look. If he noted her unconventional appearance, he didn't blink.

"That's one way to put it. The thing is—even a demon couldn't hold off nature and trading shifts," Beckford went on. "Hurricanes did a lot of damage to the plantation and the island's infrastructure. And there are other sources now for sugar, and other ways to sweeten food. The income from our sugar cane is down to almost nothing. Two months ago, my father sold the property in Barbados and everything in it that wasn't magical, and shipped the rest to our property here in Charleston."

"If the rest of your family was so keen to sign on, why are you different, Beckford?" Father Anne asked.

"Beck," he corrected automatically. "No one calls me Beckford. No one I like, anyhow." He sighed. "My father wanted out of the curse, but he didn't really wise up until he'd already accepted the ring and the demon. He was determined it would stop with him. So, to try to save me from the curse, he sent me to boarding school in New England from the time I was twelve. He asked me to cut all ties with the Pendlewoods. But…then he died, and it turns out I'm still cursed."

"What makes you think so?" Father Anne pressed. Father Anne could kick ass and kill monsters without losing a beat, but out of all of us, she was usually the one who tried the hardest to see if the monster deserved a second chance.

"I didn't think anyone except my father knew where I was," Beck said. "My mother died when I was little, and my cousins are all jerks." I was pretty sure he would have used a stronger word but guessed he was trying to be polite. "But one day, a box arrived with his ring in it. That's how I knew he was dead. There was a message in the package from my oldest cousin. He made it clear that if I didn't accept the ring and the demon, someone else would."

He swallowed hard. "I ran. I've been running since then."

"You said something about a 'lost demon' that wanted vengeance," Chuck growled. "Can we get back to that?" I elbowed him with a reproving glare, but Chuck didn't really look sorry.

"The demon—Ornias—is trying to tempt me to continue the legacy. Threaten me, really, because if I don't, he and my human cousins will kill me to take up the ring and keep the legacy going. While we lost our holdings in Barbados, there was plenty of money stashed in Switzerland and the Grand Caymans. More than enough for some people to sell their souls for." No one could overlook the bitterness in Beck's tone.

"That's why I came looking for Sorren," Beck said. "I want to break the curse, once and for all, and send the demon back to hell. But the sugar chest where the demon is bound has gone missing. And Ornias is getting impatient with me for holding out. If I die as the last direct heir, with the curse unbroken, my oldest cousin could claim the ring and the demon. And my cousin has made it clear that he's willing to kill me if I won't step up. He *wants* the curse."

He lifted his head, with a defiant glint in his eyes. "I intend for the curse to stop with me."

"I think we've all had a lot to think about," Father Anne spoke up. "And the folks here at the restaurant probably want to go home." She looked to Beck. "I can offer you sanctuary, in a warded safe house, courtesy of the St. Expeditus Society. You'll be protected, and the rest of us will have a chance to regroup and think about what to do next. Will you accept that?"

Beck hesitated for a moment and then nodded. "Yes. Thank you. Just…tell me the truth. Will I be a guest or a prisoner?"

"The truth? A little of both. We can't really let you go wandering around, considering what you've told us," Father Anne answered. "And if you've got a demon and your cousins gunning for you, you probably don't want to be out on your own. If you meant what you said about breaking the curse, I think we can work something out."

"All right," Beck agreed. "I'll go willingly. And I won't cause you any trouble."

"That's for damn sure," Chuck muttered under his breath. "Robert and I volunteer to ride shotgun to get your guest to the safe house," he added, raising his voice.

"I'll never turn down qualified help," Father Anne replied.

"Then I'll ride along too in that case," Rowan said. "It's a nice night to be out and about."

"WELL, THAT WAS AN EXCITING PARTY," Kell said when we finally left the restaurant.

I rolled my eyes. "For all the right—and wrong—reasons. I'm so happy that Anthony finally popped the question. They've been together for a while now. But the whole thing with Beck—"

"Yeah. That's quite a story." He drummed his fingers on the

steering wheel. "Do you think Sorren will help him? I got the feeling Beck didn't have a lot of friends in the room."

"I think there's a lot of history there we haven't heard," I replied. "As for Sorren—I don't know. But I'm going to call him and find out."

Kell pulled up to the curb near my house. I live in a white Charleston single house that I bought from my parents. The narrow end of the house faces the street, and the porch faces a walled garden. For privacy, the door at the sidewalk actually leads onto the porch—which Charlestonians call a "piazza"—not into the main house. It's a quintessentially Charleston style of home, and I absolutely love it.

"Can you stay?" I asked.

He shook his head. "Not tonight. I'm sorry. I've got a video shoot at dawn, and I still need to pull some stuff together. But I'll bring dinner tomorrow night if you're up for it."

"Sounds like a date," I replied. He leaned over and kissed me, a long, slow kiss that let me know just how sorry he was not to be able to stay.

"See you tomorrow," he murmured.

"Count on it." I hopped out of the car and let myself in the door. I knew Kell would wait until he saw me switch on lights in the house, despite the protective wardings Lucinda and Rowan had placed on my home. Baxter was already barking up a storm when I put the key in the door. I flashed the porch light, my signal to Kell, and watched him drive away.

Bax yipped, letting me know he'd been overlooked.

"Sorry, Bax. I didn't even bring you any cake." I checked his food and water. "But I've got some treats for my good boy." I dropped a couple of goodies into his bowl, and Baxter forgot to be annoyed at me as he gobbled them up.

When I had changed into sweatpants and a T-shirt, I settled on the couch with Baxter and pulled out my phone. With the time difference, it wouldn't quite be dawn in Europe. Calling anyone else at this hour would be rude, but since vampires sleep during the day, it was prime time for Sorren.

He answered on the first ring. "Cassidy? Is everything all right?"

Sorren may be a nearly six-hundred-year-old vampire, but he looks like a grad student—mid-twenties at most. His blond hair usually rocks the latest trendy cut, and his gray eyes aren't just pretty—he can compel most people if they meet his gaze directly. Most people, but not me. It's partly an immunity that comes with the long family association, and partly because Sorren swore he would never use his magic on me. Although we look like we're the same age, he's always acted more like a protective uncle—or grandfather. And yes, he's completely up-to-date on technology. He told me more than once that vampires who can't change with the times don't last long.

"I'm fine," I replied. "Your present arrived safely, and it's at the store for Teag to open tomorrow. Anthony proposed, which was one of the evening's big surprises. And everyone at Teag's party said to say 'hello.'"

"Please give Teag my best wishes. And trust me when I say that both Archibald and I would rather be there than here."

"What's going on?" I wasn't quite ready to share Beck's story yet.

"There's been an influx of cursed artwork coming into museums and private collections," Sorren said. "Fortunately, we caught wind of it quickly, and Archibald and I have been tracking down the items and acquiring them by whatever means necessary."

Even before he had vampire strength, stealth, and speed, Sorren had once been the best jewel thief in Antwerp. Those skills still served him well. Although we did our best to try the legal way first, sometimes the only way to save the world required breaking some rules along the way.

"Bad stuff?" I had an inkling where the art might have come from, and I wondered how much Sorren knew.

"Very bad. But it's curious—many of these pieces haven't been seen for a couple of generations. We assumed that a collector with magical interests—and abilities—had bought them and locked them away. To have them come to light now, and to include a number of rather notorious pieces, it's…unsettling."

He went on before I could interrupt. "Erik Mitchell, the new owner of Trinkets up in Cape May, used to work on art theft and relic misappropriation with all the major museums. He's been doing his best to track the items as they come up—and Robert Pettis, the former owner—has used some of his contacts from CHARON and elsewhere. But every time we get our hands on one piece of artwork, two more pop up. I wish I knew where they were coming from."

"The Pendlewood estate in Barbados," I replied.

Sorren went quiet. "How do you know?"

"Because Beckford Pendlewood burst into Teag's party like a madman with a story about a curse and a lost demon in a box that might want to destroy the world."

Sorren swore in Dutch, a sure sign he was decidedly unhappy. "Where is he now?"

"Father Anne has him in a St. Expeditus safe house."

"Why was he in Charleston, or anywhere near you and our people?" Sorren felt responsible for and protective of our group of allies, despite the fact that every one of us could hold our own in a fight. He'd told me once that it came from having to outlive almost everyone around him, and recognizing how precious—and short—mortal life was. The supernatural community understood that Sorren's vengeance for hurting one of his found family would be swift and merciless.

"He was looking for you."

"For me?" Sorren sounded surprised. "Believe me, Cassidy, I'm the absolute last person a Pendlewood would ever want to see."

"His father is dead, he's the last direct heir, and he wants to break the curse," I reported. "And I think he's telling the truth."

"I've been dealing with the Pendlewoods for centuries," Sorren replied. "Dante had a lot of run-ins with their ships around the time of the Revolution. They smuggled some very dark occult pieces to powerful practitioners in cities along the coast. Dante sank several of the ships and raided quite a few more, but we couldn't catch everything. They're bad news—and highly untrustworthy."

"Rowan, Chuck, and Robert went with Father Anne to take Beck into custody," I said. "No one's taking his word for it. But...I do think it's worth hearing him out. He said the demon and his cousins are going to kill him unless he accepts the ring and the curse."

"The Ring of Ornias? He told you about it?"

I recapped Beck's story, including the soucouyant in the sugar chest, and the lengths to which he and his father had gone to end the legacy.

"So, Ellis sold off the contents of the Barbados plantation? That would certainly explain where these art pieces are coming from."

"I think there's more to it than that," I said. "Beck said that his father sold the plantation and the things in it that were magically safe. Everything else was supposed to be shipped to their Charleston holdings—but I think some of the cargo got lost or stolen along the way."

This was the first chance I'd had to fill Sorren in on the funky island ghosts, the homicidal sailor's valentine, the murderous carved dolphin figure, and the wandering walking stick. He listened in silence, staying so quiet I thought the call might have dropped.

"I'm still here," he replied. "You've been busy. Nice work. But you're right—all those incidents have a common thread. Barbados. And if Beckford is telling the truth—which is a very large 'if'—then it's possible that cursed or haunted pieces from the Pendlewood estate could be to blame. But the real question is—what really happened to the cargo?"

"Teag and Seth Tanner are working their way through the ship's manifest," I said. "But it's a big ship, and I don't know that the Pendlewood containers would have listed their true contents. Even one crate going missing could be a big problem. But if a whole container is gone…"

"It would be too much of a coincidence for random thieves to happen to pick one of their containers to steal," Sorren pointed out.

"Unless either the contents of the container…or a demon…guided their choice," I replied.

"Both of which are, unfortunately, possible."

"We destroyed the shell valentine and the coco macaque," I reported. "We still don't know what caused the rolling cow ghost and La Diablesse to appear. Rowan and the coven circled back to deal with the other killer carvings, and they have the pieces locked up. We're holding our own, but this demon box is a whole new level of crazy."

"You have no idea," Sorren said. "A soucouyant is serious trouble. To bind one requires stealing its shed skin when it changes human hosts and locking the skin in a chest with powerful magic. It's no accident Wilfred Pendlewood picked a sugar chest for the binding. Sugar is used in a lot of attraction spells—some harmless, and most decidedly not so."

"So it would be good to keep the demon in the box?" We'd gone up against demons before, and I'd rather avoid doing that again if I had a choice.

Sorren laughed, but there was no humor in it. "Yes. Because if the demon gets loose, it will indeed want vengeance for centuries of servitude, and it won't just take its revenge out on the Pendlewoods. It could do enough damage to make a hurricane like Katrina look like a summer shower."

I shivered, and Baxter nuzzled closer. "What now? Will you and Donnelly be back soon?"

"Unfortunately, no. There's no one I trust to hand off chasing down the cursed art, and Donnelly can't handle it by himself. You're going to have to run with the Pendlewood problem—and you have an excellent team to help you do that. Don't try to handle it alone."

"That, I can guarantee," I promised.

"What about the ring? Did Beckford say where it is?"

"No. Just that he'd received it, and that his cousins would kill to get it."

"Then whether or not he's being completely truthful, protecting him while we sort this out is essential."

"You think it's really that unlikely he was telling the truth?" I knew looks could be deceiving, and that master manipulators could fake sincerity, but I had a gut sense that Beck meant what he told us.

"I think that getting free of more than three centuries of a family curse is harder to kick than smoking or a drug habit," Sorren replied. "In fact, that's a good analogy. Addicts may have very good intentions, but they can underestimate the hold the addiction has on them. And make no mistake, magic is one of the most potent addictions there is. He may actually mean what he told you. But being able to hold out against the demon and the ring—and the curse—would take exceptional strength."

"Is it possible? Would he be free if we broke the curse?" Beck had been dealt a lousy hand by fate. I couldn't help hoping that might change.

"Maybe. But you—and he—need to understand that it's far more likely for the process to kill him," Sorren replied. "Removing someone's magic tears at mind, body, and soul. A curse like this one is bound at a soul level. The demon consumes the soul, in exchange for the promised rewards. Ripping it out by the roots…won't be easy, or pleasant."

"All right," I said more gamely than I felt. "We'll get working on that. I'll keep you posted."

I could sense Sorren's frustration without him needing to say a word. "Cassidy—please be careful. I know you and Teag have gone up against some very dangerous entities. But this soucouyant is as bad as the worst of those. Take precautions. You're going to need everyone on the team, most likely, before this is done."

I ended the call, feeling jittery. I wasn't going to fall asleep any time soon. Baxter climbed into my lap, and I held him close, petting his silky fur. "How about I make some popcorn, and we pick a movie?" I asked him.

I took his yip for a "yes."

CHAPTER SEVEN

"So the band played, and people started dying?" I asked, trying to make sense out of what I'd seen on the news. A beach party the previous night had hired a local steel drum band, but when the music started, everything went wrong.

"Yeah. I was there, and I still can't believe it." Darnell Evans, the bassist for Coconut Dreams, shook his head. His long braids swayed like willow branches in the wind. Strong, slender fingers gripped his coffee cup—a musician's hands. He wore a dark green T-shirt with his band's logo on it, over ripped jeans and flip flops. Two silver medallions hung from chains around his neck. I couldn't quite make out the details, but I felt sure they were both protective charms. He didn't look like he'd slept well, and he had that spacey kind of lag that often came with shock and trauma.

Lucinda and I met up with Darnell at Honeysuckle Café, my go-to favorite for good coffee. Darnell toyed with his muffin and took a sip of his coffee, but I could tell that food wasn't on his mind. "I know you talked with the police," Lucinda said. "But we come at things like this differently than they do."

"The police thought I was crazy." Darnell gave a bitter chuckle. "Hell, if I hadn't seen it with my own eyes, I'd think so, too."

"We won't," I promised. "We deal with things like what you saw. We make sure they can't hurt other people."

His dark eyes searched mine like he was waiting for a punchline. "For real? Like those guys on TV?"

"Yeah," I said. "Sorta like that. But we need to know everything."

He took a long drink from his cup—a delaying tactic—and then nodded. "Okay. You can't react worse than the cops did."

Darnell leaned forward so his voice would only carry to Lucinda and me. "I've been playing with Coconut Dreams for four years now. Malik, Jamal, Andre, and me, we started it up after we went down to the islands on spring break and fell in love with the music. We'd been trying to get a band going for a while, but nothing ever felt right. And then, wham, there it was. We heard those drums, and it was a done deal."

He sighed. "The guys bought drums—they're called 'steelpan' and drummers are 'pannists'—and I had my bass guitar. And that changed everything, once we got up to speed on the songs. We went from couldn't-get-booked to booked solid. I shoulda known that kind of luck wouldn't last."

"You were good friends with the other members of the band?" Lucinda asked.

Darnell looked down. "Yeah. We were tight. Everyone got along great."

"Can you walk us through how things went that night?" I picked at my muffin so I didn't make Darnell uncomfortable by staring at him.

"Crab Ahoy hired us to play on Saturday nights this month. It was a great gig. They paid well, their customers don't get out of hand, and we got a round of free drinks at the end of the night," Darnell said. "We did our usual set-up and were ready to go when happy hour started. But as soon as we started playing, I knew something wasn't right."

"What made you think that?" Lucinda's voice was comforting but authoritative, and it seemed to help calm the flustered man.

"Because Malik didn't seem like himself. I'm not sure how to explain it. He just…didn't play like…him." He grimaced at the difficulty to put his thoughts into words. "Malik was a good pannist. One of the best I've played with. But that night, he was better than good. Better than his best—hell, better than anyone's best. It was spooky. And the look on his face—like he was gone into the music. My nana, she would have said he played like a man possessed."

I winced, suspecting that to be more true than Darnell realized.

"And then *she* showed up."

"She?" Lucinda echoed, raising an eyebrow. This hadn't been in the story the police gave to the newspaper.

Darnell nodded, but he looked down at his coffee, probably expecting us to laugh. "An old woman in one of those loose flowery dresses, like my nana used to wear. Only this woman looked *real* old. Like a mummy. And she just shows up in the crowd, but she's not moving to the music. She starts walking, and when she touches someone, they fall down."

He took a deep breath. "I didn't know what I was seeing, at first. But then people started screaming, and we all stop playing—everyone except Malik." He shook his head. "It was like he couldn't stop. Jamal and Andre and I had to wrestle him away from the drum, and it took all of us to do it. That shouldn't have been possible—Malik was a little dude. And then, that old lady looks right at him, and she does this thing with her fingers like she's telling him to come to her. Then she disappears. Gone. And Malik, he starts shaking and goes stiff as a board, and then just like that, he's dead."

His voice caught, and he looked away, trying to get himself under control.

"We're sorry for your loss," Lucinda said.

He nodded, biting his lip. When he could speak again, he turned back with a bleak look in his eyes. "I know the police didn't believe me when I told them about the old lady." He looked away for a moment to gather his control. "Losing him...would be bad, no matter who it was, you know what I mean? But Malik—me and him, we go way back. Grew up together. He was like a brother to me. I can't believe he's gone."

"Was there anything else different about this last party you played? Anything at all?" I hated to press him since he was obviously still grieving, but he was our best lead for finding out what happened.

He shrugged. "No. Nothing—except that flashy new drum Malik bought."

Lucinda and I exchanged a look. "Tell us about the drum," she said.

Darnell seemed surprised. "Really? Okay. He'd only had it for about a week. Instruments and shi—stuff are expensive, and none of us were raking in the cash, so we're always on the computer, looking for a good deal. He found this online auction that had a steelpan that was the size he'd always wanted. And the price was good. Only, it was marked up funny. That didn't stop him. He bought it, and it came pretty quick, so he had time to practice with it at home, but this was the first time he used it at a gig."

"Marked up funny—how?" Lucinda asked.

Darnell took his phone out of his pocket. "He texted me a picture when he bought it. See, a lot of drums have markings on them, numbers or letters, to help you keep your place on where to hit the notes. Malik, he didn't need that anymore, he'd been playing so long, but he thought this one was really different because it had these weird symbols. He liked how it looked."

He turned his phone around to show us, and I felt Lucinda straighten up in her chair. I didn't need to know anything about music to recognize those symbols as magic.

"What happened to the drum?" I asked.

"It's in Andre's garage, with the rest of our stuff," Darnell replied. "By the time the police talked to us and let us go, it was real late, and after what happened to Malik and all, we just haven't played since then."

"Don't." Lucinda's tone was sharp. "That drum he bought? Those symbols are bad magic. You play that drum, you'll end up just like him, and that spirit you saw will come back and kill more people."

"Spirit?" His eyes went wide.

She nodded. "It's called an asema. A blood-sucking hag. It's a type of vampire spirit—and the markings on that drum called it."

Darnell looked from Lucinda to me and back again as if we'd lost our minds. "You think a *vampire* killed Malik and those people?"

Lucinda raised her chin. "You've got a better explanation?"

Teag had hacked the police records, so we knew that the official cause of death was extreme blood loss. That hadn't been released to the public, but it fit with what Lucinda said.

"Vampires aren't real," he whispered, but I was pretty sure he was talking to himself, not us.

"There are a lot of things out there people don't want to believe are real," I said gently. "But all those stories come from somewhere. The details might not be like you've seen in the movies, but ghosts, vampires, curses—they're real."

Darnell had a deer-in-the-headlights look. "Holy fu—dge," he said, with a glance at Lucinda like she might give him a smack upside the head for his language. Her eyes narrowed, and she gave the barest nod, acknowledging his save.

"We need to destroy the drum," I said. "It's dangerous. We don't want anyone else to get hurt."

Darnell took a deep breath and then nodded. "Yeah. Okay. I can take you there. We practice in Andre's garage all the time, so I know the code."

We followed him to Andre's house, a ranch home on the airport side of town. From the well-tended flower garden filled with lawn decorations, I figured he lived with his parents.

Lucinda and I had debated the best way to handle the drum the whole way out there, finally deciding to stick with the basics.

Lucinda had a bag of rice, and I had a large container of salt. She carried a silver knife, and I had the silver net we usually used on shapeshifters. We also had a large bag made from cloth Teag had woven, with wardings and protections in the fabric, then blessed. It was large enough for even the steelpan, and once we got the drum into the bag, its magic would make sure the asema stayed bound until we were ready to destroy the instrument.

"What are you going to do?" Darnell whispered as we stared at the drum, lying with the rest of the instruments on the garage floor.

"We're going to shut that hag down, for good," Lucinda assured him. "Just stay back, and keep a hand on those charms. If you remember any prayers, now's a good time to say them."

Lucinda turned to me. "This kind of vampire is a little OCD. If we spill the rice on and around the drum, she has to count every grain. Putting a layer of salt down over everything might keep her from manifesting, but if she does, the rice should slow her down enough for us to get the jump on her."

Just in case, I had my athame, a bottle of holy water, and a special boline knife that could kill even a vampire ghost. Lucinda had a silver knife and her protective charms.

"Here we go," I muttered, readying the salt.

Darnell stepped back from the garage door, into a little garden area alongside the house. Lucinda and I moved forward at the same time. She already had the rice bag open and poured out the grains into the steelpan and spilling over all around it. I was on the other side, sending a torrent of salt down onto the cursed drum.

The temperature plummeted in the garage, and I barely had time to realize what was going on before an ice-cold hand touched my arm, and I felt dizzy.

"Cassidy!" Lucinda charged forward with the silver knife. The asema vanished, and reappeared outside the scattered rice, on the other side.

"Behind you!" I yelled. Dizzy or not, I had a job to do, and I took a swipe with the boline knife, slashing the hag's arm as she reached out for Lucinda.

Once again the vampire disappeared, only to show up in a different place. Maybe she needed to be in contact with the rice or salt for them to distract her, since she'd been careful not to step on the grains. She came for me again, and I dodged, wobbling a bit on my feet. I already felt lightheaded, and I didn't want to get drained more.

With my left hand, I sloshed holy water on the hag, and she let out an unholy shriek, then blinked out. Lucinda and I warily circled the steelpan drum, waiting for the next attack.

"Watch out!" Darnell shouted just as I saw the asema materialize behind Lucinda and put a hand on her shoulder. Lucinda staggered as the vampire fed. Darnell rushed forward, holding the long iron pole of a bird feeder post like a lance, and ran it through the hag.

"That's for Malik!" he shouted as the sharp end skewered the vampire and she disappeared.

Lucinda stumbled, and Darnell steadied her. I gripped my athame in my right hand, ready for the next time that vampire bitch showed herself.

The asema showed up right in front of me, almost in my face. She reached for me, but I was faster, and this time, I brought up my athame, pointed at her chest, and pulled on its resonance. The blast of cold white energy lifted the hag off her feet and tossed her back onto the salt-and-rice-laden drum. She shrieked, wriggling and writhing, but she could not force herself to leave without counting all the grains. With a final angry scream, the hag vanished.

"Thank you," Lucinda said to Darnell, looking ashen but steady. I was feeling pretty pale myself, down a pint from the vampire's touch, but mad enough to finish the job.

"How about I lift the steelpan—real carefully so we don't disturb the rice and salt—and you two slip the bag over it?" I suggested.

We all regarded the drum suspiciously, but the asema did not materialize again. Working together, we got the drum into the bag and lifted it into the back of my RAV4. Once it was level, I dumped in the rest of the rice and salt for good measure.

"What will you do with it?" Darnell asked, looking at the SUV as if he expected the hag to burst free at any moment.

"Destroy it properly," I said. "We have people who know how." In the meantime, I knew Father Anne would give us some temporary space in one of the St. Expeditus Society's holding sheds.

"Are you two all right?" he asked. "I saw her touch you."

"We've had worse," Lucinda assured him.

"Thank you," Darnell said, looking from Lucinda to me. "I really didn't know what to do." He looked wistfully back at the pile of equipment. "Not sure whether the guys will still want to play. It's gonna take us a little bit to get past this, you know? But I hope maybe, in a while, we can. Malik wouldn't want us to quit."

"Just don't buy any more equipment off shady websites," I said with a wan smile. "It's not worth the discount."

"True, that." Darnell stood in the driveway, watching us leave, and gave a wave before we turned the corner.

LUCINDA RODE with me to hand off the drum to Father Anne. We called the priest when we left Darnell's house, and she met us at the drop-off point. I figured if anyone besides Sorren could lock down the drum and the asema, it would be Father Anne.

"Do you think that's the last of the cursed items from the Pendle-woods?" Lucinda asked as we drove back toward where she left her car.

"No. I wish I did." I relayed the main points from what Sorren had told me, and she listened with a grave expression.

"There's a dark side to Caribbean magic because the conditions on those cane plantations were horrific," she said quietly. "It was bad enough people were brought there against their will, but as awful as it was here in the States, picking cotton or tending rice, it was worse down there. Barbaric." She shivered. "The folk traditions developed out of some common threads. Those people wanted deliverance—and they wanted—deserved—vengeance."

"Beck admits that his family were bad people," I replied. "And I get why Sorren doesn't trust him. But what if he's telling the truth about wanting to break the curse? It sounds like he's lived away from his family and apart from their dealings for most of his life. He can't make up for all the wrong they did, but he can stop them from doing more. I feel like that deserves a chance."

Lucinda shrugged. "Well, I guess we'll see. With the group we've got, he's not going to be able to hold up a lie for long."

I thanked Lucinda for going with me to see Darnell and dropped her off at her car, with a promise to keep her updated. Then I drove back to Trifles and Folly and found a cold deli sub sandwich and a fresh pitcher of sweet tea waiting for me in the break room fridge.

"We ordered out for lunch, and figured you'd want something when you got back," Maggie explained. "And I brewed the tea this morning, so it's cold by now."

I thanked Maggie and Teag. Lunchtime was long past, which wasn't helping my lightheadedness. Once I ate, I started to feel better after the run-in with the asema. Sweet tea wasn't quite the same as getting back the blood the hag had stolen, but between the sugar and the caffeine, it was a close second.

During the lulls between groups of shoppers, I filled Teag and Maggie in on what had happened with Darnell and the cursed drum.

"Another problem with Caribbean roots? That hunch about some of the Pendlewood cargo being stolen is looking more and more likely," Teag said.

"Unless the people who 'stole' the cargo knew exactly what was in it and where to find it." An idea that had been at the back of my mind since Beck told his story finally found its way into words.

It hardly seemed possible that the birthday dinner had just been the night before. The new ring glittered on Teag's left hand, and I caught him looking at it and fluttering his fingers to make the diamond catch the light.

"You think that some of Beck's killer cousins might be behind the thefts?" Teag asked.

"It makes sense," I replied. "Beck's father wanted to end the curse. But he would have had to know how dangerous some of the family 'heirlooms' were. I mean, according to Sorren, the Pendlewoods have been in the occult smuggling business since before the Revolution."

"If his father wanted out of the family business, then he doesn't seem like the kind to just sell off those dangerous pieces," Maggie supplied. She loved a good mystery, and while she wasn't a fighter, she'd helped with logistics and central communication for several of our big run-ins with supernatural bad guys. Maggie was good at putting the pieces together, even if her Woodstock wardrobe didn't suggest that.

"Suppose Beck's father was trying to send the dangerous stuff back to the Charleston holdings, trusting Beck to deal with them once Ellis was dead," I theorized. "But the cousins know Ellis and Beck want to break the curse, and they don't want it to end—after all, it's the source of their money."

Teag nodded, following my train of thought. "Since they're family, they could probably find out what was being shipped, when it was going out, and what boat it was on. I doubt Ellis packed the crates himself. Maybe the cousins even had an insider in Barbados who tipped them off to the best crates to steal," he added.

"Hell, maybe they worked with the insider to identify the pieces they knew would be easiest to sell off," I said. They listened while I recapped my phone call with Sorren, and told them about the problems he and Donnelly were having with cursed and haunted artwork over in Europe.

"Yeah, that's too much to be a lucky coincidence," Teag agreed. "Especially if the cousins are willing to kill Beck to keep the demon in the family."

"That would explain how the expensive pieces got to Europe," I mused. "And cargo containers full of haunted stuff might trigger the sightings we've had here in Charleston—like La Diablesse and the rolling cow ghost. But what about the things like the shell valentine and the steelpan drum? I can't see Beck's posh cousins running a Darke Web eBay."

"Maybe they weren't the only ones who stole from the cargo container," Maggie suggested. "It's got to happen a lot on those big ships."

"You'd think a family like the Pendlewoods would have wardings and spells on the container," Teag argued.

"Could they really, when it's being handled by regular people on a big ship?" I countered. "It would have to be handled by so many different groups to get it on and off the ship, inspected by customs, put into storage. That might make it hard to put strong magical protections on it, because you don't want to accidentally have it zap people who have a legitimate reason to be moving it around."

"Well, Seth and I are making progress on the manifest," Teag said. "It's just that there were a lot of containers on the *Caribe Queen,* and the Pendlewood cargo descriptions weren't exactly precise. I mean, who's going to list 'vampire-haunted steel drum' on a bill of lading?"

Business picked up in the two hours before closing, so we didn't get more time to talk. By the time we locked up, I was feeling the effects of the day—including the unwanted blood donation to the vampire hag.

"You look worn out," Maggie fussed.

"I think the fight with the asema took more out of me than I wanted to admit," I said.

"Is Kell coming over for dinner?" Teag asked.

I checked my phone to make sure I hadn't missed a text about a change of plans. "He said he would when he dropped me off last night."

"Good. I'm glad you're not going to be alone. There's too much weirdness going on right now," Teag replied.

"Speaking of which, how's Anthony taking all of this?" I asked.

Teag shrugged. "You know, he's made a lot of progress. He not only believes the supernatural is real, but to tell you the truth, the whole thing with Beck showing up and telling his story didn't freak Anthony out like I thought it might."

A couple of years ago, Anthony hadn't even known about the work we did for the Alliance. Then we fought an epic battle against some really powerful bad guys, and Teag almost didn't survive. Anthony found out, and Sorren laid down a challenge—learn to accept the work we did and the reality of the threat, or Sorren would wipe his memory of everything, including Teag. Faced with that choice, Anthony picked Teag. And the rest, as they say, is history.

"Good," I said. "Kell took it in stride, too."

Teag gave me a look. "Yeah, but Kell started with an advantage. He's a ghost hunter. He already believed."

"There's believing, and then there's having the truth shoved in your face and trying to kill you…on more than one occasion," I replied. Kell had gradually earned his way into our little group of "supernatural vigilantes," as Anthony once called us. He might not have magic, but he had courage, and he and his SPOOK team had played important roles in shutting down some scary stuff.

"Then I guess we've both gotten lucky," Teag said with a cute little smile that told me, as if I needed to be reminded, how over the moon he was about Anthony and this next step in their relationship.

"Ah, youth," Maggie said with an exaggerated sigh. "I wish you both a great evening. I'm going home to my cat and putting my feet up with a good book." Maggie had been widowed for a number of years and seemed to be perfectly content as a solo act. We walked out to our cars together, and she gave us a wave before she drove off.

"Anthony's working late, so I'm going to work with Seth on the manifests again," Teag said. "And since Sorren's got Erik Mitchell involved with the haunted art issue, I pulled in Erik's main squeeze, Ben Nolan, on the legit parts of the shipping research. He's still got his P.I. license, and I think he likes keeping his hand in the game."

"Whatever works," I said. "Let me know if you find anything." Teag promised that he would, and we headed our separate ways.

Baxter met me at the door, bouncing and yipping. I swept him into my arms, juggled the mail and my purse, and headed to the living room to tidy up before Kell arrived. My phone rang, and I plopped down on the couch with Bax, expecting it to be Kell saying he'd be running late.

"Cassidy? It's Chuck."

"Hi, Chuck. What's up?" Chuck and I worked well together, and I respected his skills, but we didn't call each other to chat.

"You know that when I was in the army, I worked for CHARON," Chuck said. I didn't know much about the shadowy supernatural special ops group that was an off-the-books military program, but what I did know made me decide I really never wanted to come up against them.

"Yeah," I replied, not sure where he was going.

"Uncle Robert worked for them, too, back in the day. And he also had a stint after that, working for Archibald Donnelly and the Briggs Society."

That, I didn't know. Donnelly was our resident necromancer, but he also ran the Briggs Society, which was a repository of dangerous magical items and historical artifacts that—for one supernatural reason or another—couldn't be allowed into mundane hands. I'd been there once—and ended up in a fight against a fallen angel who had stepped out of a cursed painting.

Robert must have been a real badass in his day. Or maybe he still was.

"Okay." I drew out the syllables, inviting him to get to the point.

"Between the two of us, we still have connections," Chuck said. "Neither of us has any love for CHARON—they aren't the good guys they want you to think they are—but we both know people who know things because of those ties. And I put out some feelers about soucouyants and demon boxes and that sort of thing."

"Did anyone know anything?" Teag and Seth worked their hacker magic. Chuck was playing it old school.

"I got an earful about the Pendlewoods. They've been under surveillance since at least the Civil War. Of course, that didn't stop the powers-that-be from asking them for favors now and again—like helping our side when Hitler got interested in occult objects. But you know by now that nobody's pure in this game. Not for long."

His cynicism made me sad, but Chuck was right. Just in the short time I'd been part of the Alliance, not only had I seen things that stripped away innocence, but I'd done things—In the course of saving the world—that could land me in jail for the rest of my life.

"Yeah. I know."

"That demon box can't be allowed to get loose," Chuck warned. "Beckford said it was 'lost.' That's the supernatural equivalent of losing a nuke. Not only could it get into the hands of occult terrorists, but it wouldn't do anyone any favors if CHARON or the Sinistram got a hold of it."

"Sinistram?" That was a name I hadn't heard before, but it didn't sound good.

"Vatican black ops. Ninja priest-sorcerers. That's the group Travis Dominick up in Pittsburgh used to be part of before he walked away. And somehow, managed to stay alive."

Interesting.

"Travis is a psychic medium ex-priest who still hunts demons. He's teamed up with a former FBI agent, Brent Lawson, who has some special skills of his own. Rumor has it Brent keeps turning down CHARON's recruitment offers," Chuck added.

"I called Travis to see what he could turn up. He's managed to stay out of the Sinistram, but he still has access to the hidden occult archives at Duquesne University. If there's anything there that might tell us how to find and neutralize the demon box, Travis will let me know," Chuck said.

"What would happen, do you think, if CHARON found out about Beck and the Ring of Ornias?" I knew it wouldn't be anything good.

"You know how in the movies, the government goons show up in black helicopters and a convoy of SUVs? Yeah, well, I was one of those goons. Except in real life, it's not that showy. CHARON would be in and gone before you ever saw them coming, and they'd take Beckford and his demon ring with them. And where they'd send him? They'd rendition his ass somewhere that makes Gitmo look like summer camp."

CHAPTER EIGHT

The next morning, while Kell made French toast and bacon, I took Baxter out to the walled garden to take care of business. My phone buzzed, which was odd considering it was still before eight o'clock.

"Simon?" Of all the people to be calling at this hour, I didn't expect to hear from my cousin.

"Hi, Cassidy. Hey, I really need to talk to you. Dante won't leave me alone until I do."

"Dante?" I echoed. "You mean dead ancestor privateer Dante?"

"Yeah. After he helped me stop that killer pirate ghost, we've sorta gotten to be besties."

"Wait. Not before coffee," I protested. Baxter trotted back inside, ready for his breakfast. Kell noticed my phone and gave me a questioning look.

"I need all the coffee to deal with this," I mumbled. Kell pulled out the biggest mug we had and filled it to the brim. I put the phone on speaker and set it on the table.

"It's Simon," I told Kell.

"Hi, Kell. Tell Cassidy you two need to come up and spend some time at the beach. Vic and I would love to show you around." Simon loved his adopted home of Myrtle Beach.

"That would be fun," Kell agreed. "What's up? I've got to warn you—she isn't caffeinated yet."

"I'll take my chances," Simon replied. "Dante won't shut up about 'evil in a box.'"

Kell mouthed, *Dead Dante?* I nodded.

I got comfortable and took a sip of coffee. I suspected I might need the whole pot by the time we were done with the call. "All right. I'm fortified. Spill."

"I talked to you a while back when we had those murders that seemed to be linked to an old pirate treasure," Simon began. I remembered. Simon's boyfriend, Vic D'Amato, is a homicide detective with the Myrtle Beach Police Department, and Simon often works with the police as a consultant when cases get weird.

"I'm not sure I ever told you how that all got resolved, but the short version is, in order to push a really dangerous relic that was trapped in a shipwreck deeper into the ocean, I had to let Dante's ghost possess me so he could use his water magic. We kind of hit it off, and he's hung around since then."

Kell just gave me a blank stare, like he'd blown a brain fuse. I had to admit, that was a lot to process, even for me.

"Okay," I said, very slowly because the coffee hadn't really kicked in yet.

"Hey, psychic medium here," Simon reminded me. "And anyway, Dante's pretty cool, considering he actually remembers the American Revolution. And he's got some powerful water magic—he just needs to be in a body to use it."

I knew that gifted mediums like Simon and our friend, Alicia Peters, could allow a ghost to possess them during a séance or a private reading. That didn't make the idea any less creepy.

"Go back to what you said about 'evil in a box.'" I gulped my coffee and held out the mug for a refill. Kell obliged and handed it back.

"He told me that I needed to warn you because he's felt the brush of that spirit before," Simon replied. "Back when he was alive and chasing down occult items on the high seas in the Caribbean."

I inhaled the smell of the coffee, and tried to figure out a plan of what—and how much—to tell Simon. He somewhat knew we got bad supernatural things out of the wrong hands. I'd tapped into his extensive knowledge of myth and lore on situations before.

But for his own protection, I'd never told him quite how big some of our incidents had been. Like, saving-the-world-big. Nephilim. Demons, The Wild Hunt. Norse demi-goddesses. Hell, I hadn't even told him that my business partner was a vampire. And now it sounded as if Simon, maybe out of the same misguided protectiveness, had omitted a few important details from his stories, too.

"He did," I replied. "It's a soucouyant from Barbados, trapped in a sugar chest by a family of witchy smugglers Dante played cat-and-mouse with many times. There's also a cursed ring that binds the demon to the chest. And at the moment, the demon box is, uh, lost."

"Lost?" Simon echoed.

"We've got the ring and the last direct heir," I said, although it wasn't my fault the box had gone missing. "That counts for something, right?"

Kell scrubbed a hand over his eyes and cast a longing glance toward the cupboard where I kept the whiskey. I sympathized.

"Cassidy, what's going on?" I heard the sincerity in Simon's voice, and I knew I had to come clean.

I told Simon about Beck crashing Teag's party, passing along an only lightly-edited recap about the Pendlewood family and the malicious ghosts we'd encountered with links to Barbados. Since I didn't want to totally fry his circuits, I figured the whole vampire-boss discussion could wait for another time.

"My business partner and a colleague are over in Europe, tracking down cursed artwork, with Erik Mitchell's help," I said. "Teag and I and our…friends…are trying to track down cargo we think was stolen—or intentionally rerouted—from the old Pendlewood plantation in Barbados."

"Well, that explains why Seth Tanner got suddenly interested in

Caribbean magic," Simon said with a sigh. "I take it he's helping Teag?"

Simon had the benefit of being on good terms with the local police. After all, he was sleeping with a detective. We'd never been that cozy with the Charleston cops and didn't have an insider on the force. I definitely didn't want to say anything to implicate Teag or Seth for their hacking.

"They're both trying to figure out what came in on the ship and where it went," I replied.

If Simon read between the lines on my comment, he didn't press for details. "I'm sure Dante will remember the Pendlewood name. I recognize it from some of the lore I looked up for Seth. They were—are—bad news. Is there anything I can do to help?"

Simon was a gifted psychic, and he knew a lot about folklore and myth, but I wasn't sure he was powerful enough to deal with what we had on our plate, and I'd never forgive myself if he got hurt.

"You'll help a lot by digging up whatever you can find out about the Pendlewoods," I replied. "And that includes asking Dante what he recalls. You never know which detail might turn out to be exactly what we need."

"Okay," he agreed. "But if you need more than that, just call. Vic and I can be down in less than two hours."

Vic was another reason I hadn't been completely truthful with Simon. I knew that Vic had started out being extremely skeptical about Simon's abilities and anything that seemed to be "woo-woo." From what Simon had told me, Vic had come a long way, but exposing him to the level of weirdness we were dealing with would be throwing him in the deep end.

Not to mention that beating the bad guys often entailed bending—or breaking—a few laws. I didn't want to put Vic in an awkward position, between his oath as a cop and saving the world.

"Will do," I said, crossing my fingers behind my back. Kell saw me and rolled his eyes. "Take care, and let me know what you find out. And—thank you."

"Any time," Simon assured me. "That's what cousins are for."

When the call ended, Kell leaned against the counter and gave me a look.

"What?" I asked, feeling judged. "I can't ask him to get involved in this. We have no idea what we're up against."

"Sure we do," Kell replied. "And we can use all the help we can get."

I glared at him. "I don't want Simon to get hurt. Or to scare Vic off."

Kell chuckled. "From what you've told me, I don't think Vic is the kind who scares easily. Simon sounds like he's got a connection that might be really valuable—Dante."

"You think I should have told him to come?" I knew I sounded defensive, but I felt torn between wanting to protect Simon and knowing that we had a big fight in front of us.

Kell held up a hand, palm out, in appeasement. "All I'm saying is, the time might come when we really need his help. It needs to be up to Simon to make the choice. You need to be willing to accept that."

I nodded. "You're right. Simon's an adult. And I get the feeling he might not have told me everything about what they've been dealing with, either. He might have more experience than I'm giving him credit for."

"You think? Cassidy, that whole bit about being possessed by a ghost water witch to push a haunted relic into the deep ocean sounded epic. That sounds like major league material to me."

Kell was right, and I knew it. "It's just…Simon's very special to me. I guess it goes with being an only child. He's the closest thing I've ever had to a brother—other than Teag. I don't want anything to happen to him."

"Simon's older than you, isn't he?"

"Yeah. Early thirties. Why?"

"Because you talk about him like he's your kid cousin. He's closer to Anthony's age."

"And your point is?" I wasn't quite done being grumpy yet. Kell refilled my cup. He knows how to handle me, and I love him for it.

"At some point, you have to trust people to make their own decisions. The business you're in—the *real* business—is dangerous. You accept that for yourself. But Anthony and I…we have to trust you and Teag to do what you need to do and hope you come home safe when it's over," Kell said quietly. "It's a little like loving a soldier—or a cop. What you do is important. And we have to let you do it. Even if it scares the hell out of us."

I looked up and met his gaze, seeing a vulnerability he'd never let me see before. Damn, I'd never really thought about it that way, and I felt bad about that. "Kell, I'm sorry—"

He shook his head. "I didn't say that to put a guilt trip on you. I just don't want you to turn down help we might need for the wrong reasons."

I drank my coffee, hiding behind my mug as I worked through what Kell said, and struggled with how I felt about it. Finally, I set the cup down and took a deep breath. "You're right. Thank you. I just…"

Kell closed the distance between us and pulled me into his arms. "Even total badasses are allowed to worry about people they love. It's okay."

I hugged him back, knowing what we were up against, and hoping as hard as I could that it really would be okay.

We were slammed with a steady stream of tourists at the shop almost from the moment we opened the door, which let me avoid thinking about bigger problems while I rang up purchases and wrapped packages.

I loved seeing the joy in a customer's face at finding the perfect gift for someone or a piece that was on their own wish list. Because everything we sell is an antique, the items can't be found easily elsewhere—and might be one of a kind. That just adds to the excitement when a buyer finds what they're looking for—it's more like a quest than a shopping trip.

Technically, Trifles and Folly exists as cover for what we do with the Alliance. But the store has been in my family for more than three hundred years, and I take pride in running it like a real business and making a profit. Days like this certainly help pay the bills. Yes, Sorren would cover expenses if need be, but it meant a lot to me to have the store pull its own weight. After all, we had a reputation to uphold.

Things finally slowed down around lunch. Teag and Maggie and I hadn't had a chance to say more than "good morning" to each other, except what was necessary to take care of customers. I felt like we'd been caught in a whirlwind by the time we had a break in the traffic.

"That should make up for the week it rained every day," Maggie said when the door closed behind the customer she had just rung up.

"I'll say—and then some," I agreed. We went into the break room to eat the salads that had been delivered an hour ago. I stayed in the doorway so I could see if anyone came in.

"We might have a lead on the missing cargo," Teag said in between bites of his spinach, chicken, and Gorgonzola salad.

"Oh yeah?" I asked over a mouthful of bibb lettuce. On busy days, I'd learned the hard way that if I didn't shovel the food in while I had a chance, odds were good I'd end up going hungry when the onslaught resumed.

"Seth and I pooled what we learned with Ben Nolan, and together we've started tracing that Darke Web auction site through a series of shell companies," Teag said. "Someone knew how to cover their tracks. But we'll get to the bottom of it. And with the three of us working together, we figured out which cargo container was breached and which crates were probably taken. Whether the contents listed on the manifest were accurate—that's a different matter."

"That's great," I said. "Admit it—you and Seth have been enjoying trying to out-hack each other."

Teag flashed a sheepish grin. "Yeah. I mean, it's like a big puzzle. That's half the fun."

"What did Ben make of it?" Maggie asked.

"He took it pretty much in stride," Teag said. "Of course, after the stories he told us about a cursed hotel up there that he and Erik had to deal with, it sounds like he's up to speed with the spook stuff."

"Any leads on the demon box?" I asked. If Dante was pestering

Simon about the soucouyant, I figured that might be the bigger problem.

"Beck's cousins seem like the likely suspects," Teag replied. "If we find them, odds are good we find the box. That's what we're working on when we need a break from chasing down cargo."

"I know you're doing all you can, but I can't shake the feeling that we're running out of time," I replied. "I don't think we've heard the last of that stolen cargo—or Beck's cousins."

CHAPTER NINE

They never get all the blood out of the sidewalk.

Even bleach couldn't completely remove the dark brown stain, especially where the blood had seeped into the cracks between the pavers. In the past two days, three men had died violently here, yet all around us, life went on as usual. Would the workers that bustled around the gangways still be on the job if they knew how their fellow dockworkers died?

Probably not, which is perhaps why the police hadn't released the details.

Teag, Chuck, and I stood near the dockyards in the shadows beyond the reach of the overhead lights. Even well after midnight, supply trucks unloaded essentials, maintenance workers made the most of ships' brief time in port, and dockworkers brought loads on and off the huge cargo carriers that would be gone by morning.

"This place never sleeps," Chuck muttered. "How in the hell did something bring down three men and carve their hearts out without being seen?"

"Because the men weren't killed over there," Teag replied, with a jerk of his head toward the well-lit, busy gangways. "Each report says that they were last seen heading back to their cars at the end of their shifts in that parking lot." He pointed to a dark expanse a distance away from the docks, where the security lights were woefully inadequate for the amount of open space.

"I still think it's a werewolf." Chuck sounded surly, but I'd learned he always sounded that way. It didn't really mean anything. Deep down, he was a good guy—and someone you wanted at your back in a fight. We stood close enough together I could hear the watches ticking under his jacket.

"You saw the autopsy photos," Teag argued. "The wounds weren't right for a werewolf."

Reading coroners' reports was a skill that came with hunting monsters. The police, of course, hadn't said much at all—just a warning to be extra careful in the area after three nightshift workers were found dead by suspicious causes.

"Suspicious causes," in this case, meant having their hearts carved out of their chests.

"Maybe it's a more civilized were-," Chuck replied. "Didn't want to get blood under his nails."

"Next you'll say he brought a knife and fork." Teag's dark humor somehow made the awful details bearable.

"Good manners count." Chuck smirked, enjoying the banter.

"Well, it wasn't a robbery. And the security cameras were too far away to be much help," I said, worried and frustrated. Teag had hacked into the morgue's database, and we'd had a look at the reports and photos ourselves. Grisly as they were, the death wounds were clean, almost surgical. I'd seen the damage a werewolf inflicted with its claws. If it had been a were-, the corpses would have looked mauled, clawed, and bitten. They didn't.

"It didn't move like a werewolf," I said, remembering the strange, shadowy shape that had been barely visible on the grainy security camera footage. Werewolves loped on two legs or ran like a wolf on four. This figure glided, feeding our suspicion that it was an entity, not a creature.

"Yeah, but did it move like this 'Heartman' you heard about?"

Chuck sounded skeptical. "Because I found bupkis in the lore about it, except that it's from Barbados, and it carves out hearts."

"No idea," Teag admitted. "But we know what works on most entities, and that's a good place to start."

Chuck muttered something about how having an actual plan would be nice, but Teag and I ignored him. He knew the score when he agreed to come hunting with us tonight. And while I would have liked a lot more details on this Heartman—or even a folk painting or two for reference—the Barbados connection was too likely to overlook.

If we were right, the cops couldn't handle this. Hell, they wouldn't really be able to deal with a werewolf. Something that I suspected could shift from solid to spirit and back again—like the asema—would either get away from the police or cause a bloodbath.

Maybe we could prevent that.

We'd had Simon, Travis, Lucinda, and Rowan on a conference call earlier in the day, trying to figure out how to kill the Heartman. While there were legends about how the monster killed, and some debate over whether he ate the hearts or gave them as a gift to the devil, none of the tales or the lore suggested a way to kill him.

Lucinda wondered whether the monster was a Petro Loa under another name, with a story that had gotten twisted in the retelling.

Rowan suggested an angry revenant, the real-life version of a slasher-film ghost.

Simon thought the Heartman might be a serial killer role-playing a movie monster.

Travis had found an obscure journal by a long-ago priest in Barbados that mentioned similar attacks but gave no suggestions on how to fight it, other than prayer.

We'd all agreed that "thoughts and prayers" weren't gonna be enough.

"Everything dies," Chuck grumbled. "We killed those demon sons of bitches and sent the Nephilim packing. I'm not about to run from a Freddy Krueger wanna-be. Let's get this show on the road."

The next shift change wouldn't be for several hours, so if the Heartman was hungry, we might look like tasty bait. Teag, Chuck, and I spread out, walking across the parking lot in a row, combing from one side to the other. Chuck and Teag were on the outside, and I walked down the middle.

We were armed to the teeth. Silver and salt, iron and holy water, all the tools of our trade. I had both my athame and the walking stick Sorren had given me that had its own special power. Teag carried his fighting knives and a long staff carved with sigils, and a wicked coiled silver whip hung from his belt. Chuck might have left CHARON, but he still had shadowy sources for off-the-books weapons that weren't for sale to ordinary people. I figured he had some of those hidden under his jacket, and that thought reassured me. We might not know exactly how to kill the Heartman, but we sure weren't going in blind.

And then there had been the side trip to the craft store for a few boxes of empty glass ball ornaments that we filled with decidedly non-holiday substances.

The crunch of our footsteps sounded loud as we walked slowly across the dimly lit parking area. The lot closer to the docks was full, so the drivers of the few cars parked in this section had been unlucky enough to arrive late. We were just far enough from the main lot and the docks that I doubted anyone on the wharves could see or hear us. That made it a perfect hunting ground for the Heartman. The question was—would he take the bait?

"You smell that?' Teag asked in a hushed voice.

The commercial docks had a lot of odors, few of them good. Brine, dead fish, hull paint, and exhaust fumes formed a noxious funk. But now I could pick up the smell of cigarette smoke and rum, scents that hadn't been present seconds ago. Game on.

Between one breath and the next, the Heartman materialized in front of me. He must have been seven feet tall, a figure made of darkness. His outline looked like a man in a long coat with a broad-brimmed hat, but the arms were too long to be human. Glowing red eyes fixed on me, and the Heartman glided closer.

I raised my athame, drew on its resonance, and sent a blast of cold energy right through him.

The Heartman kept on coming.

Teag's blessed staff sang through the air, raining down a blow on the figure's shoulders that should have felled anything living. The staff hit resistance, but it passed through without stopping the manifestation, who still headed right for me.

I pulled a filled glass ball from my pocket and hurled it at the Heartman's feet. It shattered, scattering rice, salt, and iron filings in the monster's path. The creature vanished.

"Son of a bitch!" Chuck growled.

"Cassidy, behind you!" Teag warned.

I wheeled, and brought the walking stick up, pulling on its memories, and let loose a stream of fire. The Heartman shrieked and vanished, only to show up moments later near Chuck.

"Suck salt," Chuck muttered, giving the creature both barrels of shotgun rounds filled with rock salt. This time, the Heartman's image wavered, like a bad TV signal, but he didn't vanish completely.

"Cover the area around him," Teag yelled. "If he's in the middle of salt and rice, he won't be able to blink out."

We all came prepared with glass ball ornaments, some filled with the salt/rice/iron mixture and some with holy water, and the next salvo sent broken glass flying. The parking lot beneath the Heartman was now sprinkled with holy water and covered with grains and filings, and that meant that the OCD creature couldn't leave without counting them. We had him trapped—I hoped.

Now we had to figure out how to kill him—fast.

Teag threw a silver knife that hit right where the monster's heart should have been. It sailed on through, which I guess made sense if the Heartman stole organs because he was missing his own.

"Let's light him up and see how he likes it," Chuck muttered. Teag had several of the fragile balls filled with blessed oil. Chuck pulled something from his tactical vest that looked like a modified flash-bang grenade.

Teag lobbed three of the oil balls in quick succession. I sent another blast from the walking stick, and set the oil on fire, enveloping the shadowy creature.

"Fire in the hole!" Chuck yelled and tossed in his grenade.

We heard a high-pitched squeal as the grenade went off, and then a bright flare of white light that was blinding even though we closed and covered our eyes. When we could see again, nothing remained of the Heartman but a scorched area on the asphalt.

"Someone had to have noticed that and called the cops," I said. Sirens sounded in the distance. "Let's get out of here."

We ran, glad that our black clothing blended with the night. We'd parked a few blocks away so that we wouldn't be caught pulling out of the same set of parking lots, and were out of breath by the time we reached our cars, but the sirens were going the other way, and there would be no reason for anyone to notice us leaving.

"What was that thing?" Teag asked Chuck.

"A phosphorus EMF grenade," Chuck said with a shrug as if anyone could pick one up at Walmart. "Sends an energy pulse on the frequencies most likely to affect supernatural creatures, and the phosphorus is hot enough to set the Devil himself on fire."

"Good to know," Teag said, sounding a little awestruck.

We agreed to touch base later to make sure the Heartman stayed gone, and then pulled out of the lot in two separate vehicles. Just to be careful, we didn't turn on our headlights until we were in traffic.

"Do you think it worked?" Teag asked, being very careful to observe the speed limit. We really didn't want to get pulled over.

"No idea. I guess we'll know if there aren't any new missing hearts," I replied. Just then, my phone vibrated.

I glanced at the name. "It's Travis." I set the phone between us, on speaker.

"Hi, Travis. Teag's with me, and you're on speaker. We're in the car."

"We might have destroyed the Heartman," Teag said, and I could see he was still on an adrenaline rush from the fight.

"Tell me," Travis said. He'd helped search the lore for ideas on how to get rid of the creature and come up without solid leads.

Travis listened intently as Teag and I took turns telling the story. "Nice work," he said when we finished. "I'm going to add that to my lore book, in case anyone else comes across one. Have you told Simon yet?"

"Not yet," I said. "We're still fleeing the scene." A glance behind us assured me there were no cops in hot pursuit, but I wouldn't relax until we were safely home.

"Hey, I found some info on that soucouyant and the demon box. It's not good news."

"Oh, yeah?" I had a sinking feeling. Travis was the ex-priest version of Chuck—former Vatican black ops, ninja skills. Something that worried him was definitely bad.

"If the demon box and the ring aren't properly destroyed, the demon will explode in a massive firestorm," Travis reported.

"How massive?" Teag asked.

"The last time a box like that was improperly destroyed was in 1908. Ever hear of the Tunguska blast zone? The one where all the trees were flattened around a central point for miles?"

"What was a Caribbean demon doing in Russia?" Teag sounded confused.

"Different demon, same kind of box," Travis said. "You're missing the point. The Tunguska blast is estimated to have been the equivalent of two thousand times the power of the nuke that fell on Hiroshima."

"Fuck," I muttered. "That would be bad. Real bad." A blast like that would not only wipe out Charleston but most of the Southeast coast.

"Yeah," Travis agreed. "Kind of an understatement."

"So how do we destroy the box and the ring—and the demon—the right way?"

"Still working on that," he admitted. "But we know at least one way *not* to do it."

"I don't think we can afford trial and error," I pointed out. "And I don't want to be someone else's cautionary tale."

CHAPTER TEN

We had a whole day when nothing bad happened, no crazy ghosts showed up, and nobody got killed by monsters. I should have known it wouldn't last.

Anthony was working late, so Teag came over to join Kell and me for dinner. Kell had started chili in the slow cooker in the morning, and the whole house smelled fantastic when Teag and I walked in.

"Grab something to drink and sit down—everything's ready," Kell announced as Baxter came running to meet us. Bax skidded to a stop at our feet, barking all the way, then quieted as soon as Kell picked him up.

We walked into the kitchen. Kell had set out bowls, plus all the toppings—sour cream, shredded cheese, and tortilla chips with guacamole and salsa. My stomach growled loud enough for them to hear, and the guys laughed.

Teag and Kell grabbed beers, while I poured myself a glass of wine, fully intending to enjoy a peaceful dinner. The chili was as delicious as it smelled, and we all kept to an unspoken agreement not to talk about anything involving demons or murderous creatures.

That lasted until Teag and Kell got nearly simultaneous phone alerts. I exchanged a look with Bax, who might not understand what was going on, but didn't like the buzzing phones.

Both of them muttered under their breath as they read the messages. I knew nothing good could come of the texts. "What's up?" I asked, bracing for a new calamity.

"I have a computer program that checks the police scanners in the area, and uses an algorithm to identify similar incidents," Teag replied, in an offhanded tone as if it were something everyone did in their spare time. "When it gets three hits, that's enough to look for a common cause. And we just got three very unusual drownings."

Kell's head snapped up from reading his own alert. "And did the witnesses say they saw a child with no face—and backward feet?"

I finished my wine and refilled my glass because it was going to be that kind of evening.

"I won't know until I hack the police database," Teag replied. Kell and I cleared the table, and Teag pulled his laptop out of his messenger bag and got set up.

Once we had the leftovers in the fridge and the dishes in the dishwasher, Kell also logged in to his laptop and pulled up an email from his team at SPOOK.

"What have you got?" I asked Kell since I knew it would take Teag a bit to do his hacking.

"Three drownings in the past three days, all near a community dock," Kell summarized as he scanned the email. "In one case, someone was sitting on a picnic bench nearby and saw a child-sized figure without a face push a man into the current. In another, someone on a boat reported the same thing."

"Faceless child spirit with feet on backward," I mused aloud. "That's very specific—and really creepy."

"Pete had time off this afternoon, and after the third call came in on our SPOOK-line, he drove over there. Said the EMF readings were off the charts." Kell frowned. "Which is odd, because we haven't heard anything about a problem at that dock. Whatever these new ghosts are, they haven't been there long."

"Or something new gave them more juice to show themselves," I suggested, thinking about the stolen occult objects from the Pendle-wood estate.

"Let me see what I can find out about older drownings in that area," Kell said and went back to his phone.

Since both of them were now in research mode, I called Lucinda and told her what we knew.

"Douen," she said when I finished. "Another type of Caribbean spirit. Specifically, the vengeful ghosts of improperly buried drowning victims."

"Wow. You just rattled that off."

Lucinda laughed, a deep, rich sound. "Girl, after the last weirdness you called me about, I made it my business to see what I could find on Caribbean ghosts—especially from Barbados. They've definitely got some strange stuff going on. And douens are pretty common in the folklore. With the storms and boats and beaches, you can imagine."

As much as I love a surf and sand vacation, I might never look at the sunny Caribbean quite the same after this.

"How do we stop them?"

"Nothing I found said they were different from any other pissed off spirits," Lucinda replied. "They didn't get a proper burial, and they met a violent death. Father Anne is probably your best bet to lay them to rest."

"Thank you," I replied. "When this is all over, I think we all need a girls' weekend away—but maybe not to the beach."

"I hear you," she replied with a chuckle. "And sign me up. We just have to find somewhere that's *un*-haunted."

I ended the call, and Kell snagged two more beers, one for him and one for Teag. "There have been several drownings at the boat launch over the past ten years," Kell said, handing me his phone so I could see his search results. "All of them accidental. People fell off boats, chil-dren got caught in the current when no one was looking, one guy fell in and couldn't swim. Nothing that turned up as foul play."

"Any that might be more likely than others to come back as vengeful ghosts?" I asked.

"I'd put my money on the three most recent deaths," Kell replied.

"Just because their spirits would be the strongest, and have had the least time to move on. There were two last year, and one earlier this year—before the douen problem."

"The police reports say that witnesses saw an 'unidentified child' near two of the people just before they fell in," Teag reported, looking up from his screen. "The report doesn't say anything about the child pushing the victim in. But two of the write-ups say that the officers on the scene couldn't find the child, and no one claimed to know where he had come from."

"Do you think this is related to the Pendlewood problem?" I asked.

Teag raised an eyebrow. "Don't you?"

"Yeah, but I wanted to hear it from you two. I mean, Charleston's always haunted. But it's usually local ghosts."

Kell took a long pull from his beer and stared at the ceiling for a moment. "I think we've still probably got local ghosts, considering the other drownings at the site. But we might have an outside presence—or energy—powering those ghosts up, or twisting them into something dangerous. Since we don't know what all was stolen from the cargo, we don't know why some old relic might be affecting the ghosts from a distance."

"I think it's another case of bleed-over. No pun intended," Teag said, logging out and shutting down his computer. "There's no benefit to the Pendlewood cousins in drawing attention by killing random people—and the victims in all these ghost cases have nothing to do with Beckford or his family. They're just in the wrong place at the wrong time, or they bought a collectible from a skeevy source."

"Still, we're racking up a lot of collateral damage," I said, wishing my wine were something stronger. "It's not much consolation to someone that they weren't an intended target. Dead is still dead."

"I told my team to stay away from it," Kell said. "Especially with EMF readings that strong. No pictures or audio are worth putting them in danger, and we know these douen are willing to kill."

"I texted Father Anne and Alicia Peters. They must both be out, but they'll get back to me. I think having a medium with us might help. But banishing these spirits might not solve the problem, considering how many other people have drowned there." I drummed my fingers on the table, wishing I could think up a better solution.

"One thing at a time," Teag said. "Maybe Alicia can let any other ghosts that are hanging around know what's going on, get them to keep their distance. We don't know exactly how the douen are affecting the spirits, whether the ghosts have a choice about it or not."

An hour later, I'd brought Father Anne and Alicia up to speed, and they'd agreed to meet me at the community boat launch the next night at dusk.

Kell brought out the cookies he'd bought at a local *panaderia* to go with the Mexican-themed dinner, and we all dug in, because with murdering ghosts on the loose, we absolutely deserved cookies. Since Anthony wasn't home yet, Teag wasn't in a hurry to leave, so we all headed for the living room and watched a couple of episodes of the latest baking show, with Baxter moving from lap to lap on the couch, shamelessly begging for attention.

By the time Teag got the call that Anthony was on his way home, we knew more about making meringue and icing than we might ever need to know.

"Come on," Kell said, tugging me toward bed after I'd fallen asleep during the last episode. "Let's get some sleep. You've got a busy day ahead of you."

ALICIA PETERS and I rode together to the boat launch the next evening, not long before sundown. We pulled into the parking lot to find Father Anne's motorcycle already parked. She stood at the edge of the lot where she could see the launch ramp.

Today had been such a beautiful day, it seemed hard to imagine we were getting ready to square off against murderous ghosts. We'd had a busy morning and afternoon in the store, and when I walked outside, the bright sunshine made it easy to believe that all was right with the world. But we knew better, and now it was time to deal with the dark side most people never needed to know existed.

Alicia and I walked to where Father Anne stood. "Thanks for coming," I told her.

"Any time," she replied, and I knew she meant it.

"How's Beck doing in St. Gitmo?" I asked, joking about the St. Expeditus safe house.

"He's been extremely helpful. Beck seems to mean what he said about wanting to stop the family curse. He's given us names, places, accounts—we're following up, trying to make sure we can identify these 'cousins' who want to kill him and keep the curse going."

"Any luck on who might have the demon box?" Alicia made it sound like a perfectly normal question.

"Beck's given us some places to look, but so far they've turned up empty. And while we're looking for the box, the cousins are looking for Beck," Father Anne reported. "Nothing happened anywhere near the safe house, but word on the street—the supernatural street—is that there's a bounty on his head."

I gave a low whistle. "Wow. They sure aren't fooling around."

She shrugged. "When money and power are at stake—let alone a bound demon—people tend to play rough."

We'd set up our game plan the night before. Alicia would try to communicate with the ghosts of the drowning victims and encourage them to move on, or to at least stay clear of the douen. Father Anne intended to send the spirits of the dead to rest and banish the douen. I was there for back-up because when Alicia and Father Anne get to doing their thing, they're vulnerable and so if the douen manifested, it was my job to fight them off until the banishing could take effect.

Fortunately, the launch area was almost deserted at this time of day. It officially closed around sunset for safety reasons. Since dusk is a powerful time for magic—a liminal space when the veil between our world and the next is thinner—I hoped we could make quick work of the ritual and be on our way. But I knew things rarely worked out that smoothly.

We all wore our protective silver and stone amulets—in Father Anne's case, a large crucifix. I came armed with lots of salt and iron filings, some holy water, and since this was a little too public for a sawed-off shotgun with salt rounds, I had an iron fireplace poker, just in case.

Father Anne chanted quietly as we approached the boat launch. We'd done this kind of thing enough times that I knew she would warm up with the Our Father and the Hail Mary to set down good vibes, and then roll into whatever special prayers were needed. I guided Alicia by the elbow since she was opening herself up to the spirits, getting a read on which ghosts were in the neighborhood, and whether or not they were friendly.

That left me being the only one with my full attention on making sure we didn't get knocked in the water by some faceless kid ghosts with backward feet.

As we neared the launch ramp, the temperature dropped. Father Anne smoothly segued into the blessing of the water from the rite of baptism, since the lore said douen preferred to prey on the spirits of those who died unbaptized. I had no idea what the personal preferences were of the drowning victims, but if a posthumous baptismal blessing loosened the douen's hold over the spirit, I was all for it.

"The ghosts know why we're here," Alicia murmured.

"How many are there?" I asked. Father Anne kept chanting.

"Half a dozen or more, in the water," she replied in a distracted tone that let me know her attention was straddling the worlds of the living and the dead. "Some from long ago. They would like to move on. They're…curious about us. But the new spirits scare them."

"The douen?"

"Yes. The douen aren't regular ghosts. At least, not anymore." Her voice took on a sing-song quality that always sent a shiver down my spine because it no longer sounded like Alicia.

"What are they?" I stopped a few yards shy of the ramp and let go of Alicia's arm. We were all well back from the water, but the chill I felt let me know the ghosts were closer than I'd like.

"Twisted energy," Alicia replied. "They might have been human, long ago. Now, all that's left is anger. They want us to join them."

"We're not going," I said, louder than necessary in case the douen were listening.

"Let us now pray for these persons who are to receive the Sacrament of new birth…" Father Anne said and named the three latest drowning victims. I thought I saw a shimmer by the water as if their spirits recognized that they had been called.

"The douen don't like this," Alicia warned.

"Can you tell the real ghosts to fight back?" I moved forward, standing between the water and my companions. I gripped the iron poker with both hands, but the salt and iron filings were handy in my pockets.

"The douen are coming." Her soft voice was at odds with the dire message.

I blinked and found myself staring at three creepy child-sized killer ghosts. They had the form of children who might have been around ten years old, two boys and a girl—that much was recognizable from the way they were dressed. Water soaked their clothing and hair, plastering it to their bodies. The douen were dark gray and looked solid enough that—from a distance—someone might mistake them for a real child.

Except for the part about not having a face. And the feet pointing backward.

"Stay back!" I brandished the iron poker. Iron disrupts ghosts, costing them energy as they vanish and re-form. Not all of them are smart enough to recognize the danger. The douen turned toward me in unison, and somehow the lack of facial features made them even more frightening. If they used sound instead of sight, then they seemed torn between going after me or moving toward Father Anne, who had finished the baptism and went straight into Last Rites without skipping a beat.

"Deliver your servants, O Sovereign Lord Christ, from all evil, and set them free from every bond…" Father Anne continued. Her voice never faltered, but I saw that she gripped her silver crucifix with her left hand, and held a blessed boline knife in her right that could kill almost anything.

"They want our souls," Alicia said from behind me. "They want us to die. Die in the water." She sounded like she was half-awake, a dreamy-drugged tone that made my skin prickle.

"Y'all can go straight to hell," I told the douen. "Because we are not dying today."

The creepy kids had gotten too close for comfort, so I came out swinging. The iron poker slashed through two of the phantom children at once, and they vanished in a puff of mist. I lunged and sent the third spirit packing.

"Behind you!" Alicia warned, managing to snap out of her trance.

Normal ghosts need a break between popping in and out, but the douen were strong enough that they came right back.

"Shit," I muttered, pivoting just in time to keep one of the Casper children from touching me. They tried to circle me, and I didn't want to know what would happen if they grabbed me, so I swung the poker two-handed, sending them back to wherever they came from—at least for the moment.

This time, they didn't come back quite as fast. It took a moment or two longer, and that gave me an idea. If they could tire, maybe I could give them a run for their money. When they poofed in again, I threw salt with one hand before I swung the poker through them again.

"They're losing their hold on the real ghosts," Alicia said. She sounded like herself once more.

Father Anne kept on reciting the Last Rites. It's long, and it feels even longer when you're swinging around a heavy piece of iron.

I noticed that the fourth or fifth time the douen came back, they had started to fade. They weren't as solid-looking as they had been, and their color had paled from a slate gray to a dirty white.

Alicia and I tag-team attacked the douen as Father Anne rolled into the Rite of Exorcism. I wasn't expecting her to need that, but since the douen hadn't taken the hint and departed, I guess she needed to throw them out instead of just asking them to leave.

"You switched off your ghost channel?" I asked Alicia as we stood back-to-back. She had a large container of salt in one hand and a long iron knife in the other.

"We heard everything the real ghosts needed to say. The victims' spirits are fighting from their side to get rid of the douen," she told me. "But the douen are old. It's taking all of this to weaken them."

"My shoulders and arms are going to ache tomorrow."

"Better than drowning."

The douen were nearly translucent now—no one would mistake them for real children. The lag between reappearances had gotten longer every time we made them vanish. I might be tired and sore, but it looked like we were wearing out the spirits, too.

I'd heard the exorcism enough times—in both Latin and English—to know Father Anne was coming into the home stretch. The douen knew it too, and they lunged for us, two for me and one for Alicia. I tossed salt at one and swung at the other, as Alicia slashed at her attacker with the knife. The salt missed, but the poker swooshed through one of the douen, and he vanished. The other douen closed on me before I could swing again, and its fingers grasped my wrist. I gasped, as ice slithered through my veins, numbing my hand and arm. Alicia dove forward and sank her knife into the douen. The faceless ghost shrieked and blinked out.

I knew Father Anne was closing in on the end of the rite, but I wasn't sure how much more Alicia and I could take. My left arm hung at my side, useless, as if I'd slept on it wrong. One-handed, I couldn't keep swinging the heavy poker for long. When the douen reappeared, I thought we might be done for.

We'd done some damage to the spirits; they were barely visible this time. But that hadn't stopped them from being able to hurt me, and I really didn't know if we could hold them off again.

"In the name of the Father, the Son, and the Holy Ghost, I send you back to whence you came. Go!" Father Anne's voice crescendoed. She was hoarse from the long chants, but resolve glinted in her eyes, and she wore a look of fierce determination.

The douen's images wavered, faded to bare outlines, and then disappeared.

"They're gone—for good," Alicia said.

I stumbled, leaning my shoulder against a tree while I tried to massage feeling back into my left arm.

Father Anne hung back, still on high alert, and did not relax until enough time had passed that we felt sure the douen would not return.

"Are you all right?" Father Anne asked, coming over to check on me, worry clear in her expression.

"I feel like I overdid the arm weights at the gym," I quipped, wondering if I'd be able to move tomorrow.

"Can you feel this?" Alicia looked haggard from the strain of helping the drowning victim ghosts fight the douen. She lifted my numb hand and rubbed my hand and arm as if I'd been out in the cold, trying to get the blood moving.

"It's getting better," I said, but I still wasn't sure I could move either the fingers or the arm.

"Let's get out of here," Father Anne said. "The park's closed, and I really don't want to end up locked in here—just in case."

We gathered our stuff and headed back to where we had left the cars. Thankfully, we'd had the foresight not to park inside the gates. They weren't locked yet, but the park worker would be by any minute, and I didn't want to have to explain why we were there with a bag full of salt.

"Thanks for watching my back," Father Anne said as she pulled on her helmet and straddled her motorcycle. "See you soon!"

"How about I drive?" Alicia offered as we walked back to my RAV4. I nodded gratefully, not sure how well I could grip the wheel, although thankfully, my fingers could wiggle without pain now.

We passed the park attendant, who gave us a confused look, but waved when it was clear we were leaving. "Do you think he ever noticed the douen?" I asked Alicia.

"The park guy? Probably not. I think they picked their victims carefully. I kept my focus on helping the real ghosts wriggle free. But I couldn't help brushing up against the douen in my mind. They were malicious." She shivered.

"I hope Father Anne could send the spirits on to somewhere better," I said, leaning back against the headrest and closing my eyes. I felt guilty because I was sure that Alicia probably had a pounding headache from her efforts, but right now my shoulders felt like someone had tried to rip off both arms. I wanted Advil and a heating pad. Maybe I could talk Kell into a massage.

"I felt several of the ghosts slip away," Alicia said. "Sometimes they just need someone to tell them it's all right to go. Spirits are funny like that. You'd think it would be obvious to move on, but they get confused. I guess that's why there are so many stories about guides that take you to the Underworld."

Thanks to Lucinda, I'd met a few of those guides. "Psychopomp" was the formal word, and among the Voudon Loas, they were the Ghedes. Very powerful, and very scary. If someone sent a guide like that for me, I might decide staying where I was seemed like a better bet.

"Thanks for backing us up," I said without opening my eyes. "I wouldn't have made it by myself."

"The douen were stronger than I expected," Alicia admitted. "I don't think Father Anne thought it would take that much to send them away, either. It was good that all three of us came."

"How much of the douen's power might be from the Pendlewood relics?"

She thought for a moment and shook her head. "No way to know for sure, but I'm betting quite a bit. The douen shouldn't have been anywhere near Charleston, so they hitched a ride with something—or someone. To be so far from their home turf and still be strong enough to kill would require a big energy boost. The sooner we find those missing crates and the stuff that was in them, the better. I hate to think what they'll juice up next."

CHAPTER ELEVEN

"We've narrowed down where the missing crates from the *Caribe Queen* cargo might have gone, but any help you can give us would really be appreciated," Teag said. He and I sat across a farmhouse-style kitchen table from Beck, in the safe house kept by the St. Expeditus Society not far from Charleston.

"I didn't grow up around my family," Beck reminded us. "My father sent me away. I'll do my best, but I'm not sure how much help I can be."

I gave him a reassuring smile. "It's amazing what we hear when we're children that sticks. You don't even realize that you know certain things until you suddenly remember."

Beck shrugged. "Sure. I meant what I said about helping. Let's see what you have."

Only a few days had passed since Beck crashed Teag's party, but just in that short time, he looked a lot better. Worry still pinched his expression, but he had combed his hair, and a fresh change of clothing did wonders to make him look less at wit's end. His faded T-shirt and no-name jeans cost a fraction of what the expensive outfit he'd worn at the party did, but dressed like this, Beck looked like a regular guy. I wondered if he felt more like one, too.

Teag laid out a map of the warehouses near the wharves. "We've pieced a lot of hints together. And traced ownership through a bunch of shell companies and dummy corporations. Almost like someone didn't want anyone to know what they were doing," Teag added sarcastically. "But we've come up with six buildings that might belong to your cousins' side of the Pendlewood family. And we're hoping you could help us narrow that down."

Teag, Ben Nolan, and Seth Tanner had gone looking for the cargo manifests and the missing crates with the zeal of explorers in a race to find a lost pharaoh's tomb. It had gone from a task to a game to a competition, during which I wasn't sure any of them had bothered to sleep more than a few hours a night. But finally the hard work paid off —or at least, we hoped it had.

"Hawthorn Holdings," Teag said, reading the name of one of the building's owners. We both watched Beck's reaction. He just shook his head with a blank look.

"TGP Incorporated."

"If those are initials, they aren't anyone I know," Beck replied.

"Zolard Ltd."

"Never heard of them."

I found myself holding my breath. Teag and the others had been so sure they had found the right buildings. I hoped all their hard work hadn't gone to waste.

"Greer Materials."

"Maybe," Beck said, perking up. "One of my cousins is named Greer."

The name wasn't uncommon in the South, but I hoped we had a match.

"Maury Addison and Sons"

"Hold up." Beck sounded excited. "Those are the names of two of my cousins. That can't be a coincidence.

Teag marked it on his list. "How about 'Lanier Hoke Transportation'?"

Beck nodded. "Another name mash-up. An uncle and a cousin."

Teag pulled out a map and slid it across the table to Beck. "I marked where those buildings are located. You've gotten us down to three. Does anything you see on the map ring a bell?"

Beck studied the map carefully. "This could be a long shot, but when I was a kid back in Barbados, a bad hurricane came through and flooded a lot of the island. I remember overhearing the adults talking, and my uncle Lanier lost everything in a warehouse because it was ruined by the floodwater. He said he'd never own something that close to the shoreline again." He pointed to the Lanier Hoke Transportation building. "Notice that it's all the way in the back of the industrial park." He shrugged. "That might not mean anything, but…"

"No, that's exactly what we're looking for," Teag said, clearly excited for a win. "That gives us a starting place."

"You think my cousins stole some of the cargo?"

"It's possible that there are two different sets of thieves," I said. "We think that your cousins may have had an inside man arrange for them to get some high-value pieces or powerful magic items off the ship without going through customs—or having to bargain for them with you."

"And we also think that cargo thieves stole a crate thinking it was just pricey art, and that's the stuff that's showing up on the Darke Web," Teag added.

"Okay. That would make sense," Beck agreed. "And there's no doubt in my mind that Greer, Hoke, and Addison would do anything they could to get their hands on something they wanted—or thought should have been theirs."

Beck's voice had a bitter edge to it, but his eyes looked sad. I knew plenty of people with screwed up families, and had heard tales of bitter feuds over inheritances, but that all turned so much darker when the legacy involved magic. It would be awful to have family willing to kill anyone who stood in their way.

"We also came up with a name of someone who might be involved in the relic black market. Chalmers Etheridge. Ever heard of him?" I asked.

Sorren had dropped Etheridge's name when I called to catch him up on how things were going. He and Donnelly had just waged a bitter fight against a couple of pieces of artwork that were demon possessed and had several similar pieces yet to handle. That meant they weren't coming home to Charleston soon. Still, we brainstormed for more than an hour. And between the two of them, Sorren and Donnelly knew an awful lot about the kinds of creatures we were up against, and the sort of people who ran in dark supernatural circles.

"Chalmers is bad news," Beck said, unsuccessfully attempting to hide his automatic recoil at the name. "My father and the older men mentioned his name fairly often—and never in a good way."

"Is he a witch?" I asked.

Beck frowned. "I don't think so. Remember—I'm trying to piece together stuff I wasn't meant to hear, filtered through a childhood memory. I could have gotten things mixed up. But I do remember the name—it's odd. And there was never any love lost between the Pendlewoods and the Etheridges. A lot of bad blood there—some of it literal."

"If he wasn't a witch, what power did he have?"

"Besides being filthy rich? I don't think he had any supernatural ability. Even in witchy families, sometimes it skips a person. Chalmers was that guy. And I think he must have resented it terribly, because from what I remember them saying, Chalmers went out of his way to be an asshole and cross up everyone's deals," Beck replied.

"One of the things that pissed them off was that he would outbid them for relics," Beck continued. "I remember that real clearly. They'd come back from an auction or a secret sale just fuming about Chalmers beating them to something they wanted—probably just because they wanted it," Beck recalled. "He was quite a collector."

Teag and I exchanged a glance. A wealthy collector of supernatural items with a grudge against the Pendlewoods would be the perfect suspect to have stolen the demon box.

"You think he has the box?" Beck must have guessed our thoughts.

"He seems likely, doesn't he?" I replied.

"If he knew it was something we wanted, yeah. Especially if he thought Hoke was involved. I don't know the history—it was always alluded to, but not actually said out loud—but there was some real animosity between them. Whatever happened was definitely personal."

"Do you think we should have let Beck come with us?" Teag asked as we came into view of the collector's home.

"Hell, no," Chuck Pettis spoke up from the back seat. "He'd be a liability. We'd have to guard him, and if he got snatched we'd be in even more trouble than we are now."

"Chuck's right," Rowan replied. She sat next to Chuck while I rode shotgun. "I never thought I'd suspect a Pendlewood of being honorable, but I think his intentions are good. Still, we're safer without him."

Beck had argued to come with us to Chalmers Etheridge's home, but Father Anne sided with us about it being too dangerous. Beck gave in, but it was clear he wasn't used to having limits put on his activities. Then again, he'd never had a bounty on his head before. He finally agreed that he needed to stay at the safe house, but I appreciated that he wanted to help.

Teag turned his car into the driveway and stopped at the ornate wrought iron gate. We had debated whether to buzz to be let in or just have Rowan use magic. We never expected to find the gates wide open.

"I don't think that's a good sign," Teag said.

"Probably not," Chuck agreed. "But let's go in anyhow."

Etheridge's home was out on Ashley River Road, where several of the more famous Charleston plantation houses were located. It was an old neighborhood, prohibitively expensive, with many historic homes. A long driveway with an allée of live oak trees led to a big three-story antebellum house. Large white pillars, a gracious porch, and long windows with shutters confirmed my guess of its age. The dove-gray paint gave the house a ghostly look as if it might vanish if we looked away.

"Are you picking up anything?" I asked Rowan as we drove slowly toward the house.

The hair on the back of my neck prickled. Having the gate standing open was odd enough, but I couldn't imagine a wealthy collector not having security to intercept unexpected visitors. Yet we were almost up to the front steps and saw no one.

"The house has wardings, but they've been damaged," she replied. "I'm picking up a strong magic resonance, but we'd expect that if Etheridge collects occult pieces."

"Hell, yes there's resonance," Chuck added, pulling out an EMF reader that pulsed red and beeped loudly. Knowing Chuck, I felt sure it did much more than just check for spirits. "Wardings or not, that building practically glows with all kinds of energies. A lot of them are dark. No surprise, but we'd better watch our step."

"Can you tell what damaged the wardings?" I asked Rowan.

She met my gaze. "Powerful magic. It's the equivalent of forcing a lock."

"So, someone's already been to see him?" Teag asked.

"That's my guess. And they wouldn't take no for an answer," Rowan replied.

Lights blazed in the house although it was still daylight. As we pulled up in front of the sweeping steps, I was certain security would show up to demand to know why we had come, but no one seemed to notice.

We stepped out of the car, and Teag paused. "Look there. Blood." He pointed to a dark stain on the gravel. Too much to be a minor injury, and fresh enough not to have washed away with the rain.

"More, over there," Chuck added, indicating a spot closer to the steps. Maybe we did know what had happened to the security guards, after all.

"The front door's open. Might as well go in and see if anyone's home," Rowan said.

Given my touch magic, I'd been nervous about coming to the home of a famed collector of arcane objects. I had to be careful at museums and historic locations because some emotions were strong enough to seep into the floors and walls, and I'd taken a nasty turn more than once from strong, unwanted impressions.

Tonight, I'd loaded up on protective jewelry, and I carried the agate spindle whorl that had been given to Sorren by a Norse demigoddess. It held powerful protections, and also amplified my magic. My athame was already in my right hand, and in case of ghosts or anything worse, I had both silver and iron knives hidden in my jacket.

Chuck's jacket ticked quietly, and I figured he had a small armory secreted beneath it. Teag had already palmed a dagger, and I knew his jacket's big pockets could hold plenty of gear. Rowan had her magic, but I wouldn't be surprised to learn she had a few weapons as well.

We walked up the stone steps and across the wide porch. A rectangular, boxy bench sat next to the door on one side, with a topiary in an urn on the other.

Rowan pushed the door open, and we came through, weapons ready but not up, in case we'd badly misread the situation. From the vibe I was picking up, I didn't think we were wrong.

"More blood," I said, with a nod toward a wide smear on the inlaid marble of the grand entranceway. A massive oak stairway with an elaborate balustrade curved upward to the second floor. Above it hung a huge crystal chandelier that lit a foyer almost large enough to host a ball. The mosaic in the marble floor beneath our feet held a coat of arms, and I wondered if it belonged to the Etheridges, or to the original builder of the house.

The blood streak led off toward descending steps beneath the staircase. I wasn't in a hurry to follow. We'd come to talk to Etheridge and hopefully find out about the demon box. Solving a murder wasn't part of our plan.

"We'll do a room-to-room sweep," Chuck said, stepping forward. "Stick with me."

Given what we'd seen, I had no qualms about having a weapon out and ready, one in each hand. Teag had pulled two long knives, one steel with silver overlay, and one iron. He's a mixed martial arts competitor, so he's good in a fight. Chuck had a Sig in one hand and a Ka-bar in the other, and I figured both had been modified to make them good against enemies that weren't exactly human. Rowan had started a low chant. I didn't know what magic she was brewing, but I was glad to have her on our side.

The first room on the right was a richly appointed parlor, complete with an opulently carved fireplace surround, and an oil portrait of a stern old man above the mantle. Nothing looked amiss, but then again, none of the furnishings or decorations looked at all unusual, and certainly not arcane. As we made a slow sweep of the room, I opened up my abilities, looking for anything cursed, haunted, or magical. Nothing pinged my radar. Even the leather-bound books on the shelves were classic literature—not a grimoire among them.

"Maybe it's his mundane receiving room," Rowan said. "Somewhere he can meet with people who aren't like us."

We followed Chuck to the next doorway, which opened into a lavish dining room. Just a glance told me that the custom-made mahogany dining set was not only the work of a master craftsperson, but it had been extravagantly expensive. But here again, I didn't catch even a hint of magic—dark or otherwise.

The farther we went into the mansion, the more I felt the tug of old power. Etheridge might have had a few rooms where he could meet with those outside the supernatural community, but now that I'd moved toward the heart of the house, the magical resonance was strong and impossible to ignore.

"Over here." Chuck waved for us to join him and we crossed behind the staircase to a room that took up the whole left side of the house.

Huge leather chairs and dark wainscoting gave the room a decidedly masculine feel, as did the floor-to-ceiling bookshelves. The room reeked of magic, much of it old and sullied. A wired skeleton of a strange, bird-like cryptid sat on one side table, while a taxidermied form of a large black Shuck reared as if to strike in the far corner of the room.

Just walking into the collector's suite forced me to draw on the positive memories that powered my athame, which I used to help me shield myself from the stained resonance of the room. The faint smell of cigar smoke and bourbon lingered in the air.

The place had been trashed. And near the hearth, a man sprawled face-down on the floor. Chuck moved in to check the man's pulse, keeping his weapon drawn all the while.

"Dead," he announced. "Not completely cold. Rigor Mortis hasn't set in. Whatever happened here didn't happen long ago."

"Etheridge?" I asked.

Chuck carefully turned the body over. I expected blood, but the man's white shirt was spotless. The look of utter terror on his face was unmistakable. "Yeah. And I don't think he just had a heart attack," Chuck said.

Someone had obviously been searching for something. Books were pulled from shelves, the desk drawers had been emptied onto the floor, and decorative items lay smashed on the carpet. Several empty wall brackets and table stands suggested that whoever killed Etheridge had also helped themselves to some of his treasures.

"Do you think they got the box?" I asked.

Chuck shrugged. "Hard to say."

Rowan shook her head. "I doubt it. It looks like they searched the room, and then started smashing things out of spite. But whoever it was had magic strong enough to kill. I can feel the remnants of power."

I glanced around the room. "For a famous collector, it's not quite as cluttered as I expected. Do you think there are more rooms like this? Maybe the killer overlooked something."

"Hard to miss a sugar chest," Teag said. "All the ones I've seen have been a good size."

Back when only rich people could afford sugar, special boxes were created to lock up the luxury item, which came in large, solid cones. Many of the chests could hold the big cone plus the tools used to break off pieces of sugar for use. That meant the chests were often the size of a nightstand or bigger, a locked box on feet. But I'd seen chests that were just large boxes, easily stored inside a sideboard, and that was how I expected the demon box to look.

"It could be smaller," I said. "A full sugar chest with feet would be awkward to travel with, and I don't think the Pendlewoods went far without it. So keep your eyes open, it might not look like what you expect."

"If it was out, the killers took it," Rowan replied. "This had to be done by Beck's cousins, looking for the box."

"If they recognized it," I said. "Beck couldn't give us a good description, so maybe they hadn't seen it in a long time, either."

The downstairs held a kitchen and small office that were entirely unremarkable. Teag and I searched the kitchen from top to bottom, thinking it a logical hiding place, but found nothing. The upstairs held four bedrooms—one of them obviously belonging to Etheridge—and other rooms that had been turned into displays for the man's collections. They, too, had been left in disarray, so we knew the killers had been thorough. I stayed alert, using my abilities to triage the pieces we found.

"The guy liked odd stuff," Rowan observed as we cautiously explored the second of the collection rooms.

"It reminds me of the storage rooms at the museum," I replied. Come to think of it, those had been creepy, too. Where the museum's overflow had been trays of preserved insects, taxidermied birds, and personal items owned by famous people from Charleston's history, Etheridge's more esoteric collections included old grimoires and suspicious parchments, containers etched with protective runes, and case after case of magical weapons and jewelry. Other glass domes held odd bones, creepy poppets, amulets made of twigs and hair, as well as some pieces I couldn't identify.

"It's dangerous leaving all this stuff here, now that Etheridge is dead," Teag warned.

"I'll let Sorren know. He can call his Alliance contacts and get someone to take away the dangerous stuff," I said. "We don't have the space to store all of this or the manpower to box it up. Does Etheridge have family who might be showing up to claim his collectibles?"

"Chalmers Etheridge has two brothers still living, one deceased," Teag replied. "And an older sister. All of them are, reportedly, witches of some power. They might have legal claim on his belongings, but everything I found suggested Chalmers wasn't close to anyone. It might be a while before someone notices he's missing. He wasn't a well-liked guy."

"I'll get Sorren to ask our guys to hurry. They don't have to take everything—just the stuff that shouldn't be in the wrong hands," I replied. "And the wrong hands definitely include the Etheridges and Pendlewoods."

We finished the upstairs, checked for secret passageways or hidden rooms, and also scoured the basement utility rooms. That's where we found the bodies of four guards—all of them unmarked, but with frozen expressions of terror on their faces.

"Nothing," Chuck muttered as we left the house. "All that for nothing."

We headed back to the porch, and I accidentally bumped into the rectangular box bench beside the door. It rattled, and I hesitated. "Does this look fairly new to you?" I asked the others.

"Just because he's a collector, everything he owns doesn't have to be unique," Teag said. "Maybe he just wanted a place to take off his boots."

I shook my head, knowing I'd seen a picture of a box like this before. When I looked more closely, I saw that part of the top was a locked panel. "It's a package safe," I announced, feeling a surge of triumph. "A place for a delivery person to leave a package, so it doesn't get stolen off the porch."

"You think, way out here, he was worried about porch pirates?" Chuck growled. "He had a gate, you know."

"I doubt he was the trusting type," I replied. "And he probably got shipments all the time of pieces that were rare and valuable. Maybe he didn't even trust his own staff."

I was already picking the lock, a skill I'd found surprisingly useful. The panel popped up, revealing a parcel-sized hole beneath it. "It's like those box drops at the post office," I said, kneeling next to the bench. I shone my flashlight into the hole and let out a whistle.

"There's a big square package in here."

"How did the cousins miss it?" Teag asked.

"Maybe they'd never heard of a package safe. If the box that's in there is what we're looking for, then the odds are good it was delivered after the murders—when the cousins had already searched the house and found nothing."

"How do we get it out?" Teag looked concerned. "If it's what you think it is, you definitely shouldn't be handling it."

He had a point, which I grudgingly agreed. My touch magic did not want to make contact with a demon.

"I'll get it," Rowan said. "I can do a containment warding to keep its magic inside the packaging. It has to have protections of its own, or whoever delivered it would have never made it to their truck."

The three of us were on high alert to make sure no one surprised us as Rowan took the box out of the safe. It was a large cube, wrapped in unassuming brown paper and packing tape, much smaller than some of the furniture-sized sugar chests I'd seen, about the size of an old-fashioned bread box.

"That's the box that could end the world?" Teag asked skeptically.

"We've seen before that bad things come in small packages," I replied.

Teag wrapped his silver net around the box and covered that with a big piece of fabric woven with protective spells, then we placed the whole thing in a large lead container that we had brought. It made the back end of Teag's car ride low, but that was so much better than having an active demon riding shotgun.

"What are you going to do with it?" Rowan asked when Teag slammed the trunk.

"Take it back to Trifles and Folly, make sure it really is the demon box, and put it in the safe," I replied. "The safe is spelled and warded, and it's the best option we've got until we can figure out how to destroy it—without nuking the world."

We drove back to the shop with Rowan and Chuck who refused to leave until we had unwrapped the package, seen the sugar chest for ourselves, secured the demon box in the safe, and locked the shop back up. Rowan double-checked the wardings on the safe and the shop and added a few extras for good measure. We headed back to our cars, but Chuck insisted on following Teag and me to our houses, just in case. Rowan made it clear that she didn't need a bodyguard, but she called ahead so someone would expect her to make us all feel better.

The lights were on, and I knew Kell was inside keeping Baxter company. Kell's video work often focused on editing and other tasks that could be done from anywhere, so working from my place was just a matter of moving some of his gear and setting up a workstation in my spare bedroom.

Now that we knew the Pendlewood cousins were involved, and playing for keeps, Kell had moved in with me, at least for the duration of the situation. The truth was, he spent several nights a week at my place anyhow, and we'd been talking about moving in together for a while. The more involved Kell became in our real job with the Alliance, the more I worried about him being kidnapped or hurt as leverage, since he didn't have magic of his own. And now that he knew more about what we really did, he worried a lot about me, which was kinda nice. I didn't know if we'd make the move-in permanent once the crisis was over, but I figured we were going to give it a try sooner or later.

That meant Kell was already there when I trudged in. The smell of lasagna filled the house. He looked up from his computer when I opened the door and waited for Baxter to greet me with his psycho-dog barking and bouncing. Then Kell came over to give me a greeting of his own with a soft kiss.

"How'd it go?" he asked. I gave him the short version, and he high-fived me when I told him we had found the demon box.

"That's good, right?"

"Yes, in that we've got the box, and the Pendlewood cousins don't. No, from the sense that we're sitting on a magical nuke at the shop. And I imagine that Beck's cousins aren't going to stop looking for it."

I followed him into the kitchen, where the aromas made my stomach growl. "Sit down," he said. "I bought a bagged baby spinach salad and the lasagna's in the oven, so everything's done. Except the wine." He opened a bottle of red wine and poured a glass for each of us.

"Thank you," I said, feeling the stress from the day. Even though we hadn't had to fight our way out at the Etheridge house, finding five dead bodies didn't make it a pleasant encounter.

"Glad to help," he replied and came to stand behind me, massaging the tight muscles in my shoulders where I always got knots.

"Mmm," I murmured. "I could get used to this."

"That's the idea." He bent down to kiss me on the temple and then went to check the lasagna.

The lasagna tasted as good as it smelled, and the salad was a perfect addition. Between the pasta and the wine, I ended up relaxed and sleepy. It didn't take long to clean up, so Kell and I ended up taking a second glass of wine to the couch, where Bax wriggled between us as we watched a couple of episodes of a home improvement show that was blissfully ghost-free.

"I got a call from Pete," he said as we snuggled on the couch. Pete was the audio guy with SPOOK, one of Kell's long-time investigators. "You know that our group does regular swings past places we've investigated, to see if the levels have changed?"

I managed a sleepy *uh-huh*, although I figured he was going somewhere with the story.

"Well, he went past Creedmoor, one of the old, abandoned plantations. Last time, it had been mildly haunted—some activity, but no big manifestations. Today, the readings were off the charts. He didn't try to get too close, but even so, he saw orbs and felt temperature drops—and picked up some very weird audio readings."

I sat up a little straighter. "Is that happening everywhere?" We knew the stolen relics from the *Caribe Queen* were causing problems with juiced-up ghosts near the wharves, but I hated to think what would happen in Charleston if something riled up *all* the spirits. We'd had something similar happen not too long ago and barely averted a catastrophe.

"No, thankfully. At least, not yet. But I thought you'd want to know because Creedmoor is the old Pendlewood family plantation."

I sighed and let my head fall back. "Of course it is. And we've got three crazy cousins loose as well as a bunch of stolen occult relics. So why not ghosts?"

"Wasn't Brent Lawson going to see what he could dig up about the Pendlewood cousins?" Kell asked as I took a long sip of the wine.

"There's got to be dirt if they'd hijack cargo from their own uncle's shipment."

"I don't know how far Brent's gotten," I said. "I wouldn't be surprised if the cousins scrubbed their records clean, especially considering how hard we had to dig to find out the shell companies they used to buy those warehouses by the wharves."

"You know as well as I do that nothing's ever really gone on the internet," Kell said. "If it's there, Brent will find it."

Brent was the hunting partner of ex-priest Travis Dominick, who was already helping us with lore from a secret church archive, thanks to Chuck making introductions. Brent was ex-military, ex-FBI, ex-cop —and now had his own private investigation firm in Pittsburgh. He understood the supernatural and the stakes of what we were trying to stop.

"We've pulled in almost everyone on this, and we still haven't fixed the problem."

"No, but you've made good progress," Kell pointed out. "I didn't mean to harsh your mellow, but when I found out that Creedmoor had a connection to the Pendlewoods, I figured you'd want to know."

"I do, and thank you. I'll get a group together to go out tomorrow. Just make sure your SPOOK folks steer clear. If the cousins are involved, I don't want anyone getting in the crossfire."

"I will. And you need to promise you'll take plenty of backup."

"Promise."

"Okay, then. No more shop talk," Kell said as a new show came on. "Drink your wine, let's watch the show, and we'll just forget about the rest—at least for tonight."

CHAPTER TWELVE

OVER THE YEARS, I'VE TOURED ALL THE CHARLESTON PLANTATIONS that are open to the public and been invited to see a few that aren't, given what we do at Trifles and Folly. But I'd never gone to Creedmoor or heard anyone say much about it. I'd read somewhere that originally it had grown indigo and rice, but beyond that I wasn't sure what to expect. Some of the famous local plantations are partial ruins, from damage done during the Civil War. Others got handed over to nonprofit organizations to manage, and they struggle with upkeep since old houses are expensive as hell to maintain. And still more have enough of a trust fund that they're probably in better shape now than they were when the family lived there.

Creedmoor looked like the Pendlewoods just walked away and left everything to rot.

"The family wasn't happy with the way the war ended," Teag said as he, Alicia, Chuck, and I drove up the overgrown driveway. "They effectively left Charleston and pulled back to Bermuda and Barbados. They kept some business properties—like the warehouses we found— but the family hasn't lived at Creedmoor since the end of the War."

"What happened here?" Chuck asked as we looked out over the

land surrounding the old house. "There are all kinds of dips in the ground like someone buried a lot of bodies."

"For once, that's not why," Teag replied with a dry chuckle. "The Pendlewoods didn't intend to ever come back, so they leased the land to phosphate miners in the 1880s who dug the place up and paid dearly for the privilege. When they'd gotten all they could, they filled in the holes, sort of."

"And the house?" Alicia asked.

"It's the way they left it," Teag said. "Minus any furnishings, which were removed when the family took off. There's a caretaker who replaces broken windows and sees to anything that might be structural damage. Otherwise, it's all original—and worse for the wear."

"Why bother with the caretaker doing even minor repairs if they meant to abandon it?" Chuck asked.

"I was wondering the same thing," I said. "Maybe the house is some kind of anchor, even if they don't want to live there anymore."

The old home had a grandeur, even in decline. Solid brick walls no doubt helped it survive storms and time. The lack of heat and air conditioning to even out humidity and temperature swings had probably gone hard on the interior, but I knew how well the historic homes had been built. Heavy plaster on the interior, solid wood floors, stone foundations, and thick walls were made to last. As long as doors and windows kept out animals, vandals, and the weather, Creedmoor might last another century.

"Let's find out." Chuck got out of the back and pumped his shotgun as if daring the ghosts to bother us.

Beck had told us everything he could about Creedmoor. Considering that he hadn't been to the homestead since he was a child, that wasn't a lot. He had gone inside the house back then and said that while the staircases, molded plaster ceilings, and elaborate fireplace surrounds were still impressive, everything else showed its age. Faded paint, cracked plaster, and weak spots in the floor where the roof had leaked left Beck with a melancholy memory of faded glory.

"Beck said that the family never talked about getting rid of Creedmoor, although they didn't intend to return and live here," Teag said. "To me, that suggests it factors into the family's magic, somehow."

We'd come in daylight because there was no reason not to. Creedmoor was well off the main road, down a long driveway so overgrown we had nearly missed our turn. The property was bounded on three sides with woods, and the fourth side opened onto the Ashley River. No one was going to see us by accident or wander past.

"What are you picking up?" I asked Alicia.

"I'm still tuning in," she said, as we picked a spot midway between the cars and the old house. "There are definitely spirits here. Not happy ones."

"Workers? Or family?" Teag asked.

Rice plantations required hard labor, and working in waterlogged paddies made the risk of mosquito-borne diseases like malaria and yellow fever common. Mining was also a dangerous profession without any safety precautions. I didn't doubt that there were plenty of graves somewhere on the land. And probably more than a few restless spirits.

"Some of both, I think. They're…surly," she said.

"Surly?" I echoed.

Alicia nodded. "They're not coming close enough to talk just yet. But the ghosts of the workers are rightfully angry about how they were treated during their lives. And the family is…well, what you'd expect from the way Beck described them. Entitled, snooty. They're close to telling us to 'get off their lawn.'"

We all came armed, in case we happened to cross paths with Beck's murderous cousins—or the pissed off ghosts of his ancestors. I had both my athame and my walking stick, as well as iron and silver knives and all my protective gear. In addition to the silver, onyx, and agate— and the spindle whorl—I wore woven bracelets Teag had made that included spells for safety. We had jack balls and gris-gris bags in our pockets, courtesy of Mrs. Teller, for another layer of Hoodoo protection against evil spirits.

Teag had a whip of coiled, spring-like silver that was razor sharp on the edges, several knives, and his staff, which is part of his martial arts weaponry. Chuck was armed to the teeth as usual, with all kinds of weapons that weren't regulation. Alicia didn't usually carry a weapon, but we'd persuaded her to have a knife, just in case. She'd be focused on the ghosts, so we were there to protect her.

We made a circle with Alicia in the middle. That way we could keep watch in all directions for threats from humans or spirits.

The day had been warm when we left downtown. I expected it to be somewhat cooler near the river from the breeze, but the temperature had fallen noticeably since we had gotten out of the car, which could only be due to ghosts. The wind kicked up, rustling in the leaves of the trees and bending the long grass that covered a lawn no one bothered to mow. I could have sworn that I heard low moans in the distance, and a hum of voices just out of earshot.

"Look." Teag pointed toward the shadows beneath the trees at the edge of the clearing. Greenish orbs of light danced in the near-darkness, too large to be fireflies. A gust of wind across my neck made me shiver from the cold and the primal awareness that the dead were listening.

The ghosts of Creedmoor were waking up, and I wasn't sure that was a good thing.

"Cave-in. Boat tipped over. Fever. Crushed by a wagon," Alicia murmured. It sounded like a stream of consciousness ramblings, but I knew she was relaying what the ghosts told her about the ways they died.

"Heatstroke. Got hit in the head. Beaten too bad to get over it. Stomach problems. Bad heart," she continued. "So many. Everyone left, but not them."

Alicia turned slowly until she was looking toward the water in the distance. "The river. Freedom in the river. Pendlewood men fear the water. Fear the water," she repeated.

I wished we had brought Father Anne, but she had obligations at her church today, and we hadn't thought we should put off coming here. I made up my mind to come back with her when all this was over and help these poor souls move on.

"They're running away," Alicia said in that sing-song tone that meant she was between worlds. "Oh. Bossman is coming. Told me I should leave. He's not a good man. He's here."

Alicia's breath hitched, and her manner changed. I didn't know whether she planned to channel anyone, but the thought of being temporarily possessed by a Pendlewood made my skin crawl.

"You're not welcome here." The body was Alicia's, but the voice didn't match. Her tone had dropped, and from the way she held herself, I guessed the speaker was an older man who was used to giving orders. "Shouldn't be here. Get off my land."

"We want to know about the demon box," I said, looking Alicia in the eye and hoping the spirit got the message that we weren't going to turn tail because he said so.

"You're crazy."

"We know about the deal with Ornias," I replied. "It's brought nothing but death and ruin to your family. How do we destroy the box?"

A cold, cruel laugh came from Alicia, and her expression twisted with malice. "Destroy it? That isn't going to happen. Ever. That box is our future. Our legacy. And that demon is in our blood. It made us who we are. So don't talk nonsense. That box isn't going anywhere."

"Your legacy?" Teag countered. "Have you looked around lately? Your mansion is a ruin, and your plantations in the islands are bankrupt. Your demon lied. It's a curse. How do we break it?"

"That deal can't be broken, not while there's a Pendlewood with breath," Alicia said in the deep voice that wasn't hers. "It would take a god to break that contract, and God's been scarce in these parts if you hadn't noticed."

"Get out of my head." Alicia's voice sounded strained, but it was her own.

"Make me."

Alicia cried out and fell to her hands and knees. Her body twisted and jerked as she tried to force out the Pendlewood ghost that did not want to leave.

"Cover me," Teag said, and dropped to his knees beside her. He laid a hand on her shoulder, letting her draw from his magic, and loosened one of the knotted cords that hung from his belt, that he used to store extra power. His hand glowed where it touched Alicia's shoulder.

She shrieked in fury—I didn't know whether the rage belonged to her or the ghost—and then slumped and would have fallen if Teag hadn't caught her.

"I'm…all right," Alicia said, but she sounded spent.

"We've gotten what we came for," I said. "Let's go."

Teag helped Alicia to her feet and let her lean on him as we headed back to the car. The walk seemed longer going back than it did coming in. Now that we had woken the ghosts of Creedmoor, I hated to turn my back on the place, but walking backward to the car would have been impossible. I had the feeling that the old manor and its ghosts were watching us, unwilling to have us stay, and yet not entirely pleased that we had slipped their grasp.

"You have no business here." Three men stood in front of a black SUV that had parked behind Teag's car on the road, blocking us in. They all appeared to be in their early to mid-thirties, two brunets and a blond, broad-shouldered and fit. Reasonably handsome, if it weren't for the entitled expressions on their faces and the malice in their eyes.

I was finally going to meet the Pendlewood cousins.

"Just went for a walk," I said, meeting the blond man's stare. I could see a bit of resemblance to Beck in their faces.

"I doubt that very much," the blond said. I tried to remember who was who from the pictures Teag had found online.

"Hoke, Addison, and Greer Pendlewood," Teag said in a cold voice. That made the blond speaker Hoke, and the two dark-haired men Addison and Greer. Addison was the tallest of the three, and possibly the oldest. He had a muscular build that I might have thought meant ex-military if I didn't know better. Hoke also looked like he spent time at the gym. Greer, on the other hand, was the shortest of the three, with a lean build that I knew didn't mean he was weak. But if they were Pendlewoods, they didn't need brawn—they had magic.

"You're not just hikers," Hoke said.

"You already knew that," Chuck replied. "Now how about getting the hell out of our way so we can leave."

"Not so fast," Hoke shot back. I knew from the look on his face that he thought he had us trapped, and was enjoying it.

Alicia shifted, taking her weight back from Teag. Her body shielded the cousins from seeing Teag unhook his silver whip from his belt. I let my athame slip down my sleeve into my right hand, and tightened my grip on the walking stick in my left. Chuck crossed his arms, which let him reach into two pockets on his vest at once.

We wouldn't start a fight, but we'd do our damnedest to finish one.

"Where's the box?" Addison demanded.

"What box?" I kept my gaze level.

"You know damn well which box!" Addison snapped. "The one Beckford must have stolen because it wasn't on the ship."

Interesting. They're blaming Beck, but apparently it was Chalmers who pulled the switcheroo.

"No idea," I lied. "Maybe you should keep better track of your stuff."

Greer muttered something and started forward. Addison flung out his arm to hold him back.

"We know who you are," Hoke said. "You run with that bloodsucker, Sorren. Not the first minions he's thrown in our way; probably won't be the last. You're going to lose, but you don't have to die. Just give us the box."

I knew he was lying. Box or no box, Hoke and his bully cousins intended to kill us, because they were Pendlewoods and figured it was their due. Screw that.

Alicia had been quietly murmuring under her breath. I felt the temperature fall. Off to the right, I saw gray forms take shape and begin to glide toward us. I wondered if there had been an old slave cemetery or worker burial ground back among the trees. If so, the wronged ghosts might not care which generation of Pendlewoods they got their vengeance on.

"Hoke…" Greer said, noticing the ghosts.

"Shit, one of them's a medium," Addison growled. He raised a gun and aimed it at Alicia. "Make them go away."

Everything happened at once.

Teag snapped his wrist, sending out the razor-sharp silver whip. It coiled around Addison's gun hand, biting deep into his flesh and making him drop the gun as Teag jerked it back.

"Fuck!" Addison yelled in pain, grabbing his bleeding wrist.

I brought up my athame and shot a blast of cold white energy at Hoke, who was the nearest to me. The power hit him in the chest and sent him reeling backward.

A shot rang out. Alicia screamed and dropped to the ground. Greer had a gun in his hand, but so did Chuck. Chuck fired, an electronic squeal shrieked from the pocket of his jacket, and Greer dropped, bucking and jerking as if he were being electrocuted, then stopped moving. The smell told me he'd pissed himself.

Chuck ran forward and kicked the gun from Greer's hand, as Teag knocked Addison's weapon out of the way with his staff.

Addison came up swinging, despite his bleeding wrist. Teag spun his staff and caught him on the side of the head. Addison dropped with a thud and lay still.

Hoke was struggling to his feet from where my blast of power had thrown him.

"That's far enough," I said, and this time, I loosed a stream of fire from the walking stick, aimed just in front of where Hoke was crouched. He stayed where he was. Smart man.

"Alicia, are you all right?" I asked, not taking my gaze off Hoke. Chuck retrieved something from Greer, and both he and Teag closed on Hoke. That's when I saw Hoke's lips move.

"He's casting!" I shouted.

Chuck raised his weapon again, and Hoke went down just like Greer before he could finish his spell.

"I hope he has a change of pants when he wakes up," Chuck said as he walked up to the unconscious man and retrieved two metal pins.

"You Tasered him?" Teag asked.

Chuck shook his head. "It's a little more high tech—matches the EMF frequency of the jolt to the level of magical energy the target gives off. The stronger the witch, the more juice hits them on the same frequency as their magic."

"Wow," Teag said, looking at Chuck with admiration and a little uneasiness. "You're a scary dude."

"Thank you."

I had Alicia up on her feet. "Are you hit?" I asked. She'd scared the crap out of me when she screamed and fell.

"I'm fine. Figured you could use a distraction. I don't know where Greer shot, but it missed all of us," she said.

She didn't look "fine." Her pinched expression told me that evicting the unwanted ghost had taken a toll, and I suspected her head was throbbing.

"Come on. Let's get out of here. If they weren't out for blood before this, they will be now," I said, helping her to the car.

"How long do you think they'll stay down?" Teag asked as he backed up, maneuvered around the SUV and the bodies, and took off down the lane.

"Long enough for us to be gone," Chuck replied. "I hope we weren't trying to be stealthy because we've kicked over the hornet's nest now."

Alicia's pallor worried me, and she didn't seem to be getting better. I pulled out my phone and hit the speed dial for Rowan. She listened while I explained what happened.

"I'll meet you at your house and take Alicia back to the coven with me. When a medium has an unwelcome possession by a malicious spirit, it can create ghost sickness. It's a malady of the soul that no hospital can fix," Rowan said.

"That sounds really bad," I replied. Teag glanced over his shoulder at me, worried.

"It can be, if not cared for properly. I promise you that my coven sisters and brothers will do right by her. We consider Alicia one of us," Rowan said.

"Thank you," I said, feeling the adrenaline start to fade. "I really appreciate it."

"Any time. And Cassidy? You got lucky if the Pendlewoods relied on guns this time. Now that they know what you all are capable of, they won't make the same mistake twice, and they'll use magic. You didn't just get away from them—you humiliated them. If they weren't out for blood before, they will be now. Be careful."

We were quiet on the way back to town. Alicia had been the only one wounded, but that was plenty, and we were all worried about her.

"Those sons of bitches aren't going to win," Chuck said. The ticking of the watches inside his vest seemed louder than usual in the confines of the car. "We'll send their snooty asses all the way back to Bermuda, or wherever the hell they came from."

"Did you ever hear back from Sorren about getting the dangerous items out of Chalmers Etheridge's house?" Teag asked.

"I got a text that said 'clean-up handled,'" I replied. "I was planning to call Sorren with an update when I got home. The situation over in Europe must be pretty bad. Normally, this is the kind of thing Sorren would be here to handle."

"If the problem in Europe is straining Sorren and Donnelly, I'm kinda glad we're not in the thick of it," Teag said. "Think about it. They're our two heavy hitters. Whatever's going on must be catastrophic."

"A demon box that could nuke the East Coast isn't a walk in the park," I said, but I knew he was right. As much as I wanted Sorren and Donnelly here for backup, Sorren couldn't be everywhere, and I had to trust his judgment that he was where he was needed most. I also knew that he'd never leave us on our own if he had a choice.

But we weren't really on our own, not anymore, not since we'd put together a family of people with awesome abilities. None of us individually might have the same power as Sorren or Donnelly, but together, we were some badass mofos. Realizing that made me smile, despite everything.

Rowan was waiting when we got to my house. Alicia had gotten back some of her color, but she still seemed listless, and I thought her skin was too cold to the touch. Rowan threw a shawl around Alicia's shoulders and helped her into a big black car with a driver, then whisked her off. I didn't know whose car that was or where they were going, but I trusted Rowan, and I knew she'd make sure Alicia was all right.

I looked at Teag and Chuck. "Rowan's right—it's going to get nasty, especially when the cousins realize we really do have the box. It might be safest if we hunkered down at my place. I've got spare rooms. We should bring Maggie in, too. She and Kell can run the HQ, and the rest of us can figure out what needs to be done."

Before either of them could argue, I kept going. "Bring your Uncle Robert," I told Chuck. "And Anthony," I said to Teag. "It's better to be a little crowded than have someone be vulnerable. Father Anne and Beck are at the safe house—they've got the St. Expeditus people to watch out for them. Alicia's with the coven, and I wager that Rowan and her group can take care of themselves. I'm going to invite Lucinda, Caliel, Mrs. Teller, and Niella, but I won't be surprised if they figure they're safe where they are, considering the protections they have in place. With luck, it'll only be for a few days."

"All right," Teag said. "I'll drop you off and text Anthony, then swing by our house to pack. And we just got groceries. I'll bring whatever I can fit in the car."

"I'll go get Robert. He'll probably think it's fun. He's been reliving his glory days, getting pulled in on this," Chuck said, shaking his head. "He's started telling stories and whoo-boy! I thought I was a hardass, but he just might have me beat. If half of what he's saying actually happened, the man has balls of steel."

"TMI!" I protested, but it made me chuckle, a welcome relief after our day. "I laid in extra groceries this week, too, and I guarantee that Maggie will show up with at least one casserole, fixings for a huge pot of something, and a batch of cookies."

"I'll raid the liquor cabinet," Teag promised. "For medicinal purposes," he added with a wink.

I felt better knowing that our friends would be together. Once Teag dropped me off at my house—and waited to make sure I got inside the wardings—I texted Father Anne to let her know what happened and to batten down. She assured me they were secure.

That left Trifles and Folly. The store was solidly warded, and the safe was as secure as anything we could come up with for the demon box. But I didn't want to put our customers at risk if the Pendlewood cousins decided to make a move on us. That had happened before, and people got hurt. My next text was to the owner of the neighboring store, asking her to put a sign on the door to Trifles and Folly saying that we were closed for a few days due to a family emergency and would reopen soon.

With that out of the way, I headed inside. I could hear Baxter from the garden and saw that Kell was watching from the window.

"Problems?" he asked, folding both Baxter and me into a hug.

"We got jumped by the Pendlewood cousins out at Creedmoor," I said. He drew back in alarm, checking me over for injuries. Baxter must have sensed the tension because he growled protectively.

"Thank you, Baxter. Heart of a lion, body of a guinea pig." I gave him a kiss on the head. He looked rather pleased with himself.

"Everyone's okay?"

I nodded. "Yeah. Or, Alicia will be. She got hit the hardest. I'll tell you all about it. But the short version is, the Pendlewoods will be out for blood when they wake up, and so most of our crew is moving in with us until the crisis is over."

"Makes sense," he said, kissing me on the forehead. "I guess that means we should tidy up, get out the spare blankets, and I should use the big pot for a double batch of ham and bean soup."

I squeezed him hard enough Baxter gave a little yelp. "I love you. Thanks for rolling with it."

Kell shrugged. "It makes sense. This is the best warded place. Sort of like heading to high ground in a storm. And in between the moments of heart-stopping terror and mortal danger, it might even be fun."

CHAPTER THIRTEEN

I called Sorren and filled him in on what had happened since our last conversation. I knew as soon as he answered that something had gone wrong on his end.

"Archibald was badly injured last night. A curse breaking didn't go the way we thought it would. He'll recover, but if he and I weren't basically immortal, we'd be dead," Sorren said. "As it is, we should be back to work in a day or so, but we've got to tackle the same object again and get it right this time."

"I'm sorry you two were hurt," I said. "It sounds like the stolen items that went to Europe were too dangerous to put on the market."

"Of course they were," Sorren replied, sounding unusually curt. "Sorry. I don't mean to be short with you. I just haven't been this drained for quite a while." I knew that feeding would help him heal and restore his energy, but I didn't know what his options were where he was. Sorren usually fed from willing donors, or in a pinch he could take enough from someone without causing harm. In an extreme situation, he might drain someone he had to kill anyhow, but I knew he did his best to avoid that. Once, when he'd nearly been destroyed by a demon, Sorren had fed from Teag. But I had no idea how he could help Donnelly regain his strength.

"Do you think whoever stole the items knew exactly how much chaos they would cause?"

"I've been wondering that," he said. "It's almost like a terrorist strike meant for disruption. And it's tied Donnelly and me up far more than I like."

"The ghosts at Creedmoor said something about the Pendlewood men being afraid of the water, and that only a god could destroy the demon box," I pointed out. "Teag's got Simon and Travis working on figuring out what that means."

"Good," Sorren said. "I feel bad that we're not in Charleston to help, but you've got a good team with all the right skills. If you work together, you can do this. I believe in you."

I knew he did, or he'd have found some way to come back, even if it resulted in casualties on the European side. I didn't want to cause that, and if Sorren thought we had it covered, then I trusted him to know what he was talking about. Even if it didn't feel like we were on top of things to me.

One by one, the others drifted in. Everyone brought food, alcohol, and distractions—movies, cards, dice, tabletop RPGs, even old-fashioned board games. I didn't know how long we'd have a full house, but it looked like we were set for a siege.

"I did a little cooking before I came over," Maggie said, as Teag and Anthony both helped her carry in a slow cooker, containers full of baked goods, and two insulated double-casseroles.

"It all smells wonderful, but you shouldn't have gone to so much bother!" I said, although I knew how good her cooking was and really didn't mind.

"Hush," Maggie said. "An army moves on its stomach. It's like hunkering down for a bad storm. With good food, good friends, and plenty of booze, it becomes a party!"

I appreciated the sentiment, but unfortunately we weren't just facing down a hurricane. Still, good food made anything easier to manage, and we were going to have a crowd to feed.

Teag and Anthony had swung by the store on their way and brought salads, fruit, side dishes, scotch, and wine. Chuck and Robert showed up with more whiskey, as well as some beer. Together with what I had in the freezer and pantry—and wine rack—we wouldn't be going hungry.

I had three bedrooms on the second floor and a converted attic that wasn't furnished but was air conditioned—and had plenty of room for air mattresses and sleeping bags. There might be a wait for a shower with two and a half bathrooms, but everyone had a place to sleep.

Maggie was in the kitchen plugging in a slow cooker full of the chicken and dumplings she had brought when the doorbell rang. We had decided to have that for dinner, since Kell's bean soup wouldn't be ready until late. Kell and I exchanged a look.

"Everyone's here that you expected, right?" he asked.

"Yeah. This should be it," I replied. Chuck already had his Sig out and took up a stance near the front door. "Let me see who's on the camera."

The house is heavily warded, so only people who I've cleared can come in. That includes Sorren, now that he's been invited. It's a minor inconvenience when it comes to food delivery, but well worth it for safety. Since with a single house, the public door opens onto the side of the porch, I can't really see who's there from a window, so I installed security cameras.

Two men stood outside, each carrying backpacks. One had shoulder-length chestnut hair and a lean, rangy build. The other was more muscular, with short dark hair and tribal tattoos peeking out from beneath the sleeves of his shirt.

"Do you know them?" Kell asked, peering over my shoulder.

"Yeah," I said, totally surprised. "That's my cousin, Simon, and his boyfriend, Vic."

I went down to the door to greet our unexpected visitors. Kell insisted on following, I guess in case something evil tried to drag me into the street. Chuck came out onto the porch, gun drawn but held low.

I opened the door and held up a hand for them to wait. "Gotta tell the wardings you're okay," I said and murmured the short spell Rowan had taught me that let the magic know Simon and Vic could be trusted.

Simon seemed to take that in stride, but Vic gave me a skeptical look. I waved for them to come in. Vic's expression didn't change, but I saw a flicker of acknowledgment on Simon's face.

"Simon!" I threw my arms around him and hugged him tight. It had been too long since we'd seen each other in person, although we talked and video chatted often. He hugged me back, enveloping me against his larger frame.

"Hey, Cassidy. I, uh, hope you don't mind, but Dante won't leave me alone, and he said we absolutely had to be here."

"There's a man with a gun on your porch," Vic said, his voice cold and flat. "Can you ask him to put it away?"

"Chuck! Stand down. It's okay. They're family."

I heard Chuck mutter that family wasn't a reason not to shoot, but he headed back inside.

"Sorry about that. We're kind of in crisis mode," I said. "Oh, and Simon, Vic, this is Kell."

Kell shook hands, and Simon gave him a once over that was very much a big brother protective thing.

"And this is Vic," Simon introduced his partner. I wasn't sure how Vic wanted to be greeted, but I was pleased when he pulled me in for a firm hug.

"Big Italian family," Vic said with a grin. "We hug. The aunts kiss. Gotta watch out for them."

"Come on in," I said, leading the way. "You know just about everyone here, at least by phone and email."

"You said crisis mode?" Simon asked as we headed for the main door.

"I'll tell you more inside. But Dante has good timing. I think we're going to need you."

We walked inside, and there was a surreptitious but noticeable rustling as weapons were put away. Teag slipped his knife back into its sheath, and Robert lowered his Glock. Maggie replaced a frying pan on the stove as if she'd just been about to cook something, not use it as a cudgel. Even Anthony slipped his gun into the waistband of his jeans.

"What the hell?" Vic said. "Why are we walking into an armed camp?"

Kell moved to the sideboard and came back with two glasses of good scotch. He handed them to Simon and Vic. "You might want this," he said with an apologetic smile.

Introductions were traded all around. Simon and Teag greeted each other like old friends since they had talked so often by phone and online. Chuck was his curmudgeonly self, but he did shake hands, as did Robert. Maggie fussed over both newcomers and told them we'd have dinner soon.

Vic came up short when Teag brought Anthony over for introductions. "I've seen you," he said, and his cool demeanor slipped. Simon put a hand on Vic's shoulder. I wondered what the hell was going on. "You came to help Simon when I couldn't."

Anthony nodded. "I'm happy I could assist."

"Thank you," Vic said, his voice suddenly rough with emotion. "That was a bad situation, and anything I might have done would have made it worse. But I owe you, big time."

"Simon is Cassidy's cousin. Teag is like a brother to her, and Teag's my fiancé. That makes you and Simon family."

Simon's gaze dropped to the ring on Anthony's left hand. "Are congratulations in order?"

Anthony grinned as Teag came up beside him and waggled his fingers, showing off his own ring. "Just a few days ago, for Teag's birthday. Don't worry, you'll get an invitation to the wedding. Once we know when that will be."

Simon and Vic sat down on the couch. Robert had dragged a dining room chair near the window and sat there on watch, although his view of the street was limited. Chuck left and headed down the hall, presumably checking the perimeter. Maggie bustled about in the kitchen, pretending to get things ready for supper. I knew she was just giving us privacy, but listening all the same. Kell sat next to me, perching on the arm of my chair.

"I might not have let on about the full extent of what we do with Trifles and Folly," I said, wondering how Simon and Vic would react.

Sure, Vic had come to accept Simon's visions and his ability as a medium, and according to Simon, they'd seen some strange creatures, but that was still tame compared to what we'd come up against. I'd always wanted to keep Simon safe. Explaining was going to be awkward.

"You get cursed and haunted objects out of the wrong hands, so no one gets hurt," Simon replied. "And you and Teag research occult problems."

I cleared my throat. "That's part of it. The truth is…we're part of an Alliance of mortals and immortals who protect the world from supernatural threats."

"Mortals and immortals?" Vic echoed incredulously.

"Yeah. It's…complicated. And I'm sorry I didn't tell you the whole truth before now, but I didn't want you to get hurt."

Simon just stared at me, not as surprised as I expected. "Go on."

"My business partner, Sorren, founded Trifles and Folly the same year that Charleston was chartered."

"That's impossible," Vic scoffed. "He'd have to be—"

"Immortal," I replied, meeting Vic's eyes. "He's a nearly six-hundred-year-old vampire."

"Vampire." Vic just looked at me, like the people do in TV shows when someone breaks it to them that monsters are real.

"She's not joking." Robert stood and walked over. "I'm Robert Pettis."

Simon looked up. "You just sold Trinkets to Erik Mitchell, up in Cape May."

Robert nodded. "How old do you think I am?"

Simon cleared his throat. "I wouldn't attempt to guess."

"You're too polite. So I'll just tell you. I'm one hundred and twenty."

"That's…not…possible," Vic protested.

"Side effect of working with a vampire," Robert said with a shrug. "I knew Cassidy's Uncle Evann, the one who sold her the store. He was a lot older than he looked, too. Extended lifespan is a side effect of the job—if something doesn't kill you before you have a chance to die of old age. Apparently, ninety is the new sixty," he added with a smirk and walked back to his chair.

"As I was saying," I said. "We've ended up dealing with some very bad players over the years."

"The Mob? Cartels?" Vic asked, going into what I thought of as cop-mode with narrowed eyes and a sharper tone.

"No. Nephilim. Gregori. Demons. Not to mention some nasty creatures like Perchten and Redcaps."

Simon's eyes widened. Vic looked like he was waiting for the punchline to find out this was an elaborate prank. "You're serious," Vic said. He turned to Simon. "Is she serious?"

Simon nodded. "I…suspected. But you didn't say, and I didn't want to pry. You've asked me about all those creatures over the years, and after a while I figured it wasn't just academic interest."

"You were just finally embracing your gifts," I told him, meaning his psychic abilities and mediumship. "And we had people here in Charleston who were experienced with those things, so I didn't want to drag you in. It's not the sort of thing you can unsee."

"I understand," Simon replied. "So, you have a group of people with skills, like the Fellowship of the Ring?"

Kell snorted at that, and I couldn't help laughing. "No elves. But oddly enough, this time around we do have a demonic ring…"

"Oh, God," Vic said and covered his eyes with his hand. "Please tell me you slipped something in my drink."

Simon shoulder-checked him. "You think I'd roofie a cop?"

"Not roofie. Maybe something trippy…I'll forgive you."

"Sorry," I said. "No drugs. Reality around here is strange enough."

Vic knocked back his whiskey in one shot. Chuck refilled his glass.

"The Fellowship, huh?" I couldn't help smiling.

Simon shrugged. "I call my team the Skeleton Crew. Long story. Go on."

"Right now, we've got powerful witches, a Voudon mambo and houngan, two Hoodoo root women, and a talented medium who's unfortunately injured at the moment. Plus, Chuck and Robert, who were supernatural black ops."

"Ex-CHARON," Chuck said. "Nasty bunch of bastards."

Simon's eyes narrowed. "They're the ones who want to get their hooks into Brent Lawson."

"That's why it's 'ex,'" Chuck said with his usual gruffness.

"Yeah," I added. "And a priest who is part of the St. Expeditus Society."

"I thought they were just a legend," Simon countered.

"Nope. They're real. Like vampires, werewolves, and necromancers."

"Really?" Vic was still trying to digest what we'd told them.

"The necromancer is in Europe with Sorren, handling some really nasty cursed artifacts."

Simon looked a bit shell-shocked, but not as much as I expected. "Wow. I mean, I thought you were doing more than you told me, but I didn't really expect…"

Vic met my gaze, all cop. "What are we up against? Because this Dante ghost—"

"Our ancestor," I interjected.

"—won't let Simon have a moment's peace. He said Simon had to come here, that really bad things could happen. So…"

I didn't pull any punches. "We have the heir to a dynasty of dark witches who wants out of the family business. His cousins want to keep things going—and they'll kill to do it. The family's power comes from a bound demon—"

"The soucouyant you asked me about," Simon said, closing his eyes and sighing as he put the pieces together.

"Which is controlled by a bespelled ring. The demon box was stolen, but we found it. Now we have to figure out how to destroy it because if we don't do it right, it sends off a fireball like the one that flattened a forest in Russia and wipes out the East Coast."

Simon paled. "Tunguska?"

"Yeah."

Vic's eyes widened. "Holy shit. You're not kidding."

I shook my head. "I wish I were."

"How does this go down?" Vic slipped back into his role as a homicide detective. "These cousins—they're human. They're not the Jersey Devil or the Mothman. So if you intend to stop them, and they're as powerful as you say, it's going to get bloody. Because in my experience, people who are used to power don't just give it up—and if you fight them and people die…that's murder."

"Well…the actual charge would depend on the situation," Anthony hedged.

Vic looked up sharply at him. "You're a lawyer. How are you even listening to this conversation? Couldn't this get you disbarred?"

Anthony shrugged as Teag came to slip an arm around his waist. "If you think lawyers don't make unholy deals, you haven't been watching enough TV. Lawyers take plea bargains and offer immunity to 'monsters' all the time to catch bigger monsters."

Anthony looked away. "If it helps, I did transfer out of prosecution to business law. But even there, I'm coming to understand how many of the city's old families have supernatural connections, some of which are deeply unsavory. And that old family money was the result of slave labor. No one has clean hands."

"I'm from New Jersey. No one there does, either."

I couldn't read Vic's expression, but he hadn't bolted for the door, so that was in his favor. And from everything Simon had told me about his boyfriend, Vic was a good guy. It had taken Anthony a while to come around, too, in the beginning.

"Isn't there some sort of authority that handles this sort of stuff?" Vic asked. "Like that CHARON group you mentioned."

Chuck growled. "You don't want them involved. They're not the good guys. They'd roll in with their black SUVs and choppers, piss all over everything, probably cause the box to nuke the coast, and then they'd rendition all these fine folks, and no one would ever see them again. CHARON would want to study them or turn them into weapons. Those movies where the secret government agency gets everyone killed and is run by psychopaths? Not really too far off the mark. That's why we're *ex*-CHARON."

"I'm surprised they let you leave," Vic said.

"Sorren and Donnelly pulled strings. Long story. Proves that even the boogeymen are afraid of someone." Chuck went to sit by Robert, his moment of sharing obviously at an end.

"Okay," Vic said, clearing his throat. "For the record, having dealt with some SOBs in the FBI and NSA, I understand jurisdictional turf wars. Just, without magic."

"It's all about to hit the fan," I said, bringing the conversation back to the original point. "The cousins are out for our blood, the heir is on lockdown, the demon box is in a warded safe, and now all we have to do is figure out what the ghosts meant about the river and a god."

"A river god?" Simon's head came up.

"Maybe," I said uncertainly. "One ghost said the Pendlewood men feared the water, and another said it would take a god to destroy the box."

"Pendlewoods? Fuck—they're real?"

Simon hadn't really batted an eye when I'd listed off angels and demons, but a dark warlock family caught his attention.

"Unfortunately, yes."

Vic looked at his boyfriend, tilting his head as if he picked up on something I had missed. "That means something to you? Your wheels are turning."

Simon frowned. "I think so, but I need to research. Actually, it would help a lot if I could get Travis on the phone. It might be nothing…but I want to look into things before I say more."

"Sure," I replied. "Call Erik Mitchell too, if you think he can help. He's been providing intel to Sorren on the European side of this." I pointed toward the hallway. "If you need someplace quiet, you can use my office."

Simon gave Vic a peck on the cheek, grabbed his messenger bag, and headed down the hallway. Vic watched him go, then turned his attention back to me. "Will it screw up your…wardings…if I go sit on the front porch for a bit? It's a lot to process."

I smiled, thinking again how lucky I was that I hadn't needed to explain the basic supernatural part to Kell. "Sure. Just stay inside the walled area. Protections are strongest closest to the house. And don't let anyone in."

Vic rolled his eyes. "Cop, remember?" I watched him go, hoping he could make sense of everything because we needed Simon's help, and Simon needed Vic. Plus, I was betting Vic was good in a fight.

Robert, Chuck, and Teag had wandered back to one of the guest rooms, where I could hear Simon on the phone. Maggie had made herself comfy in a chair with a book, waiting for the chicken and dumplings to heat and things to calm down so we could eat. I wasn't sure where Anthony had gone.

Kell slipped up beside me and gave me a hug. "Are you doing all right? There's a lot going on."

"I'm fine…well, as good as can be expected under the circumstances," I amended. "And I'm thrilled to have Simon and Vic here. I think we're going to need them. I just can't imagine what's going through Vic's head right now. Simon, actually, didn't seem too surprised."

"Before I knew you, when we were just starting SPOOK, I was on the fence with being a skeptic," Kell admitted. "I wanted to prove to the world—and myself—that ghosts were real. Or prove they weren't. Then we started running into stuff that way too real, and we met you and Teag."

He gave me a kiss on the forehead. "Kinda crazy, huh? But you didn't have to convince me about the supernatural aspect. And once I accepted that, it wasn't a big stretch to believe magic was real and all the rest."

"That's only part of what's got me worried," I confided. "Vic's a homicide detective. And he's right to worry about the legalities. Greer, Hoke, and Addison have wealth and power in addition to magic. Going up against them won't be viewed as self-defense by any rational jury if —when—someone gets killed. And with guys like that, I don't know that we'll have a choice about how to handle it if we win. They're too dangerous to just let them roam around out there."

"I know." The somber look in Kell's eyes told me he was on the same page. "Vic—and Anthony—are going to have to work that out for themselves. Maybe they sit out the fight and stay here with Maggie and Robert."

I snorted. "You think Robert is going to stay behind? We'll have enough trouble convincing Anthony and Maggie. You saw her with that cast iron pan. She was ready to defend the ramparts." I thought about what he said, and his meaning dawned on me. "And you—"

"I'm coming with you," Kell replied in a tone that said the matter was settled. "I'm all in. If I could get nuked in the fireball, then I get a chance to make sure it never happens. Don't even try to talk me out of it."

Chuck and Robert didn't have magic, but they had serious skills and lots of training. Kell could shoot, but he would be the least able to defend himself. Vic didn't have magic either, although if he went with us, he still had a cop's training. But could he reconcile what had to be done with the oath he'd taken to uphold the law?

A timer went off, and Maggie headed into the kitchen. "Dinner's ready," she called out. "Send everyone in to eat while it's hot."

"I'll go get Vic," I said to Kell. "Why don't you let Simon and the others know to come out as soon as they can?"

I headed for the door, expecting to see Vic in one of the white rattan chairs on the porch or sitting on the steps. I worried for a moment that he hadn't heeded my warning to stay inside the brick walls of the enclosed garden. Then I saw him near the birdbath, talking with Anthony.

They looked deep in conversation, so I didn't want to shout. I headed toward them, somewhat screened from view by a stand of bamboo.

"How do you do it?" Vic said. "You and Teag. I know that Simon's abilities are real. But it scares the shit out of me that things could hurt him, and I can't protect him from them." He looked down. "I saw him let Dante's ghost possess him to fight off a bigger bad. I was really afraid he might not still be…him…after it was over. Even so, he was hurt and I felt useless." His voice trailed off.

I didn't mean to eavesdrop, but now didn't seem to be the best time to ring the dinner bell, so I stayed near the bamboo.

"When you go to work, Simon can't protect you from the dangers, either," Anthony pointed out. "And as a lawyer, even though I'm not handling criminal cases anymore, death threats aren't uncommon. So Teag and Simon have to live with the same kind of fear, too."

"I was an ass to Simon when he first tried to convince me his gifts were real," Vic confessed. "How did you accept everything so easily?"

Anthony chuckled ruefully. "I didn't. Teag didn't tell me the whole truth for a long time. I knew about vengeful ghosts and haunted objects, but not the other stuff. And to be honest, I didn't press. I didn't really *want* to know. Plausible deniability and all that."

"What changed?" Vic sounded earnest, looking for answers.

"I came home one night from working late, and Teag had left me a letter on the kitchen table—along with his will and a copy of his power of attorney. They were going up against the Nephilim and Gregori that Cassidy mentioned—and Teag didn't think he'd make it back." Anthony's voice tightened with emotion.

"I came over here, scared witless, demanding to know what was going on. And I walked into a war zone," Anthony went on. I remembered that night all too well. We had barely managed a victory, and everyone had been wounded in the process, Teag worst of all.

"Everyone was bloodied, like in a disaster movie. And Teag—" His voice broke, and he had to pause. "I didn't think he was going to make it. He was hurt so badly. Sorren had called a doctor—someone he trusted—and Teag was on an IV, but I was ready to start throwing punches to get him out of there."

"What happened?" Vic asked, in a hushed voice.

Even though I was there, just hearing Anthony tell the story from his perspective made my heart ache. I'd been exhausted and in shock when it all went down, and my memories were honestly a little fuzzy on the details.

"Sorren confronted me and told me Teag would die in a regular hospital because they didn't understand the magic involved. And he gave me a choice. He could make me forget everything I'd seen, everything about the supernatural, and I could go back to my normal life none the wiser. But that also meant forgetting Teag. And that's when I knew. I'd throw it all away to keep him safe, everything, but I couldn't leave him. I made my peace with the tradeoffs and the costs, and here I am." He gave a sad laugh. "The deniability isn't so plausible, anymore."

That was the break in the conversation I'd been waiting for. I cleared my throat. "Dinner's ready," I announced.

I doubted that either Vic or Anthony really believed I hadn't overheard their conversation, but they didn't ask. They followed me back to the house. Anthony looked deep in thought, and I didn't know Vic well enough to guess what was going through his mind.

By the time we came inside, Teag had pulled out the long folding table and chairs we used at Thanksgiving and set it up in the living room. Two plates of homemade cornbread sat on the table as well as plastic utensils, cups and two pitchers of sweet tea. Maggie handed us bowls of steaming chicken and dumplings, and Teag and I tag-teamed getting them on the table, while Vic headed to the restroom, and Anthony went to fetch the others.

"Maggie, you're the best organizer for the end of the world anyone could ever have," I said as we all praised her cooking.

"Just because we're having a cataclysm doesn't mean we can't have good food," Maggie joked. "And that bean soup Kell's got cooking will make a great late-night snack."

Teag opened some bottles of wine, Anthony brought out the scotch, and Chuck snagged a beer from somewhere. Maggie passed a plate heaped with freshly baked cookies, and we all helped ourselves. If we might get blown sky-high, a few more calories weren't going to matter.

"I think we're on to something," Simon announced when we were lazing in a food coma. "Brent Lawson called. He was looking into the Pendlewood holdings and the cousins' U.S. business dealings. It took some digging and P.I. skills, but he followed the money, got copies of documents, and recorded eyewitness testimony. They're dirty as hell— no surprise. Tax evasion, smuggling, customs violations, relic misappropriation—Erik Mitchell helped on that part—art theft, blackmail— the list reads like something out of those big mobster trials in the Nineties."

Vic and Anthony exchanged a look. "Brent has real evidence? Something that could be shown to a judge?" Vic asked.

Simon nodded. "Yeah. Brent knows his stuff. He thinks it's enough to get them on a slew of charges, maybe even RICO. We talked it over, and decided he should turn over what he found to a friend in the FBI—one who understands about the supernatural," he added. "If we destroy the demon box and break the curse, the cousins are ruined with no magic and the feds on their tail."

"And if, in that process, someone should go missing, a paper trail like that suggests plenty of suspects," Chuck added, not afraid to put into words what the rest of us were thinking.

Anthony paled but said nothing.

Vic opened his mouth then shut it again, crossing his arms over his chest.

"That's great. Really great," I said. "But how about the demon box?"

Simon grinned. "That's where we hit pay dirt. You mentioned that the ghost said Pendlewood men were frightened of water, and needing a god to destroy the box. I couldn't place the memory of something I'd read, but when we conferenced in Travis and Lucinda, among the three of us, we figured it out."

"Don't keep us in suspense, son. Spit it out," Robert snapped and knocked back his scotch.

"Mama Wata," Simon said.

"Say what?" Kell looked confused.

"Mama Wata is a powerful Caribbean spirit. A demigoddess at least, maybe more. She's the protector of rivers, and can take the form of a sea monster," Simon replied. "And she is an eater of demons."

"Doesn't do us much good if she's in the Caribbean and we're here," Vic said.

Simon shook his head. "She's an entity. She can go where she pleases. Lucinda and Travis think that we—meaning me, Caliel, Lucinda, and Dante's ghost—can summon her to the river behind the old Pendlewood plantation. With Dante's magic and Lucinda's, we stand a good shot at getting Mama Wata to eat the demon box and the Ring of Ornias. That would destroy them, end the curse, save Beck, and leave the cousins as plain old ordinary white-collar criminals." He smiled, deservedly pleased with his revelation, while the rest of us all looked a bit slack-jawed.

"Of course, he'll have backup," Chuck said. "Robert and I were discussing munitions. We've got some stuff that should even the odds with those cousins, buy Simon and Dante some time."

"We ran the plan past Rowan, Beck, and Father Anne. They think it has a shot—and they don't have a better suggestion. Father Anne said Beck needs to be there. She thinks that the magic that binds the ring and the demon box to him as the heir will need him present to break the curse."

Vic looked at us as if we were all crazy. I didn't envy the way he'd been thrown into the deep end with us. "I'm glad there's a plan," Vic said, a low current of anger barely restrained beneath his words. "But did any of those folks hazard a guess on the odds of you coming back alive, after you let Dante possess you to bargain with a fucking *goddess*?" His voice rose on the last words, and I could see the cords standing out on his neck.

Simon reached across the table and took Vic's hand. I thought for a moment Vic might snatch his hand back, but he didn't, although from his glare, I could tell he wasn't mollified.

"What are the other choices?" Simon said quietly. "If we try to destroy the box ourselves and screw up, we Nagasaki the East Coast, and none of us come back. This way, we have a chance."

What he didn't say, didn't need to say, was that we might have a chance, but it didn't guarantee that any of us would come back alive, even if we won. Kell took my hand under the table and gave it a squeeze, letting me know he was in. I saw the expressions on the faces of everyone around the table as they processed the strategy, the threat, and the odds. One by one, they nodded, even Anthony, who slipped an arm around Teag. I understood the need to be close to someone you loved when you were thinking about walking into an impossible battle.

"Vic?" Simon sounded tentative.

Vic swore under his breath. "I don't like it, but I don't have a better plan. I'm in. I love you, and I can't live without you. So you'd better plan on living through it—and that goes for the rest of you, too," he added, glowering at us.

"I love you, too, and I have every reason to want to live to a ripe old age with you," Simon assured him, threading their fingers together. "I'll do my best to make that happen."

I silently seconded that thought and hoped that when it was over, we could gather back around this table to celebrate—all of us, alive and kicking. It was asking a lot. But this seemed to be the day to bet on long odds.

CHAPTER FOURTEEN

We planned our arrival at Creedmoor, the old Pendlewood plantation, so we could be in place well before noon the following day. Noon and midnight were liminal hours—times when the veil between this world and the next thinned. We still weren't entirely sure Mama Wata would show since we could hardly do a dry run. That meant we wanted every advantage we could muster.

"You could have stayed back at the house," Simon told Vic as we parked near the old manor. "This could be rough without magic."

"Hell, no," Vic replied in a voice that wasn't open to argument. "If you're here, I'm here. End of story." He'd left his personal sidearm at my house and carried two guns that Chuck provided. To his credit, he didn't ask questions about registration and Chuck didn't volunteer information.

"I'm glad Anthony didn't try to come with us," Teag said quietly as he and I walked behind Simon and Vic. "If everything goes to hell, no amount of deniability is plausible if he's found at the scene."

"It's going to do more good for him to strategize with Brent Lawson on the legal angles to take down the cousins, before they go to Brent's FBI contact," I replied.

"Yeah," Teag said, sounding wistful. He and Anthony had a lingering goodbye, and I understood the unspoken promises and fears.

Kell walked on my other side, close enough to bump shoulders. He had a shotgun and plenty of shells filled with rock salt, as well as salt, holy water, blessed oil, and some useful magical objects that would help him protect us from malicious ghosts. Like Vic, he insisted on backing me up, and I loved him for it even though I wished he was safely far away. He and Vic took turns carrying the heavy lead container with the demon box inside—safer since neither of them had magic.

"Did you check your earpieces?" Chuck's perpetual growl pulled me out of my thoughts. "It'd be a real bitch to be in the thick of things and find out they don't work."

Teag, Chuck, and I dutifully took a moment to make sure the communication devices worked. Chuck provided the tech, and I knew from how heavy his gear bag looked that he'd brought a lot of unpleasant surprises for anyone who dared try to interrupt our efforts.

"Are you sure Robert knows how to use them?" Vic asked.

Chuck snorted. "Robert knows. He'll keep an eye on CHARON and the police scanner, and let us know if we've got unwanted visitors on the way."

"I don't even want to know," Vic muttered, wisely doubting the legality of those monitoring efforts.

"Maggie'll keep an eye on him," I joked. Maggie planned to have Sorren's doctor on standby and our exceptionally well-provisioned medic kit ready, setting up for a returning party that could be injured and hungry.

"That's Lucinda's car," I said as we passed a blue SUV parked off to one side. "She and Caliel must be here."

"And there's Father' Anne's ride," Kell said, noting her motorcycle next to the SUV. "Do you think she made Beck ride here on that?"

"Beck doesn't strike me as the biker type," I replied, noting two helmets perched on the seat. "I bet that was interesting."

I glanced behind us. Mrs. Teller and Niella headed down the road away from the manor then worked their way back, liberally sprinkling the center of the driveway with goofer dust and making a large "X" from side to side with a mix of secret ingredients to jinx and cross anyone who followed us—namely, the cousins. We could walk out safely on the edges of the road, assuming the situation went our way. That was a big assumption.

I looked around, wondering whether Rowan and her coven were nearby. She had promised to come and bring backup. Alicia was still recovering from the ghost possession, so she was sidelined, and some of the coven had promised to watch over her.

For most of the threats we'd dealt with, we would have been way over prepared. But since we didn't know what we'd face from the cousins or the demon box, we erred on the side of overkill.

Beck had explained more about the family's Solomonic magic before we came. He couldn't use it to control Ornias without accepting the curse and using the ring. The cousins couldn't control Ornias so long as Beck was the heir—and alive. Beyond that was the native Pendlewood magic. Beck hadn't spent enough time with his cousins to know exactly what they could do, but he warned me that he expected them to be of at least middling power as witches, and completely willing to use magic to curse and kill.

As for the limits of his own magic, without Ornias's help, Beck wasn't sure. He said he'd tried to do very little magic in order to hide from his cousins and blend in. That made him an untrained wild card, which could be dangerous in its own way.

I felt relieved when we neared the riverside without spotting the cousins. Father Anne and Beck were waiting for us, and so was Rowan, who stood with two other women I didn't know. They were talking with Lucinda and Caliel. The two Voudon practitioners were dressed in white, showing they were ready to be ridden by the Loa they called upon for power. We'd left ourselves time to prepare, because demons and gods were nothing to fool with, and didn't give do-overs.

Chuck had stopped a few times on the drive in to place monitoring devices along the road that would give an audio warning via the earpieces, and provide video to the feed Maggie was monitoring.

"I wish you'd have let me bring those witch-bang grenades," Chuck muttered.

"Those would take down Rowan's coven and maybe everyone with magic, not just the cousins," I reminded him. "The benefit from keeping our allies outweighs whatever the grenades might do for us."

He harrumphed in response but didn't argue.

Witches were a tricky enemy. Silver and holy water didn't work on them. They were human, so that made killing them hard to explain away. We didn't dare do anything that might deaden all magic temporarily since we planned to summon a god. That put us at a disadvantage.

When we reached the riverbank, Vic and Chuck stood guard while the rest of us laid down three concentric circles of salt, iron filings, Four Thieves vinegar mixed with brick dust, and holy water. We needed to make sure the ghosts of Creedmoor couldn't disturb the ritual or try to harm us because once we started, stopping wasn't an option.

Inside the smallest circle, nearest to the river, Caliel and Lucinda set up small shrines on either side, one to Papa Legba and the other to Baron Samedi, a powerful Loa and Ghede. Simon would be between them when he and Dante summoned Mama Wata.

In the next circle, Mrs. Teller and Niella had black candles for more Hoodoo curse work. Father Anne and Beck would wait with them, in case Beck's magic proved key to getting rid of the ring and the box.

"We're in here," Kell said to Vic, indicating for him to step over the salt line. "Welcome to ghost patrol. Shotguns with salt rounds," he said, pointing to two guns and a pile of ammo, "along with iron swords, and a bag of rice, in case we get one of those OCD monsters again."

I could tell from the look on Vic's face that he wanted to be right beside Simon, but he accepted his role. We figured that also avoided putting him in a situation where he might have to fire on living people.

Chuck and Teag conferred in low tones and then distributed some of Chuck's dirty tricks tech across the approach area, which included laying out a wide mesh of fine wires that had a nefarious purpose.

"Your people are in place?" I asked Rowan when I realized her coven sisters were nowhere to be seen.

She gave a curt nod. "We're all shielding now, to keep from tipping our hand. Beck's given us an idea of what to expect, and what kind of magic he believes his cousins are capable of, but he doesn't know for certain."

Chuck, Teag, Rowan, and I were the first line of defense, after the tech and jinxes. It was our job to hold off the cousins long enough to have the goddess destroy the box—if she agreed to help us.

My phone's timer buzzed, reminding me we were nearing noon. "It's showtime, folks."

Kell met my gaze. We'd said everything last night, and sealed those promises with slow lovemaking. Vic and Simon shared a look as well, silently communicating. I could tell that Simon was doing his best to look brave, but I saw Vic's fear for his partner's safety in the cop's eyes.

Robert's voice crackled in my ear. "Get going. There's a car approaching the lane."

"Roger that," Chuck replied.

"I keep telling you, it's Robert," the old man snarked.

"Incoming!" Teag yelled. "Let's get this party started!"

"Simon, are you ready?" I asked.

When Simon turned, I knew immediately that he was channeling Dante's ghost. His features hadn't changed, but something in the eyes was different—older and scarred. "Yes. We are ready," Dante spoke through Simon. "It is good to see you again, Cassidy." He turned to Vic. "I will do my best to return him unharmed."

"Damn well better," Vic muttered. "Now go kick some demon ass."

I heard Caliel and Lucinda begin their chants, as they lit candles and made their gifts, asking for Papa Legba and Baron Samedi to intercede. A faint whiff of cigar smoke and the distant barking of a dog told me that Papa Legba had heard Caliel's petition, and would open the

Veil. Whether the Baron would accept Lucinda's plea and refuse to dig our graves remained to be seen.

I couldn't take my eyes off Simon. Everything about his stance was different, and I felt a chill go down my spine realizing our long-dead ancestor had possessed him. Simon threw his arms wide facing the river and lifted his face to the sky as my phone buzzed to tell me it was noon, the "other" witching hour.

"Mama Wata! Hear us! We have a rich meal for you!" Simon called out. Even his voice was not his own. I glanced at Vic, who had a stricken expression at the change.

I didn't fully understand Dante's water magic, but I knew it continued beyond the grave. Dante had guided Simon in creating the spell to summon the Caribbean goddess, and as Simon spoke the words, a frisson of power made me shiver. I felt a charge in the air, a warning that something powerful approached.

"Look!" Kell shouted.

The temperature had dropped rapidly, and the ghosts of Creedmoor were waking up. Foxfire-green orbs hovered and flashed. Indistinct gray shapes took form, looming and hostile. As the ghosts became more clear, I saw that some were dressed as workers, while others wore the fine clothing that indicated they were the masters of the plantation, the Pendlewood ancestors.

An old man in Seventeenth-Century finery stalked toward Beck, and I wondered if this was Wilfred Pendlewood himself, the man who had made the deal with the demon and cursed his descendants for centuries.

I expected Beck to shrink back, but he stood his ground. Even without words, the ghost's malice was clear in his expression, and the way he lunged toward Beck, held at bay by the salt circle.

"I'm ending this, Wilfred," Beck shouted defiantly. "The curse ends right here, right now."

Wilfred lunged again, and a shotgun boomed. Kell's shot struck the ghost in the chest, and the revenant vanished.

"He'll be back," Beck warned. "We're a stubborn lot."

"We've got trouble," Chuck muttered. I glanced toward the road and saw three men approaching. Hoke, Greer, and Addison Pendle-wood strode toward us, looking more like prep school frat boys than powerful witches. Their choice of button-down shirts over expensive jeans suggested that after they murdered the lot of us and took the demon for themselves, they intended to stop off at a country club for cocktails.

I held my breath as they approached the portion of the road where Mrs. Teller and Niella had laid down their crossing. Addison gestured, and a strong wind swept across the gravel driveway, carrying away the goofer dust and graveyard dirt that held the jinx.

"Seriously?" Hoke smirked. "Root magic? You've got to try harder than that."

"Beckford!" Greer called out. "What the hell do you think you're doing, boy? Stop this nonsense, and we might let your friends walk away from this ill-considered effort." His voice dripped with entitle-ment, the tone of someone who took for granted they would be obeyed.

"It's over," Beck shouted. "Leave while you still can."

"You think too highly of yourself, little cousin," Addison drawled. "I believe we need to adjust your attitude and teach you some respect."

"What my brother means is, once we flay your friends alive in front of you, we'll feed you slowly to the demon," Hoke said. "Or you can surrender, and we might kill you quickly."

"Go to hell," Beck shot back.

"What do we have here?" Greer asked, stretching out an arm to keep Addison from walking closer. "Traps only work when you don't see them coming." He made a grasping gesture with one hand, and the wire mesh Chuck had carefully laid went flying, to land in a heap to one side.

Addison clenched his fist, making Teag, Chuck, and me double over in pain. Rowan muttered a word of power and made a sweeping gesture. The pain stopped abruptly, and Addison stumbled backward as if shoved.

Behind me, I heard Simon beseeching Mama Wata to grant his plea. I caught the flare of candles and heard Mrs. Teller and Niella murmur the names of the cousins as they dropped bits of paper bearing those names into each black candle's flame.

Hoke fell to his knees and started to retch. Greer's expression suggested he wanted to puke as well. Addison looked unwell and furious. He shouted a word that seemed too slippery for me to hear and made a tearing motion in the air. Hoke got back up with a glare that promised revenge, and Greer straightened his shoulders and went to stand beside his brother.

"You have pushed my patience to the limit," Addison growled. "Beckford—stop this foolishness. I will not be merciful."

"Fuck that shit," Chuck muttered with a nod to Rowan.

Rowan flicked her hand, sending the tangle of wires from Chuck's trap flying toward Addison and hitting him in the chest.

"Let me help with that." Chuck pushed a trigger. The wire mesh glowed blue and sent Addison staggering. I leveled my athame and blasted cold power at Greer, which made him stumble into Addison, and the two cousins went down in a pile atop the glowing wires. That left Hoke.

Another shotgun blast rang out. Hoke cried out in pain, and his shirt blossomed with spots of red where the salt blast caught him full in the chest, dropping him on his ass. Vic racked another shot as if daring Hoke to try getting up again.

"What's with the glowing wires?" I asked Chuck.

"It's like that EMF Taser I used the last time, but bigger," Chuck replied. "Disrupts their magic—for a while."

Simon's invitation to Mama Wata had shifted into a spell to summon the goddess. Caliel and Lucinda sang and chanted, keeping the connection open to the Loa. The scent of candle smoke and incense mixed with the tang of plants and powders that the Tellers added to their black candles.

Maybe Addison hadn't been able to sweep away all of the effects of the goofer dust and crossing dirt, or perhaps the curse candles were working their spell, because the cousins' skin mottled with boils, and their bodies trembled and jerked. The other two witches from Rowan's coven had emerged from their hiding places in the forest and closed in, forming a triangle around the downed men.

Teag and Chuck jumped over the salt barrier, heading toward the Pendlewood cousins and becoming the fourth and fifth points of a pentacle that reinforced the coven's containment magic. Chuck might not have power of his own, but apparently, he'd been fine with lending some of his essence to Rowan in a fight.

"Teag! Careful!" I cried, but his curt nod told me he knew what he was doing. Teag had pulled a large rope net from his gear bag. I knew he had woven his magic into the knots and mesh.

Chuck held a gun on the downed cousins, while Rowan and her coven sisters made the air spark with power, focusing their magic on the Pendlewoods.

Teag dropped the rope net over the three men, and Chuck squeezed the remote in his left hand just for good measure, sending another jolt through the wire mesh. Then he tossed an egg-shaped object to land beside the captives.

"That EMF grenade has a five-foot radius, which will cover all of you," he told Addison, who glared at Chuck with murder in his eyes. "If I set it off, it will blast on your magical frequency, and you'll think every nerve and cell in your body has exploded. Don't push your luck."

Rowan, Chuck, Teag, and the coven sisters took hands, encircling the prisoners. The three coven members invoked a spell, Teag's net flared with power, and the men trapped beneath it slumped.

"Are they dead?" Vic asked, sounding less disturbed about the possibility than I expected. He and Kell still had their shotguns racked and ready.

"Not yet," Rowan called back. "But if something happens to us and we don't reverse the spell, they will be. Consider it an insurance policy."

The wind picked up, cold and cutting. Orbs and spirits gathered in growing numbers across the open land and near the ruins of the plantation house.

"Come back inside the circles!" I shouted.

Teag and Chuck sprinted back, and to my surprise, so did Rowan and her coven sisters.

The sky over the river had grown dark, and the air crackled with power. The smell of incense and candle smoke had grown cloying, and choppy waves troubled the surface of the water as if something from the depths disturbed its flow.

Hundreds of ghosts instantly surrounded us, and all of them wanted blood. They swarmed against the salt barriers, as Kell and Vic fired again and again into their midst. I blasted them with the cold power of my athame and streams of fire from Alard's walking stick. With the way the wind had kicked up, I worried that the salt lines might not hold.

"Do something!" I yelled at Rowan.

"Working on it!" Teag pulled the witches together, quickly explaining what he meant to do, as the shotguns blasted and I sent fire and energy crackling through the air, blowing holes in the ghostly assault.

A gossamer curtain of power rose from the salt lines, and Teag stretched out his hands, fingers moving as if he were knotting rope, weaving his magic together with that of Rowan and her coven sisters to fashion a stronger wall between us and the ghosts—but I knew it couldn't last long.

"Is it working?" I shouted to Simon, who had continued his invocation. All of the magic expended around me threatened to overwhelm my psychometry, but I thought in that babble of energy I could make out Dante's water magic, a somehow familiar psychic signature.

"She approaches," Simon replied in a voice that wasn't his own.

Caliel and Lucinda remained fixed on keeping the connection with the Loa. Simon stood in the maelstrom as the wind whipped his hair and tore at his clothing. I felt power building, and I knew that something strong and old and not of this world had joined us.

"What the fuck?" Vic muttered, his tone a mix of horror and awe.

An iridescent form rose from the murky water of the river, growing clearer and more solid as we watched. The ghosts, driven to frenzy only seconds earlier, vanished as if they feared the gathering power, or did not dare presume to stand in the presence of a goddess.

Mama Wata unfolded her thick, snake-like body from the river, black and glistening. A woman's face beheld us with glowing red eyes, and while the features were human, dark as the rest of her scaled skin, something in the shape of the head warned my primal instincts to be careful in the presence of a viper.

"Why have you summoned me, sorcerer?" The goddess's voice made me quake, and I forced myself not to turn away or fall to my knees, overwhelmed by the force of the power that held us in her gaze.

"We offer you tribute, and a rich meal," Simon shouted, standing tall and strong before Mama Wata. "The demon Ornias, bound in his box, and the ring that binds him. Yours to consume, and to remove forever from this world."

"Why should I wish to do so?" Her sibilant voice sent shivers through me and made the ground tremble.

"You are the only one who can take his power, m'lady," Simon coaxed. "Only a god can break the curse, only a river god."

I had no idea what the others sensed, but my gift screamed with the overload of sensation. Vic's wide-eyed expression of fear wasn't for himself, although we had no way to ensure Mama Wata wouldn't strike us all dead for the hubris of waking her. I felt certain Vic's terror was for Simon, at the center of the storm, bargaining with a god.

"Interesting," Mama Wata mused. "But not sufficient. I desire a sacrifice. Someone delicious. You, perhaps?"

Vic started forward, and Kell grabbed him by the arm, stopping him from intervening and possibly killing us all. Vic gave him a deadly glare but stayed where he was. I found myself holding my breath.

"Take me." Beck stepped around Father Anne. He bowed low, then straightened to his full height, head raised, shoulders back.

"I am Beckford Pendlewood, the last direct heir of Wilfred Pendlewood," Beck shouted above the wind, his voice strong, clear and determined. "Wilfred summoned the demon Ornias, bound him in the box, and used the ring to control him, bringing a curse and destruction on our family for generations. I accept responsibility for the evil done by those of my blood. Take me, and the demon, and let the others go."

Nobody moved. Teag's eyes were wide, and even Chuck looked spooked. Father Anne stayed next to Beck, silently supportive, and clasped one hand around her crucifix as her lips moved in silent prayer to a different deity, no doubt asking for our deliverance.

The barking of a phantom dog and the strong smell of pipe smoke reminded me that Papa Legba kept the doorway to the Veil open, aiding Mama Wata's presence. I couldn't see the Baron, but I sensed a dark, grave-cold presence where Lucinda swayed in a trance. Rowan and her coven sisters had gone still, like prey avoiding notice of a predator.

"I accept your supplication," Mama Wata said, fixing her terrible attention on Beck. "Surrender your enslaved soucouyant and supply the ring, and I will siphon what I desire from the essence of your soul."

Beck paled, and I saw how his hands shook as he lifted the sugar chest that bound Ornias from the containment box and pulled a velvet pouch with the ring from his pocket. He took care not to disturb the salt line as he crossed from his circle to step in front of Simon. Once more, he made a deep bow.

"Here I am, m'lady, with all that you requested. Do with me as you wish."

We stood in the presence of a power that could obliterate us with a thought. My heart thudded in my ears, and I didn't dare breathe. I wasn't ready to die. There were far too many things on my bucket list. There had been no real choice about summoning Mama Wata, not when the alternative meant killing millions of people in a supernatural fireball. But even if we died at the hand of the goddess and spared those people who would never know our story or our names, our lives would not be lost in vain.

Mama Wata's powerful body coiled until her head was level with Beck and Simon. Simon, channeling Dante, remained deep in a trance, with Dante's magic keeping the connection with the goddess.

"First, the soucouyant. Then the ring," Mama Wata opened her mouth, and unhinged her jaw, stretching impossibly wide.

Beck placed the box inside her maw, and then the pouch with the ring. I braced myself for her to pull him in as well, but he drew back, and she permitted it.

Mama Wata's mouth closed, and the muscles in her throat worked as she swallowed down the demon and its ring. Red light flared from inside her body, outlining every scale. The surface of the river trembled, and the land beneath our feet shook. Beck dropped to the ground with a scream, writhing in pain as Mama Wata tore away her tribute. His hands scrabbled in the dirt and his back arched. The wild winds howled around us, scattering salt, but we knew that if Mama Wata wished to destroy us, nothing we could do would stop her.

The red light vanished, the water stilled, and the land quieted. Beck stopped moving.

"I accept your sacrifice, Beckford Pendlewood, of your slaved spirit and your sorcery. The curse is sundered. And I will spare your life."

Mama Wata turned from Beck to Simon. From this angle, her face appeared far more snake-like, with nostril slits and holes where ears should be. Nictitating membranes blinked sideways across her red eyes, and her cold gaze had no pretense of being remotely human.

"Release me, sorcerer. I have answered your summons and supplied what you wished. Do not presume to press your luck."

Simon gave a low bow. "As you wish, m'lady. Thank you." He raised his arms once more, and spoke the spell again, shouting above the wind. Lightning cracked, thunder rumbled, and the river churned. Papa Legba's dog barked wildly, sounding much closer now though still invisible, and the smell of the Loa's pipe smoke filled the air. I shivered, feeling the disquieting rift between the world of the living and the place of the gods. Simon released the magic that summoned the goddess, and her form grew less distinct, then translucent, until she vanished altogether.

The sky cleared, and the river regained its flow. Simon dropped bonelessly to the ground. To my relief, I could see Beck breathing, but he was far too still and pale.

"Simon!" Vic moved forward, but Teag grabbed his arm. "Let me go!"

"It's not over yet," Teag warned.

Caliel's prayers and swaying quieted. He bent forward, adding a few items to his small altar, thanking Papa Legba for opening the Veil. But my attention was on Lucinda. Her eyes still had the glazed look of deep trance, and just in front of where she stood, another form began to take shape.

Baron Samedi, tall and slender, wore black tails and a top hat, and a pair of sunglasses missing one lens. His ebony skin had been painted white to resemble a skull. The tip of a cotton plug protruded from each nostril, in the islands manner of burying the dead. A fat cigar canted from his mouth, clenched between his teeth.

His gaze swept over us, like the hand of death. For an instant, when his attention fixed on me, my heart quaked. He appraised each of us before moving to the next. If he demanded our souls, we had no recourse against the Ghede of the crossroads.

Then he lifted his head as if he had seen what he needed. The Baron gave a solemn nod, touched the brim of his top hat, and disappeared.

"What just happened?" Vic's voice cracked.

"The Baron refused to dig our graves today," I told him. "We live."

Vic ripped his arm free of Teag's hold and ran to Simon, feeling for a pulse and murmuring his name. I went to aid Caliel, knowing he would require food and drink after being the Loa's horse. Rowan did the same for Lucinda, pressing a bottle of water and a protein bar into her hands as soon as she completed her thanks and offering to the Baron. Father Anne knelt beside Beck, checking to make sure he was all right and helping him sit up.

"It's gone," Beck said, in a tone that held confusion, loss, and wonder, his voice roughened from his screams. "My magic. It's gone."

Chuck and the coven sisters walked over to the unconscious cousins. "Well?" Chuck growled.

The two witches circled the prisoners, stretching out their hands to sense any remaining magic. The taller of the two women shook her head. "Their magic is also gone."

Chuck pulled out his remote, and pressed the button again, making the tangle of wire flare blue and causing the cousins' bodies to jerk.

"What the hell?" Kell asked. "Didn't you hear her say they don't have magic anymore?"

Chuck shrugged. "Insurance," he muttered and walked away.

Caliel drank and ate, then nodded to let me know he was all right. Rowan gave me a thumbs up from where she knelt with Lucinda, to tell me the mambo was also recovering. With Vic's help, Simon sat up, and while he appeared pale and dazed, I knew from his expression that Dante's ghost had departed, and Simon was fully himself once more.

"Are you okay?" Kell pulled me to my feet and kissed me, saying everything that needed to be said about fear, worry, and relief.

"Yeah. At least, I will be. And, we're all still here," I said, a little gobsmacked that our crazy plan had worked.

Vic held Simon close, one arm around his shoulders, and his right hand cupping the back of Simon's head. I couldn't tell for sure, but it looked as if Vic was holding Simon up, taking most of his weight. I didn't envy Simon the aftermath of magic worked on that scale, and I was glad to see Vic also had water and food stuffed in his pockets to help with Simon's recovery.

"Beck's going to need to disappear," Father Anne said, standing beside the last Pendlewood heir. "He's rid of Ornias, but there will be humans out for his blood—including his cousins. The St. Expeditus Society can protect him."

I nodded. "Good." I met Beck's gaze. "Are you okay with that?"

I could forgive Beck for looking a little dazed. "I…don't have any other plans. I guess I hadn't thought I'd live through all this. So, sure. Maybe I can even help, if you'll have me." He gave a self-deprecating smile. "I know a lot about dead languages and occult relics. My job options are limited."

"You might be surprised," I said, glancing in Simon's direction. Simon had put his doctorate in folklore and mythology to use providing research for hunters and giving ghost tours to tourists. Beck seemed like a bright guy. He'd figure something out.

Caliel and Lucinda were nearly finished packing away their altars, while Kell gathered up the weapons and ammo.

"Heads up, everyone!" Chuck shouted, with one hand to his ear as, I assumed, Robert relayed information. "CHARON's figured out something big just went down. We do not want to be here when they arrive. Move it, move it, move it!"

"What do we do with them?" Kell asked, with a glance toward the Pendlewood cousins, who were still unconscious thanks to losing their magic and a solid jolt of electricity.

"Can you leave them for these CHARON people?" Vic asked.

Chuck shook his head. "Too dangerous. Not that I'd object to anything CHARON wanted to do to those assholes, but they'd serve us up on a platter to save themselves, and I've got no desired to be pulled back in."

"The coven owns a place," Rowan replied. "We can hold them there until Sorren and Donnelly get back."

"I'll come with you, make sure they're not a danger," Chuck offered. As he spoke, he cuffed each of the downed men with silver cuffs etched with binding runes, and retrieved his EMF grenade. I thought he looked a little sad and figured it was because he didn't get to set it off. The cousins wouldn't easily escape, assuming they regained consciousness and hadn't been addled by Chuck's EMF weapons or Rowan's incapacitating spell.

In minutes, nothing remained to show that we had been there except for trampled grass. We made our way back to the cars, while the coven and the Tellers did their best to cleanse any residual magic. I doubted they could fool CHARON into thinking nothing supernatural had happened here—calling a goddess into the mortal sphere left traces behind—but perhaps they could remove any identifying magical signatures to keep CHARON from knowing exactly who had called the power.

We piled into our vehicles and headed in separate directions by prior agreement. I knew everyone would end up at my place, as soon as the goons in the black helicopters and government SUVs cleared out.

"You need me to drive?" Kell offered. "I got off easy, just shooting things."

Teag shook his head. "I'm okay. But thanks." He met my gaze. "Maggie and Anthony know from the comm link that we're heading in. They'll be ready."

I looked into the back as Vic steadied Simon to climb in. "He's shaky, and I'm pretty sure he'll have a hell of a headache, but he's going to be all right," Vic told me, answering my unspoken question. He kept his arms around Simon and spoke quietly to him all the way back into the city. Kell got in on the other side and slipped his hand up to my shoulder. I reached for it and twined our fingers.

"I think we'll skip checking on the ghosts at Creedmoor for a while," Kell said as Teag headed back for the main road. "I imagine they're going to hold a grudge for a very long time."

I leaned back in my seat and closed my eyes. We had summoned a goddess, destroyed Ornias, the ring, and the demon box, captured the cousins, and lived to tell about it. If the worst that came of it was some pissed-off ghosts, I counted it as a huge win.

/

CHAPTER FIFTEEN

"I'M SORRY I DIDN'T TELL YOU THE WHOLE TRUTH." I SAT ACROSS THE kitchen table from Simon and Vic, a few hours after the showdown at Creedmoor.

As I expected, everyone circled around and eventually made it back to my house, once they were sure they weren't being followed. Maggie had dinner ready, a hearty chicken-corn chowder, and we had eaten with gusto. Robert had assembled all the alcohol on a sideboard and proved to be a very competent bartender. Fortunately, we hadn't needed the doctor Maggie'd had on call, but we all looked a little worse for the wear.

Beck and Father Anne had gone back to the St. Expeditus safe house. Chuck had escorted Rowan and her coven sisters—and the unconscious Pendlewood cousins—to a bunker the witches could protect, then came back to join the rest of us. Lucinda and Caliel had both poured themselves rum drinks and were lounging on the couch. Anthony had looked so relieved when we walked in; he'd pulled Teag off to one side to greet him properly and confer in low tones. Baxter had finally stopped barking, but he circled continually begging attention—and treats.

"I don't think I really would have been ready to hear it, until now,"

Simon replied and swirled the whiskey in his glass. Vic sat shoulder-to-shoulder beside him, with two fingers of the same brown liquid in his tumbler. Kell had opted for a beer, but I'd wanted scotch, neat, after what we'd been through.

"I'd kept my abilities locked down for so long, back when I was at the university, and before that at home, it took me some time once I got to Myrtle Beach to learn how to use them," Simon confessed. "I'd almost let my parents and Jacen convince me that my gifts weren't real."

I'd forgotten the name of Simon's ex-fiancé. Good riddance, I thought. Just in the short time I'd known him, I liked Vic much better.

"While I was writing the ghost books, I learned everything I could about visions and being a medium," Simon went on. "I've made some friends who helped. A *bruja*, and a root woman like Mrs. Teller. And I've tried to help some of the younger people who have gifts and never had training. That can really mess someone up, make them think they're crazy. My Skeleton Crew," he added with a chuckle.

I had to laugh, because Simon's in his thirties, about six years older than I am, so I suspected that some of those "younger people" were probably my age.

"I could have told you the truth, too," Simon confessed, meeting my gaze. "But I didn't want you to worry, either."

He and Vic had told me about what kind of creatures and threats they had dealt with, and I was suitably impressed. "I've got to say, I envy you your connection to the police. We don't have that here, at least not since I've had Trifles and Folly. It makes things…complicated."

"We're lucky Captain Hargrove is a reluctant believer," Vic replied. "And after Simon busted that supernatural serial killer, it was hard to dispute the evidence that his gift was real." He looked chagrined, and I got the feeling that there was a story there, and perhaps the captain hadn't been the only skeptic. Simon took Vic's hand and rubbed his thumb across the back.

"Hey. That's water under the bridge," Simon said quietly. "It all worked out okay." Vic repressed a shiver, and a haunted expression crossed his face before he locked the feelings away.

"Anyhow," Simon went on, returning his attention to me. "Now that we both know what's going on, maybe we can help each other out more often. In fact, I think you'll be getting a visit from some hunter friends of mine, Seth Tanner and Evan Malone, before too long. They've got some unfinished business in this area, and I doubt they'd turn down a helping hand."

I was just about to ask more about that when I heard Chuck swearing.

"Son of a bitch. Those goddamned CHARON bastards found us." He and Robert were glued to the video feed from the camera on the corner of my house that faced the sidewalk. We all hurried to join him, and my heart sank as I looked at the screen.

Four black SUV's with dark windows were parked along the street. Two guys in black suits who were built like bar bouncers paced by the door, held back by wardings.

"Shit," I muttered. "What do we do now?"

"I was afraid of this," Chuck muttered. "Once those SOBs sink their teeth into you, it's hard to shake them off."

If CHARON raided us, assuming they could get through the protections on the house, they'd have several of the more senior members of Charleston's magical community—and the Alliance—in one swoop.

"Who's that guy?" Simon asked, pointing to the screen as a tall, slender blond man came seemingly out of nowhere. A moment later, he was joined by a large, broad-shouldered man with craggy features and Victorian-style facial hair.

"Whoever he is, he's got brass balls," Vic muttered. "He's giving the Feds shit, and they're taking it."

One of the men in black argued heatedly, and even without hearing the conversation, I could see him posturing and no doubt threatening to rendition the newcomers' asses to Gitmo.

He hadn't figured out yet that he was about to be totally owned.

"Wait a second," Simon said, and his eyes widened as the fed-in-charge suddenly straightened. The fed stopped arguing, but everything about his posture said he was still extremely pissed. A moment later, he shouted to the others, gave his colleague a shove toward their SUV, and we watched as the convoy cleared out.

"What the fuck?" Vic muttered. "Who are those guys?"

A knock at the inner door—the one to the house instead of the porch accessible only to my most trusted friends—made Simon and Vic jump.

Baxter ran toward the door, yipping frantically, then abruptly stopped a few feet from the entrance, sat down, and tilted his head, looking a little glazed.

I went to greet our long-overdue guests. Sorren and Archibald Donnelly came inside. They cast worried, appraising glances over the crowd in my living room, then seemed reassured by the lack of blood. Sorren stopped to scratch Baxter's ears, and the dog gave him a befuddled look of admiration.

"What's with Baxter?" Vic asked.

"Vampire glamour," Teag replied. "I wish I could learn that trick."

"Simon and Vic, I'd like you to meet Sorren, my business partner, and Archibald Donnelly, of the Briggs Society," I introduced.

Simon looked like a deer in the headlights, and even Vic seemed at a loss for words. "You're Sorren," Simon managed. "And you're a…"

"Yes," Sorren replied. His expression gave little away, but I knew him well enough to see a hint of a smile on his lips. He let the tips of his fangs show, just a bit. I took that to mean he was amused by their reaction. He has a dry sense of humor—it probably comes with immortality.

"And I'm Archibald Donnelly," the big man beside Sorren said, reaching out to shake hands and pumping the handshake vigorously. He leaned in. "I'm a necromancer, if you didn't know," he added in a conspiratorial whisper.

"We've heard good things about both of you," Sorren said, taking pity on the two gobsmacked newcomers and withdrawing his fangs. "Miss Eppie speaks highly of the work you've done. That counts for a lot in my book."

"You know Miss Eppie?"

"Mrs. Teller knows Miss Eppie, quite well, in fact. And I hold both ladies in the highest regard," Sorren assured them. Finding out that his root worker friend knew more than she had let on just made Simon shake his head.

Donnelly slapped Simon on the back with one of his huge hands, nearly knocking him off his feet. "I don't know about you, but this whole business has caused a powerful thirst. I need a drink."

As Donnelly wandered off looking for whiskey, I glanced at Sorren. "How did you get rid of the CHARON goons out front?"

Any trace of amusement left his expression. "I reminded them of the accords between the Alliance and his upstart group of mercenaries. Accords I personally negotiated with people far above his level. Charleston is off-limits. Always has been. It is *protected*. Their presence is not desired."

That explained why Chuck and Robert had chosen to retire here, now that I knew Sorren had something to do with "liberating" them from their ex-employer.

"And I offered to raise that insufferable agent's ancestors from the dead and send them to shamble over to his house," Archibald shouted from the makeshift bar, sounding like he'd enjoyed the confrontation tremendously.

"You finished up in Europe?" I asked, changing the subject. I decided that the less I knew about CHARON, the better.

He nodded. "Archibald and I got rid of the worst of the lot. What's left can be handled by our people there. Nasty business. I'm sorry we weren't here, but I take it your plan went well?"

"We'll be glad to tell you, but I agree with Donnelly," I replied. "I'm going to need another drink first."

I walked over to the bar as Donnelly greeted Robert with a hand on the shoulder. "Robert. It's been a long time. We miss you at the Briggs. Good work there. Although I understand why you wanted to take that Trinkets shop up in Cape May for a while. Gods, man, how long has it been since we did that's little caper in Monaco? Was it in Sixty-two? Sixty-three? You're looking very good."

"It was in Seventy-four," Robert said. "Quite a while ago. And you don't look a day older, yourself."

Simon sidled up to me. "What is the Briggs Society?"

"It's complicated," I answered. "But it's a building that comes unstuck in space and time, offering sanctuary to explorers who have become lost from their own eras, and serving as a repository for objects that are too dangerous to keep here and can't be safely destroyed."

"Oh," Simon replied, getting a glazed look much like Baxter. "Okay, then."

I patted his arm. "Just take it in small bites," I reassured him. "It's a lot to accept all at once."

Simon poured double shots for himself and Vic and wandered back to where his partner waited near the wall. As everyone gathered in the living room, I gave a recap of what happened at Creedmoor, only slightly edited for Anthony's sake. Sorren and Donnelly filled us in on the hunt for the stolen Pendlewood artwork, and although I knew he was understating the dangers they faced, even the redacted version made me shiver.

"We've got some news, too," Anthony announced when things grew quiet once more. "Brent Lawson and I spent the afternoon hammering out the case against Hoke, Greer, and Addison Pendlewood. He found the evidence we need to take to the FBI on a slew of felony charges, including RICO. I think it'll stick, too." He looked rather pleased with the outcome.

Teag had been checking something on his phone and looked up. "That Darke Web auction house that supplied the killer objects from the stolen cargo containers has been shut down, and the site owners have been doxxed to the feds," he added, with an innocent expression I didn't buy for a moment.

"Coincidentally, Erik Mitchell used his old contacts to sic Interpol on the ones who were selling the cursed artwork in Europe. And the real kicker?" Teag continued, with a grin that suggested nothing had been a matter of chance. "None of them were witches or even supernatural. Just a couple of longshoremen with itchy fingers who thought they saw a way to make a big score."

"So it's over?" I thought about all the people who had been hurt and killed by the stolen relics, the ghosts and monsters set loose by the dark magical cargo, and the damage done by the Pendlewoods.

"It's over," Sorren confirmed. "The Alliance has already sent people to clean out Chalmers Etheridge's collection, as well as the Pendlewood cousins' warehouses, and gather up any of the dangerous objects in those cargo containers that came into port. I don't know what the bloody hell Ellis was thinking, shipping them like that."

"And Beck?" Teag asked. "Is the Alliance going to come after him? He did right by us, down at the river."

I nodded in support. Beck couldn't help who his family was or what they had done. Despite my initial misgivings, I liked the guy.

"Father Anne and Rowan have recommended him for protective custody," Sorren replied. "Not as a prisoner, but as a witness. The Pendlewoods made a lot of powerful enemies. Without his magic or the demon, I'm afraid he wouldn't last long, on his own."

"Supernatural WITSEC," Teag muttered under his breath. "It does exist."

I looked around my living room at everyone who had fought side by side, staring down a goddess, and felt a warm surge of pride. My friends kicked serious ass. But more than that, despite their many differences, they had also become family. My family. I couldn't ask for any better.

"Who wants cookies?" Maggie announced from the kitchen doorway. "Chocolate chip, fresh from the oven. Eat up. Calories don't count when you've just saved the world. Get 'em while they're hot."

AFTERWORD

Among the Shoals Forever, one of the individual short stories featuring Dante (included as a bonus story in *Trifles and Folly 2*), was the first short story I ever wrote for publication, and it first appeared in an anthology of tales featuring pirates and magic. If my friend hadn't been editing and asked me personally for a story, I probably wouldn't have gotten up the nerve. I wrote a second Dante story, *The Low Road*, for the sequel anthology.

That was before there even was a Deadly Curiosities series (which, oddly enough, came about because a publisher asked for a modern story with magic, and then not only published the story *Buttons* but offered me a contract to do a series based in the world of the story).

Dante features prominently in *The Rising*, a Badlands novel written under my Morgan Brice pen name. Simon and Vic are the main characters in the Badlands series, and they've got their hands full with supernatural dangers in Myrtle Beach.

Erik Mitchell (former art theft investigator, bought Trinkets from Chuck's uncle) and Ben Nolan (ex-cop, private investigator, Erik's boyfriend) also star in their own series, Treasure Trail (also Morgan Brice). Seth Tanner (white hat hacker) and Evan Malone are the main characters in my (Morgan Brice) series Witchbane. All of the Morgan Brice series are urban fantasy MM paranormal romance.

Travis Dominick (ex-priest, former Sinistram) and Brent Lawson (ex-army, ex-FBI, ex-cop private eye demon hunter avoiding CHARON) also have their own urban fantasy series, the Night Vigil under my Gail Z. Martin name.

Since all of my Gail Z. Martin and Morgan Brice urban fantasy series cross over, there's a whole big world for you to explore!

The physical description of Creedmoor was very loosely inspired by Drayton Hall, near Charleston, although the family history, dark aspects, and magic are entirely my invention! That plantation is open to the public, as are many others—if you're visiting Charleston, you might want to stop in!

The ghosts and monsters in this book were inspired by folklore from Barbados and the Caribbean Islands, although authorial license was taken to fit the creatures to the needs of the plot. I enjoyed working with legends that aren't as familiar as many other monster stories, and I always love the research aspect of a book, which is where I discover new information and cool ideas.

I hope you enjoyed this book, and that you'll look for new adventures from Cassidy and her crew as well as perhaps exploring some of the other tied-in series. There will be lots more stories yet to come!

ACKNOWLEDGMENTS

Thank you so much to my editor, Jean Rabe, to my husband and writing partner Larry N. Martin for all his behind-the-scenes hard work, and to my wonderful cover artist Lou Harper. Thanks also to the Shadow Alliance street team for their support and encouragement, and to my fantastic beta readers: Amy, Andrea, Anne, Annmarie, Barbara, Beth, Candi, Carra, Cheryl, Chris, Chris, Christi, Christy, Darrell, Diane, Donald, Karolina, Laurie, Lisa, Manda, Mary, Mindy, Nica, Patti, Raven, Sandra, Sarah, Shannon, Sharon, Shirley, Tekna, and Xochitl, plus my promotional crew and the ever-growing legion of ARC readers who help spread the word! And of course, to my "convention gang" of fellow authors for making road trips fun.

ABOUT THE AUTHOR

Gail Z. Martin is the author of *Vengeance*, the sequel to *Scourge* in her Darkhurst epic fantasy series, and *Sellsword's Oath*, the sequel to *Assassin's Honor* in the new Assassins of Landria series. Be sure to check out the rest of the Deadly Curiosities urban fantasy series, with *Deadly Curiosities, Vendetta, Tangled Web*, and two collections, *Trifles and Folly* and *Trifles and Folly 2*, set in Charleston, SC. *The Shadowed Path* and *The Dark Road* are part of the Jonmarc Vahanian Adventures series. Co-authored with Larry N. Martin are *Iron and Blood*, the first novel in the Jake Desmet Adventures series and the *Storm and Fury* collection; and the *Spells, Salt, & Steel*: New Templar Knights series (Mark Wojcik, monster hunter), as well as *Wasteland Marshals* and *Cauldron: The Joe Mack Adventures*. Gail is also the author of *Ice Forged, Reign of Ash, War of Shadows, Shadow and Flame* and *Convicts and Exiles* in The Ascendant Kingdoms Saga, The Chronicles of The Necromancer series (*The Summoner, The Blood King, Dark Haven, Dark Lady's Chosen*) and The Fallen Kings Cycle (*The Sworn, The Dread*).

Under her urban fantasy MM paranormal romance pen name of Morgan Brice, she has three series (*Witchbane, Badlands*, and *Treasure Trail*) with more books and series to come.

Gail's work has appeared in more than forty US/UK anthologies. Newest anthologies include: *The Weird Wild West, Gaslight and Grimm, Baker Street Irregulars, Journeys, Hath no Fury, Legends, Across the Universe, Release the Virgins, Tales from the Old Black Ambulance*, and *Afterpunk: Steampunk Tales of the Afterlife*.

Join the Shadow Alliance street team so you never miss a new release! Get all the scoop first + giveaways + fun stuff! Also where Gail and Larry get their beta readers and Launch Team! https://www.facebook.com/groups/435812789942761

Find out more at www.GailZMartin.com, on Twitter @GailZMartin, at her blog at www.DisquietingVisions.com, on Goodreads https://www.goodreads.com/GailZMartin and on Bookbub https://www.bookbub.com/profile/gail-z-martin. Join the newsletter and get free excerpts at http://eepurl.com/dd5XLj

Support Indie Authors

When you support independent authors, you help influence what kind of books you'll see more of and what types of stories will be available, because the authors themselves decide which books to write, not a big publishing conglomerate. Independent authors are local creators, supporting their families with the books they produce. Thank you for supporting independent authors and small press fiction!

Inheritance

Trifles and Folly

Trifles and Folly 2

Assassins of Landria

Assassin's Honor

Sellsword's Oath - *Coming soon*

Night Vigil

Sons of Darkness

C.H.A.R.O.N. - *Coming soon*

Other books by Gail Z. Martin and Larry N. Martin

Jake Desmet Adventures

Iron & Blood

Spark of Destiny - *Coming soon*

Storm & Fury: Collection

Spells, Salt, & Steel: New Templars

Spells, Salt, & Steel: Season One (Collection)

Night Moves

Wasteland Marshals

Wasteland Marshals

Joe Mack: Shadow Council Archives

Cauldron

Other books by Larry N. Martin

Salvage Rat